D1054789

Second Time Around . . .

His mutinous hands brushed nothing but cloth. His tongue touched bare gums; where were his dentures? The air smelled of hospital; that part of his guess was probably right.

Below his middle was a warm wetness; whatever his ailment, it included incontinence. He felt depression; maybe his state was worse than he had thought.

A new sound came; in the blurred distances, something moved. Vaguely seen, a huge face loomed over him and made soft, deep clucking noises. Then he understood.

Reincarnation, by God! They'd always said you don't remember; well, somebody was wrong. Either he was the exception—some kind of fluke—or else all babies remembered at first and lost the recall later. He didn't want to lose his.

—from the F.M. Busby story ROAD MAP

Other books by F. M. Busby

ZELDE M'TANA

The Rissa Kerguelen Saga

YOUNG RISSA
RISSA AND TREGARE
THE LONG VIEW

GETTING HOME

F. M. BUSBY

ACE BOOKS, NEW YORK

GETTING HOME

An Ace Book/published by arrangement with
the author

PRINTING HISTORY
Ace edition/August 1987

All rights reserved.
Copyright © 1987 by F.M. Busby.
Cover art by Tom Miller.
This book may not be reproduced in whole or in part,
by mimeograph or any other means, without permission.
For information address: The Berkley Publishing Group,
200 Madison Avenue, New York, N.Y. 10016.

ISBN: 0-441-28267-9

Ace Books are published by The Berkley Publishing Group,
200 Madison Avenue, New York, NY 10016.
The name ''Ace'' and the ''A'' logo are trademarks
belonging to Charter Communications, Inc.
PRINTED IN THE UNITED STATES OF AMERICA

10 9 8 7 6 5 4 3 2 1

Previous copyrights on materials in this book are as follows:

Columbia Publications, Inc.: "A Gun for Grandfather," 1957. Renewed © 1985 by F.M. Busby.

Ultimate Publishing Co., Inc.: "Of Mice and Otis," "The *Puiss* of Krrlik," "Proof," and "The Real World," 1972. "Once Upon a Unicorn," 1973. "I'm Going to Get You," 1974.

Robin Scott Wilson: "The Absence of Tom Leone" (under the title "Here, There and Everywhere"), 1972. "Road Map," 1973.

Robert Silverberg: "Tell Me All About Yourself," 1973.

Terry Carr: "If This Is Winnetka, You Must Be Judy," 1974.

Mankind Publishing Co.: "Three Tinks on the House" and "2000½: A Spaced Oddity," 1973. "Time Of Need," "Retroflex," and "Misconception," 1974. "The Signing of Tulip" and "Advantage", 1975.

UPD Publishing Corp.: "The Learning Of Eeshta," 1973.

Mercury Press, Inc.: "Getting Home," 1974.

For all the writers who have pleased me,
and the readers I hope to please.

Contents

Introduction

At "WRITERS' EVENTS," people tend to ask "What do *you* write?" When I specify science fiction, they want to know why. Generally I say: "Because it gives me room to breathe."

Consider. Mainstream writing is limited to what could have happened in the past, may be happening in the present, or (within this known framework and using very few wild cards) might happen in our near future. The setup leaves *some* room to swing a cat, but one must be awfully careful not to bash the dear creature's head against the genre's confining walls.

Science fiction, on the other hand, can deal with pasts and presents that never existed and never can, plus many interesting futures, some less likely than others. Also, the mainstream writer is restricted to characters belonging to known, existing species; SF can deal with sentient creatures from differing evolutionary backgrounds, resulting in strange physical and sociological characteristics, and (above all) new and unfamiliar ways of thinking and reacting.

Aliens are fun to do: not merely inventing them physically, but giving them the "tones of voice" that make them distinctly *other*, and then showing how their differences from ourselves may lead to unexpected, sometimes dangerous complications.

Ever since storytelling first began—I envision a small group sitting, listening, illuminated by flickering light from the fire that guards the cave's entrance—the basic plot has been: Joe gets his fanny caught in a bear trap; now how does he get it out again (preferably, though not necessarily, all in one piece)?

It seems to me that mainstream's range of bear traps resembles the available selection of groceries at the local

7-11, compared to SF as the Food Giant up the street. How many ways can anyone treat the problems of A who is married to B but has the hots for C, so he does something stupid that gets him into worse trouble, and how will it all end? Certainly this plot is still popular: each month the bookstands are loaded with variations on the theme. But I'd rather write where the ruts aren't so deep.

Science fiction lets me put characters into predicaments which haven't been shown to exist in our mundane world and which may seem to be categorically impossible—until the story itself proves such a snap judgment premature. An interesting thing about SF is that it can force us to stretch our assumptions: just because a certain improbable event or condition has never become known to us, how do we *know* it could never occur? All the SF writer has to do is show that the apparent impossibility can't be proved—and this also can be fun to do. Especially in what I call ''identity'' (or, possibly, paranoid) stories.

The essence of science fiction is to avoid predictability: that's why I'm giving no further clues here. After all, why should I tip off my own punchlines?

So please read on and see what we have on the menu. I wish you much enjoyment.

—F.M. Busby
Seattle, WA
December 1986

A Gun for Grandfather

"I'M NOT KIDDING you at all, Phil," Barney insisted. "I *have* produced a workable Time Machine, and I am going to use it to go back and kill my grandfather." Certainly his pale, determined face showed no sign of concealed humor. He hadn't sounded mirthful on the phone, either, asking me to come over to his lab right away.

"But, Barney—what on Earth *for*? In the first place—"

"Oh, don't bother telling me about the paradox. If I kill grandpa before papa is launched, I won't be born, so I can't go kill grandpa, and so forth. I don't know how that part will work out."

"But what's the point? Is this just another go-to-hell Barney Feldman gesture, or what?" Barney had made plenty of those—leaving school a week before graduation to enlist in the Air Force, getting courtmartialed for refusing to shoot down an unarmed enemy transport plane, quitting a highly-paid government job for reasons he refused to state. But this didn't fit.

"I just had a physical checkup," he said. "I've been getting sicker lately—maybe you've noticed, maybe not. Well—seems I have about three years to live, and the last two mostly under sedation."

"Barney, I . . . ." There isn't much you can say. If I looked as shocked as I felt, it probably got across all right.

"I don't like that, Phil—I don't like it at all. The doctor gave me a lot of talk about faulty genes and linked characteristics. Says this particular form of dry-rot's only recently been identified as a syndrome—and if I had brown eyes instead of blue, I wouldn't be having it." He lit one of his midget cigars—his hands *were* shaky—and blew smoke.

"Did you get a second opinion? Some doctors are a lot less willing to write off a patient."

He nodded. "Three independent reports; yesterday's was the third. There isn't much leeway between them. And finally, I checked back home with our old family doctor—you remember Evans?"

"Sure." I thought back to the small town where we'd both grown up. "But he must be ninety years old by now."

"About seventy-five, a little over. Mostly retired, but he keeps his office open for visiting purposes and hands out a few pills now and then. I asked him about my family." He scowled, blue eyes slitting under black brows. "Phil—my grandfather died slowly and painfully. So did my father—I knew *that*, of course. Now it's come up to me—and I don't like it."

"But, Barney! You can't plan, seriously, to wipe out three generations to vent your spite. I don't doubt you can do it if you want to—but it's a horrible thought."

"Oh, come off it, Phil." His voice was low, not quite a growl. "It's not spite. I'm merely going to erase a mistake that shouldn't have happened in the first place, and clear up a lot of suffering, all down the line. My grandmother, my mother, my wife . . ." He winced. "Wanda's pregnant, you know—they'll all marry other people, men with sound genes."

Now he snarled. "*I* can take it—and my forbears already have. What I *can't* take is my unborn child growing up to the same damned thing!"

I saw his point but still I had to argue. "It might not be passed on, you know—isn't there a fifty-fifty chance? And mightn't they find a cure before your child grows up?"

He snorted. "You don't know much about genetics, I guess. To show up in three straight generations the killer gene has to be a dominant, even though it's linked to recessive blue eyes. Not only that—it's getting worse every time. Grandpa was weak and shaky—and hurting—for more than twenty years, but he could still get around. From the time the thing started bothering dad, it took eight years to kill him. With me it's three years, they say. And it's *striking* earlier each time."

He leaned back in his chair. "In the ordinary way, I suppose I'd just go through with it. Certainly I couldn't kill myself and the child, after it's born—I couldn't do that to Wanda.''

"Then how can you—''

He overrode me. "But this way—with this Time Machine I hoped to get a Nobel Prize for—it won't hurt Wanda in the least. She won't ever have met me. Probably she'll marry that boneheaded fullback I rescued her from. Can't knock off *his* grandpa, though—I'd be doing the school out of the only All-American it ever had.''

"Barney—why bother to tell me all this?'' He looked hurt, so I explained. "I mean—if you succeed, you won't exist. *I* won't ever have met you—and won't remember this, because it didn't happen.''

"Because I don't *know* what's going to happen, Phil. If someone else were trying this, I'd want to know about it beforehand—so that *maybe* I could check on the results. You and I, we've been friends for a long time—if there *is* any data, I want you to have it.''

He opened a drawer and began sorting papers. "I want you to take this stuff home with you, for one thing; it's the basic theory behind the Machine, and the hardware's not all that difficult.''

"But—''

He waved a hand. "I don't know how widespread any changes will be. I had this lab building constructed for my own use—it may or may not still be here.'' He started to hand me a slip of paper, then pulled it back.

"No—use your own notebook.'' I brought out my address pad. "Now write a memo to yourself. To come to this address—no, make it just the block, the 1400 block on West Fremont—and see if there's a brick building at 1425. If so, look for a man named Bernard Feldman. Got it?'' I nodded. He said, "That may be general and detached enough to survive the collapse of causation leading to it—since you wrote it yourself, in your own notebook. Now, date it for tomorrow—yes, I'm going tonight—and staple it to your desk calendar when you get back to the office. Then tomorrow, well, see what happens—if you can.''

"Sure, Barney.'' I've seldom felt so uncomfortable. How do you say goodbye to a man who is going to pull himself out by the roots? Do you wish him good luck—or just stand silent for a moment, as when the flag passes? And blow Taps, maybe?

I thought of a question to stall the evil moment. "Barney—how come you're only going back to your grandfather? I mean . . ."

"Good question, Phil—several answers. One is, I don't know that the problem existed before his time. His father was killed in the Civil War and *his* father lived to ninety-three—obviously the gene pattern was pretty good at that stage."

"How about their wives? Could the flaw have come in that way?"

"It might; I just don't have enough information. I gather it can be passed through either the male or female line but only shows up in the males—but this is pretty theoretical. None of the medics knew for sure—there simply haven't been enough cases identified."

"You said there were other reasons for picking on your grandfather. What else?"

He grinned, his first sign of honest amusement. "Mainly on account of that's about as far as the Machine will take me." He chuckled. "The past—it's pretty damned solid, Phil. It's a little like a compost pile—fairly soft near the surface but packed hard further down, with all that Time piled on top of it. Don't work too closely with that analogy, though—it's rough enough to draw blood if it slips in your hand."

"You're beginning to sound more like Barney, Barney." The levity was a mistake; he went serious again.

"Yes—I always shape up when I have work to do." He handed me the folder he'd sorted. "You'll have to be running along, Phil—because I have work to do right now, if I'm going to be ready to step off the way I've planned it."

"Does it make a difference, what time you get into your gadget?"

"Quite a bit. I've done some experimenting—not enough to make a solid paper for the Physical Society but enough to learn that several factors are involved in getting to a specific time. For a while I thought I was coming up with a scientific basis for some form of astrology, but that didn't pan out. Luckily. The PS would have excommunicated me."

"And what will they do with you now, Barney?" I said it quietly.

His gaze flickered. "Damn you, Phil—I might have known you'd try to pull out a few stops. Sure—I can melt out of my personal life with a bearable amount of struggle, because that's going to be a net plus in human happiness. But you're right—it's hell to lose the chance to present Time Travel to the Society as an accomplished fact.''

On the arms of his chair, his knuckles turned white. "Phil—to be able to hand them that, I would gladly go through personal torture. But I will not put my kid through it.''

He lit another midget cigar, and now his hands shook more noticeably. "Okay—you had to try. Now so long, Phil. Beat it back to your knickknack shop—and thanks for listening.'' I peddle turbine generators to power companies; to Barney, that's selling knickknacks.

"Okay, Barney.'' We shook hands. "Unless the notes and memory both evaporate, I'll be here tomorrow.'' I've never tried to swallow a golf ball, but I think I know how it would feel, the way my throat felt then. "And good luck, boy—good luck, whatever happens.''

Barney just grunted something. I was outside and halfway down the block before it struck me—that I'd never know what it was, the last thing Barney Feldman ever said to me.

The rest of the day, I wasn't much good for business. Or at home, either—Dorene got irritated, the way I'd stare at her and then have no idea what she'd been saying. When my fixed gaze wasn't on her, it was on one of the kids—Laura or Timmy.

Finally Dorene's hand waved back and forth across my face. "Come out of it, Phil. What's eating on you?''

I couldn't tell her—it wouldn't make sense and would make her feel bad. Too esoteric to throw at her, all at once—and without the background I couldn't explain why I was absorbing the sights and sounds of my wife and children as though I'd never see them again.

I made a quiet resolution—to try my best never again to be "too busy'' for them. I said, "Honey—it's nothing to worry you about. A tough deal happened to a fellow I know. It may be all right, with luck, but it was a shock to me—I've been mulling it over.'' We went on to discuss something else, that I could put half a mind to. It was a safe bet that I'd never have to explain Barney's problem—not if his plans worked out.

We went to bed early, shortly after the kids were down for the night, but I didn't sleep well. I lay awake, dozed, dreamt weirdly, got up—not usual, with me—for a cigarette, and lay awake some more. In the morning, a hangover would have been an improvement.

Breakfast was a mess. The toaster blew out its element, and a fuse, besides. We were out of fuses—and I've written too many safety pamphlets to strap across them. The Dripmaster is on the same outlet so the coffee was rare; we didn't think of that until Dorene poured it, and there wasn't time to make fresh. The station wagon had a flat; the kids and I took a cab to be late to school and office.

The Crow River turbine, on its test run, had seized a bearing. It took me all morning to expedite a repair crew and round up the replacement parts they'd need. Part of the delay was our warehouse superintendent, a man dedicated to keeping his stock in the warehouse where it wouldn't get worn out or weatherbeaten. For some months I'd been promising myself a try at getting him transferred; this seemed like the right time for it. I called the head office.

There was a delay until the chief of personnel got out of conference; from there, the action took less than three minutes. I celebrated by taking my secretary to lunch, with Martinis. When we got back to the office it was 1:30—a late start on the day's business.

What was current? I looked at my desk calendar. And that was the first, all day, that I had time to think of Barney Feldman.

I remembered Barney! Without a word to anyone I was out the door and out of the building, walking much too fast for my legs and wind.

1425 West Fremont—the building was there and it had Barney's sign on it. I didn't bother to knock—I went in, through the front and then back to Barney's sanctum. There, I knocked.

"Come in, come in."

Inside, the blinds were closed. With only a desk lamp on, the room was dim. Barney sat slouched back in his chair, eyes closed. The half-filled glass in his hand matched the half-emptied bottle on the desk.

"Barney!"

"The same." He drawled it. Then he sat up and looked at me. "No—not the same, Phil. Not exactly." He wasn't drunk, I saw—just a little high.

"What *happened*, Barney? Did you change your mind?"

"Did I change my . . ." He broke off, laughing—laughing until he choked slightly and coughed it out. "Yes—you might say I changed my mind. Yes, you might." He started to laugh again—and suddenly my tension and fatigue knotted into anger.

"Damn it, Feldman—I don't know what the hell you think is so funny! Ever since you told me that sob story I've been sweating you out—is that the big laugh? Was this just a rib? If it was, I think maybe I'll . . ." I had him by the shirt front and took aim.

"No, Phil." With a gulp he recovered his voice. "No rib. Wait a minute now—I'll tell you. It's a little blurred—yesterday, I mean—*your* yesterday."

"*My* yesterday?" It still came up blank.

"Yes. Your old yesterday—it's getting a little hazy now, alongside my new one. The change seems to propagate slowly; I don't have it figured out at all."

"What *happened?* Did you go back and kill your grandfather?"

"I went back and shook his hand."

All I could do was stare.

"Last night," said Barney, "I looked through a lot of old family papers. It seemed to me I should put my affairs in order, a little—don't ask me why; it doesn't make sense, I know. But in the looking, I found grandpa's diary."

He held up the bottle and pointed to an empty glass; I nodded and he poured. The first taste helped.

"When my grandfather was thirty, he came down out of logging country with a pretty good stake for himself. He looked around farming territory, near where we grew up, Phil—it's townsite now—with an eye to buying himself a farm and finding himself a wife. He bought the farm, fixed up the house—and got engaged to a girl with eyes as dark as his own."

"But two brown-eyed people . . ."

"They were going to be married in June." Drinking or not, Barney's voice was firm. "But one day a young stranger walked up to my grandfather and put a bullet in him." He waved me to silence. "For a long time, grandpa was a sick man—it didn't look as though he'd ever recover. His bride-to-be's father moved away, and took the girl along with the rest of the family. It's a wonder he managed to live through the infections and all, in what passed for a hospital in those days. But he had devoted nursing—from a comely, blue-eyed blonde.''

"A blue-eyed blonde . . .''

"Phil—she needed a husband pretty badly. She was supporting an invalid father, who was dying in a slow and painful way. She married my grandfather and bore him a blue-eyed son—my father.'' At my blank stare, he smiled broadly. "Don't worry—I won't wind this up into 'I'm My Own Grandpa'!''

"I hope not. Pour me a little more, will you?''

He did, then continued. "On the farm my grandfather worked hard to support his wife and son. He never recovered completely from that bullet wound; for the rest of his life it pained him. And at the age of fifty-one it led to complications that killed him.''

Barney leaned forward. "I read most of that in his diary, Phil. I'd known it was around someplace but I'd never looked for it, before. And the rest, once I began searching, I found in family letters.''

"So you went back and . . .''

"Phil . . . I read about somebody shooting my grandfather. Somebody who appeared, fired a gun, and disappeared before he could be found. That was *me*, that I read about. Another me.''

"But *why*?''

He shrugged. "Maybe another variation of this same misunderstanding.''

Barney paused, sipping his drink. "I got into the Machine and went back to the date my grandfather was shot—my calibrations worked perfectly. I walked to that farm and saw him—he was hoeing, hilling up potatoes. In a neighborly way I introduced myself; we shook hands and talked a little. Naturally he thought it was quite a coincidence that we were both named Feldman. Then I went back to the Machine and came home.''

"That's all there is to it, Barney?''

"Not quite. Things started to shake and whirl when I got back into the Machine; it hadn't been that way, the first time. Somewhere along the line I passed out, and woke up here about two hours ago. I broke out this bottle and have been quietly celebrating, and waiting for you to show up.''

He grinned. "I'll be a little drunk, getting home, but I guess I can square it with Wanda. Yes—I think I can.''

He shook the bottle. "Phil—there isn't much left of this. Why don't we have one more, to finish it, and then I'll be going home."

I nodded. He poured, and we lifted our glasses. "Here's to grandpa," he toasted.

"Well, that's that." Barney rose and snapped on the overhead lights. He took his coat from the hallrack, put it on and stuffed some papers into a side pocket. Turning to me he said, "Let's go, Phil."

There wasn't the sign of a shadow in his clear brown eyes.

Of Mice and Otis

ONCE THERE WAS a man who invented things. His name was Otis, but that didn't stop him; he invented things anyway. Otis specialized in inventing machines which you could put things into and different things would come out the other end. Once he invented a machine that you could put dirty wristwatches into and clean wristwatches came out the other end. So he went into the wristwatch-cleaning business until one day when he put a lot of dirty wristwatches into the machine and instead of clean wristwatches, what came out of the other end was a lot of little-bitty gears and springs and a lawsuit. So Otis got out of the wristwatch-cleaning business with only a few minor damages and went back to inventing things.

Five years later he had invented a machine which you could put things into one end and the *same* things would come out the other end. To make it easier to carry, he built the machine in two parts, one for each end. So now he could put things into one part of the machine in his kitchen, and they would come out of the other part of the machine which was out in the barn because the kitchen wasn't very big. Otis was pretty discouraged; the machine worked fine, but it took an awful lot of walking back and forth. Still, Otis knew the machine was completed, because there were no more spare parts left in any of the little bins under his workbench. So he decided he might just as well call in the newspapers to interview him about his new machine.

The newspapers always interviewed Otis about his machines. They had interviewed him about the wristwatch machine, and before that, the machine that you put Scotch whisky into and rubbing alcohol came out. There had been a machine that you put things into and they came out larger or smaller but you never knew which it was going to be. And the one machine that really discouraged Otis: no matter what you put into it, nothing ever came out—nothing at all. So now the newspapers came to interview Otis about the machine that you put things into in the kitchen and they came out the other end just the same as they went in, but you had to walk all the way out to the barn to see for sure that they had.

There were a tall reporter and a short reporter and a fat reporter. "What do you call your machine, Otis?" asked the tall reporter.

"Well, I've been working on it for five years," said Otis, "and most of the time I've been calling it a damn money-eating clatter-barrel. But now that it works, I guess I had better think up a new name for it. Since it doesn't change the things I put into it, and since it is in two parts so as to be easier to carry, I think I will call it The Two-Piece Invariator. That sounds like a good name, don't you think?"

They all nodded, and the tall reporter wrote down "Two-Piece Invertor," and the short reporter wrote "Two-Piece Clatter-Barrel," and the fat reporter wrote, "Two-Headed Inventor." This is one of the benefits of a Free Press.

Otis also told the newspapers that this time he did not think think he would go into business for himself with his machine. He thought he would go to Washington, D.C. and sell it to the government, or else maybe he would go to New York and sell it to some big corporation.

So Otis wrote to his congressman and got back a nice letter telling Otis who to see anytime he got to Washington and that the congressman would be delighted to see Otis in person and show him around the city except unfortunately he would be out of town that week. The letter was mimeographed and signed with a rubber stamp; Otis was quite impressed.

The congressman had made a small mistake as to who Otis should see about his machine, but finally Otis located the proper Branch of the correct Division of the appropriate Bureau of the Department that is rightfully concerned with giving the brushoff to people like Otis. Since he had been carrying the machine with him from place to place, the advantage of two-piece construction was obvious. Otis was becoming round-shouldered, but not lopsided.

There were a tall bureaucrat and a short bureaucrat and a

fat bureaucrat. "What does your machine *do?*" asked the tall
bureaucrat.

"You put things in *this* end and they come out *this* end just
the same as they went in. I'm glad you folks have a nice big
office. At home I had to keep *this* end out in the barn; all that
walking back and forth got pretty tiring."

"No trouble at all, here," said the short bureaucrat. "Lots
of room."

"What sort of power does your machine require?" asked
the fat bureaucrat.

"Well, I run it off a doorbell transformer," said Otis. "I
had my nephew hook that part up for me, because I'm scared
of electricity. But you just have to plug *this* end in, and that
runs the other end too. I had to fix it like that because I don't
have any wires out to the barn."

All three bureaucrats were quite impressed with Otis' machine. Everybody had a lot of fun putting things into it, and
sure enough, everything came out the other end just the same
as it went in. Well, almost everything—seven white mice,
one after another, all went in alive and came out dead. "I sort
of expected that," said Otis. "One time I was going to make
the machine big enough so I could put *me* into it, so I
wouldn't have to walk out to the barn, but my cat jumped into
it right about then and he came out dead in the barn, so I
figured it might be unlucky for me. Especially since it was a
black cat."

All the bureaucrats, even the fat one who had owned the
white mice, said they were real glad to have seen Otis, but
none of them could see how the government could use Otis'
Two-Piece Invariator. Now if it only *did* something to things,
or if it could be miniaturized and be made easy to carry in just
one piece—but it was not even the cheapest or most efficient
way to kill mice! The tall bureaucrat left to mail some letters.
The short bureaucrat had to hurry home because he was
expecting a C.O.D. package. The fat bureaucrat sent his
secretary out to the cafeteria for some sandwiches and coffee,
and he and Otis had a nice lunch together before saying
goodbye.

So Otis took his machine to New York and carried it
around from office to office until he was so round-shouldered
he had to put roller skates under the two pieces of the
machine, but finally he got an appointment with some senior
executives of a large industrial concern.

There were a tall executive and a short executive and a fat executive. "I guess you boys must come in sets," said Otis.

He told them the name of the machine ("We'll have to change that," said the tall executive), how it worked ("We'll put Research on it and get the Full Picture," said the short executive), and that he would like to sell it or have it manufactured on a loyalties basis ("We'll put Legal on it, and that's *royalties*," said the fat executive, patting himself on his corporation which was what had convinced Otis that he'd come to the right place).

So Sales changed the name of Otis' Two-Piece Invariator to "Modextron Mark IV." Legal presented him with a handsome forty-seven page contract. Research put things into Modextron MK IV and took them out again and tested them to see if Modextron MK IV had changed them any. Then they shoved Modextron MK IV over into one corner and built Modextron MK V, which was streamlined with lots of chrome and little flashing lights. Otis was called in to see them test Modextron MK V, along with the three executives and the head of Sales, a man named Mr. Juggernaut, who glowed slightly in a dim light.

So they put an apple into MK V and it came out the same, and they put a live mouse in and it came out dead, and they put the dead mouse in to see if it would come out alive and it didn't. (Otis could have told them that; he'd tried it with the cat. But they didn't ask Otis.) So Mr. Juggernaut said all right it was time to hit the ball with this product, and he led the way to the Conference Room. The sales staff and the three executives and Otis followed, bobbing up and down a little bit in Mr. Juggernaut's wake.

"First we'll hear from M.R.," said Mr. Juggernaut. "That's Motivational Research," he told Otis (who already knew it). A man asked what does Modextron MK V *symbolize* to John Q. Public. Nobody seemed to know, so Otis said that to him it symbolized the way you can put something down for a minute and then you can't find it; it just seems to disappear. Mr. Juggernaut's glow flared, but before it blew any of his fuses, the door burst open and Research people come crowding into the room with armsful of dead mice.

It seemed that every time you put something into either Modextron MK IV or MK V, it came out of both of them. One in, two out; both the same.

After the meeting sort of went to pieces, Mr. Juggernaut

said now we'll hear from Product Impact, and a nervous little man asked, "Will Modextron MK V create technological unemployment?" Otis patiently explained all over again that his machine did not create *anything*—that you took *out* of it exactly what you put *into* it except you could not take out live mice. For a big industry, these people sure had a hard time grasping a simple fact.

So they locked Modextron MKs IV and V up *tight*, built Modextron MK VI which had a great big place to put things into, and lots and lots of the ends that things came out of; Otis couldn't figure out why they would want so *many* dead mice. And when they started making such big models, he decided that what they really wanted was dead elephants. But his contract was paying him lots of nice money, so that he could buy all the parts he wanted, and he was working on a new invention: a machine that you put something into and it threw it right back. "This will save all that walking," he said. "These people are going to have to do an *awful* lot of walking to make sure that everything they put in comes out the same in *all* those places."

Otis went to some of Mr. Juggernaut's meetings in the Conference Room, but they didn't seem to make much sense. People would say that the national economy would be paralyzed, and Mr. Juggernaut would glow a little brighter and smile and nod his head. Or someone would say that the government would go under, and Mr. Juggernaut would actually give off little sparks and say, "Just keep in mind *who* the government will go under, and we'll be all right!" This wasn't what it said in the pretty colored pamphlets from Sales. They said "Live the Modextron Way!" with pictures of beautiful people standing around the coming-out end of Modextron MK VI, looking at fur coats and steaming platters of sirloin steaks and heaps of jewelry, and everybody smiling to the ears. Otis finally got an M.R. man to explain it to him, after the man explained that M.R. stood for Motivational Research. "Yes, I know that," said Otis.

"We rent these receivers out, you see," the man said. "We charge monthly fees and key the programming to the customer's rental bracket. The set turns on and off according to what schedule he paid for, but all the sets are on for the Basic Issue, like the advertising for next weeks's Specials. We rate the Specials so that everyone has to go up a bracket to get them. Trust Mr. Juggernaut to have *that* figured!" The young

M.R. man was beginning to glow a little bit himself, just thinking about Mr. Juggernaut. "For a hundred dollars a month," he said, "a man can live with nothing but basic MK VI and a garbage can! And at least ninety-five of that is sheer gravy for Modextron, Inc.!"

Otis was confused. It didn't help that his new machine when you put things into it sometimes threw them back too hard, and sometimes just dribbled them out a little bit at a time. This was especially discouraging with mice. Otis wished that the Supply Division of Modextron, Inc., would go a little easier on giving him mice for test-subjects. But Supply Divisions give you what they want to get rid of rather than what you want, so there was no help for it; he had mice, and it was not doing either of them much good.

The nervous little Impact man confused him even more. "The farmers will starve to death," the man said, "the railroads and truckers will go broke; in six months Modextron will own everything: *Juggernaut* will own *everybody!*" Otis tried to cheer him up by showing him the new machine, but it hiccupped on the first mouse.

Some days are like that.

M-(for Modextron-) Day was on its way, though. Millions of receivers had already been rented and installed all over the country. "An *awful* lot of walking," Otis said, but nobody was paying much attention to Otis since Research had watched his new machine throw back a few mice.

Mr. Juggernaut's M-Day meeting was very impressive; the fat executive explained the Opening Ceremony: what they were going to do, he said, was to start the Modextron distribution system up with a Gimmick. The short executive said the first thing to go into Modextron MK VI would be a coupon which would entitle the holder to one item absolutely free, but the renter had to sign up for a higher bracket to actually *receive* the item, of course. Then the tall executive got up to say that the next part of the Gimmick was that there would be a Mark VI receiver set up to feed the conveyor belt which would feed *into* MK VI. Everybody went off his rocker, and even louder when Mr. Juggernaut said that with this arrangement they would print just one coupon but that every ten seconds the belt could put a coupon into at least 100 million households. "They are only good once a week," said Mr. Juggernaut, "and every time, everybody has to rent into the next higher bracket to collect." Mr. Juggernaut was glowing like a railroad flare by now, but somehow he looked pretty dim to Otis, who didn't know for sure what Mr. Juggernaut was talking about except that it didn't seem to have much to do with mice.

Otis wasn't quite sure how mice had gotten into this inventing business so much, but they certainly had; everyone seemed to be mice-conscious. For instance, the nervous little man from Impact had come around that very morning and asked Otis for a mouse. Otis liked him, even if he *did* give Otis the wheebies with all that gloom and jitters, so Otis looked for a nice fresh mouse. But the little man didn't want a new one; in fact, he didn't even want a mouse that the machine (which was doing a lot better lately) had thrown back all in one piece; he insisted on waiting for the machine to hiccup when throwing back a mouse, and then he had to carry it away in a plastic bag. But it takes all kinds, Otis always said. So he hurried off to be on hand for the Opening Ceremony.

Modextron MK VI was really fixed up very nice, Otis thought; the conveyor belt between the two parts of it was running nice and smooth, too. Mr. Juggernaut was glowing just right; not too much, and yet not all weak and flickering as sometimes happened when people were slow to agree with him in the Conference Room.

The young man from M.R. was holding the Coupon on a gold-edged cushion; he was wobbling a little from excitement: just about right, Otis judged, considering the approving look of Mr. Juggernaut.

The nervous little Impact man, though, was not making a good impression. Mr. Juggernaut was trying not to look his way very often, and when he did, he was careful to be smiling *first*. Otis knew that usually when Mr. Juggernaut looked at people *that* way, they came out not much better than some of Otis's mice. It could be, thought Otis, that Mr. Juggernaut is trying to invent my new machine on his own hook. Otis wasn't worried, though; he had a whole backlog of machines he hadn't even *tried* to invent yet.

Then people began to make speeches. And they kept *on* making speeches, but someone stepped on Otis's foot so he woke up when Mr. Juggernaut was telling all about the coupons. Otis decided that maybe he hadn't understood all those meetings in the Conference Room after all, because Mr. Juggernaut wasn't saying anything at all like what he had said before.

Finally Mr. Juggernaut finished his speech. He turned to the young M.R. man who was holding the Coupon, and said: "In the name of Modextron, I charge you to open the Modextron Cornucopia."

No kidding; he said that.

But when the young M.R. man moved up to put the Coupon on the conveyor belt, the little Impact man jumped out and kicked the young M.R. man very dirty. And then instead of the Coupon, what the Impact man dumped onto the moving belt was this scrambled mouse that Otis had given him.

The Impact man couldn't seem to make up his mind. First he stopped Mr. Juggernaut from grabbing the mouse off the belt and then he dodged back so that Mr. Juggernaut *did* fall on the belt, himself.

Otis was real surprised at how fiercely the little Impact man kept everybody away from the controls while Mr. Juggernaut kept going past on the conveyor belt every ten seconds. It was seven minutes and 35 seconds before somebody managed to turn it off.

There were a tall FBI man and a short FBI and a fat FBI man. The tall FBI man scribbled in his notebook and said, "I guess he went through forty-five times." The short FBI man said, "And roughly a hundred million receivers." The fat FBI man said, "I don't think the assets will cover 4,500,000,000 coffins, even plastic ones. "Every time the M.R. man tried to suggest turning on Modextron MK VI again just long enough to provide packaging for Mr. Juggernaut, someone would kick him, so pretty soon he kept quiet.

Otis couldn't think of anything to say, and besides he didn't think he would like to be kicked, so he went back to his laboratory and watched his new machine throw back a few used mice which were all he had left now that the government had taken over and closed down Modextron, Inc., including the Supply Division.

Otis was pretty tired of mice, and of FBI men, and of Modextron, Inc., and of executives, and of Sales, and of M.R., and of New York, but especially of mice. So he took his machine apart and used the parts to make one of his old machines—the one that had been so disappointing because nothing ever came out no matter what you put in. He put all the used mice into it, every one. And sure enough, nothing came back out. Then he took that machine apart and put all the parts back in the right bins and went down the back stairs and out of the Modextron Building and went home.

He had a new idea he wanted to work on.

The *Puiss* of Krrlik

KRRLIK THE SQUILTH surveyed and considered himself. Krrlik's self-designation, even when neuter, was always "he"; he felt it gave him an advantage in sexual combat with other Squilth. Such might occur today at Dssief's home arena; Vrilgn appeared to be approaching sexuality. Krrlik himself certainly was, though he used the normal ruses to hide his condition. The advantage of surprise . . .

It would be good to force Vrilgn into the egg-nurturing role again; it would be Krrlik's third victory over Vrilgn, and would probably lock Vrilgn permanently into egg-bearing with respect to Krrlik. Krrlik would gain much *puiss*, as well as avoiding the discomfort of egg-bearing and the pain of undischarged sperm. Krrlik remembered well the multiple agonies of sexual defeat.

He could find no fault with his bodily condition. The saclike torso suspended from the legs-juncture was richly spotted with excretory pustules oozing fragrant yellow-green wastes that flowed slowly downward, soothing him with their warmth and texture. He stroked himself with a mandible, savoring the taste and approving of the delicate balance between stickiness and slime. The oozing material clotted and hung in ropy strings from the coarse white bristles that grew in scattered clumps.

The immature pustules growing at the bases of many bristles itched deliciously. Self-indulgent, Krrlik seldom was able to let these ripen and mature naturally; all too often he would give way to the urge for pleasure and pluck the bristle, releasing excretion prematurely. The glow of sensation, as tension broke and matter flowed, was too much for Krrlik to resist.

He considered the hard darker-bristled tubes of his exoskeletal legs. Not many Squilth had ten legs functional at the same time. He had another half-grown; only one was at the bud stage. Here was more *puiss*. The more functioning legs, the better able to avoid losing any of them in group discussion.

In the matter of eyes, where the sockets formed a ring above the leg-bases, Krrlik felt he might be pushing success too far. Seven of the twelve were functional. Two were noticeably decaying; he noticed and enjoyed the odd color-values of that stage. Only three were budding; one of those could already tell light from dark. But two buds were on the same side, even adjacent. Krrlik considered crushing out two of the seven functional eyes, properly spaced around the ring, to insure new eyes growing as older one decayed. It would not do to allow a period of minimal sight. Akpt had done that, had been reduced to three. Then Akpt had lost all three in discussion, and been eaten.

To eat was pleasant; Krrlik recalled the eating of Akpt. To be eaten was inevitable but Krrlik preferred to postpone it as long as possible.

Krrlik extruded his tongue from the opening of his apex. Yes, he was well advanced into sexuality. More so than Vrilgn, he was sure. That would be another advantage. Krrlik contracted his tongue laterally and thrust it, imagining Vrilgn's dismay at being penetrated and overcome, seeded and bereft of what little *puiss* it had built since last bearing eggs.

Satisfied, Krrlik rolled carefully one last time in the ripened pool of excreta, where it was deepest at the center of his home arena. Now with the warm sticky fluids coating his torso and enriching his scent-sense, he set forth to Dssief's home arena. It was good to arrive before others; he who was in place had an indefinable *puiss* over the Squilth who was required to enter and find a place of lesser scope. It was by noting such trivial advantages that Krrlik had progressed to his present state.

The Earthman would be present today, Krrlik remembered. He wondered what it might recognize of his *puiss*, of his triumph over Vrilgn. The Earthman had not yet seen Squilth in sexual combat.

The Earthman was not to be understood. The first time it had appeared at a home arena, it had done proper homage by excreting from the opening at the front of its apex. But this act had not been repeated. Later, always, the Earthman had come sheathed in a covering that prevented the social exchange of smells and excreta, as well as true discussion. Krrlik had guessed that, having only two eyes, it feared losing them and being eaten. Its fear was not in reason; Krrlik and others had, on that first occasion, torn small bits from it and found them inedible. Further, its legs could not be detached during even the most profound discussion. But still, after that first time, the creature had worn its coverings.

Krrlik could find no signs of *puiss* in the Earthman, though a being twice the height of a Squilth could hardly be without some semblance of it. Krrlik fought his unease.

He thought of Vrilgn's story, that the Earthman had tried to rub away Vrilgn's healthy coating of excrement and seal the red oozing openings that exuded the warm flow. Krrlik did not believe the Earthman could have tried to do such a thing. The creature was strange, yes, but surely not blind to the needs and goodnesses of life.

Krrlik went his way to Dssief's home arena, along the excrement-coated path, carefully tasting the still-moist spots with his sensitive foot-pads. The pleasurable itch of a growing pustule just below one of his two decaying eyes overcame his resistance; without conscious intent, Krrlik plucked the bristle and released first a spurt and then a flow of warm rich fluid.

The decaying eye noted a small squirming lump in the flow. Krrlik was surprised: after all this time he was still releasing young from the occasion when Nfaeg had defeated him, forced him into egg-bearing. He caught and tasted the young with a mandible, then reached it to his apex and ingested it. Young were nutritious, tasty also, until their legs grew out.

As Krrlik approached Dssief's home arena, he felt the *puiss* that surrounded it. It was old; the central pool had ripened and enriched itself over many generations. Krrlik contemplated his own *puiss* before entering, building and enhancing it to meet Dssief without disadvantage.

Inside. The Earthman was present. Advantage? Doubtful. The Earthman showed no signs of understanding advantage, or any way of performing it. It was at the edge against a wall where the pool was shallow, its pitifully-few limbs folded awkwardly. Krrlik could find no sign of *puiss*, but kept watch for a time until his unease subsided.

Krrlik waited. Dssief opened idle discussion, not seriously. Krrlik disdained the bait of legs or eyes offered so casually but he did not offer in kind, for Dssief had not survived so long uneaten without much *puiss*.

Many young bobbed in the pool among the other food-organisms: Krrlik tasted and ingested several. It would not do to be uncivil, to disdain the young of Dssief's visitors, even though some were growing legs and losing in delicacy.

Others entered, and finally Vrilgn. Krrlik had nearly forgotten; quickly he rubbed surfaces with Dssief, to diffuse the scent of his growing sexuality and confuse Vrilgn as to its source. He had used that method before, but not against Vrilgn. It should still be effective.

The discussion proceeded. Krrlik paid little heed to it, except defensively. One with such *puiss* as his would be instantly overwhelmed by all if taken at disadvantage. He angled always toward Vrilgn, who seemed to be trying to avoid him. Finally Krrlik shifted to put Vrilgn directly in his path, and closed. He caught Vrilgn torso to torso, mandible to mandible, tongue to tongue, *puiss* to *puiss*. Krrlik's sperm made ready to relieve his pain.

His mandibles pulled Vrilgn's apex to his; he ignored the leg that Vrilgn was tearing away from him, but worried two of Vrilgn's, and an eye besides. Krrlik hardened and extended his tongue, forced it into Vrilgn's apex, twisted and bent Vrilgn's tongue until it softened, then tip-to-tip forced concavity on it and began the penetration that would make Vrilgn a bearer of eggs.

Oh, there would be much *puiss* of this!

Little by little Krllik forced his way. His sperm tortured him with writhing pressure; frantically he strove for release. Almost, now . . . The Earthman was making loud noises; Krrlik ignored the distraction.

A violent blow tore Krrlik away from his triumph, sent him sprawling, legs a-scrabble into the deepest part of the pool.

What had happened? The Earthman! Interfering. How could this be? How could the creature interfere in what did not concern it? But no matter, for now Vrilgn was in *puiss*, holding Krrlik down. The tongue penetrating his, releasing Vrilgn's sperm into Krrlik, making him the egg-bearer. And oh, the pain! Like being eaten.

Now the others came. Legs torn away while he was in sperm shock. Because he had had so much *puiss*, they would take it all. Now, while they could.

The eyes. They left him none. No eyes, no legs. And now, no mandibles. They would leave him alive until the eggs bore, before eating him. Because his young, those that survived, would carry his *puiss*, needed by the race.

But for Krrlik now, no *puiss* at all. All, all gone, all taken. Vrilgn would take his home arena, his rich pool, sully it with his own lesser *puiss*.

For Krrlik, only the slow warm comfort of the pustules oozing rich fluids over his sperm-shocked torso, while he waited to bear young and then be eaten.

The Absence of Tom Leone

ABRIS OF THE Hill People was soon to produce our child. As agreed at the meeting of clans she had come to live with me during this period, one of the women who came to our lowlands. At the same time my sister Fearl and others of our own women went to the hills. It is a pleasant arrangement.

Abris was a fine mate. Her voice was sweet both in speech and song; the iridescence of her skin, augmented in the child-carrying changes, were delightful. I believe that even the Terran, my friend Tom Leone, could tell that Abris was exceptional in beauty of person and activities. Certainly he always rendered her every courtesy as he understood these matters.

Leone the Terran no longer appeared monstrous to me; I knew that within the dwarfed head atop his outsized body were a mind and spirit like my own. He labored for half a year to learn to use our language with skill. Although I despair that any Terran will ever fully grasp the Wholeness, with Leone it was not for want of effort. So we came to be friends. Even the filaments of dead cells that grew here and there on his head and body no longer repelled me, nor the drab color of his skin, leathered at face and hands by our wind-driven dusts.

But on the day we first met, the day I saved his life, I thought him a monster indeed.

To say I saved the Terran's life sounds as though I had done something exceptional; it was not so. I merely repelled, by our method of projecting a deterrent feeling, one of the mindless Leapers. Although no one could stand against that voracious flesh-eater or evade its swift charge, the Terran could normally have killed it with the weapon he carried.

But Leone the Terran had fallen from a height and was unconscious. Had I come to that place only a short time later, the Leaper would have eaten him. I would have found only bones scattered around the fed, torpid creature, which I would then have killed, accepting the temporary breach of Wholeness that killing brings. But I was in time, and repelled the beast instinctively. Only then did I look to its intended victim.

I had not seen a Terran before, though quite a number of them are present at the settlements across the Roaring Straits.

So I did not know what to do to help. I spread a cloth to shield him from sun and wind and dust, and sat waiting. After a time he came awake.

We could not speak, of course, but knowing each other as Terran and Gelban respectively, and so not hostile, we could gesture and try to begin the exchange of words. He could walk without aid; I took him to my home, of which I have some pride. It is my own design, all roof and dust screens with no opaque walls except of course for the central chamber. It was not a time for me to have a mate in residence, so I put that chamber at the disposal of Leone the Terran.

Over a considerable number of days we learned to speak with each other. Others who lived at civil distances from me occasionally came to see and hear Leone also. Perhaps the most surprising thing to learn was that his activities were not entirely of his free choice. It was equally a surprise to Tom Leone, I think, to find that no Gelban does another's bidding. We of course do what must be done, I told him, but freely.

"You really don't know then, Fairn," he said to me, "what it is to agree to work for someone, to do a job and get paid for it?" I did not, and furthermore, I am not sure I understand the concept even yet.

"Well, Fairn, just take it that I hunt funny-looking rocks up in the mesas because when I find the right kind, somebody across the Straits will take them and give me something I want in exchange." We spoke no more of it. He showed me some of the rocks; they were of the kind that show patterns of creatures long dead, some ancestral to those presently living.

I was equally at a loss in trying to show Leone the Wholeness, the way of seeing All That Is. It is such an obvious thing, almost instinctive with us, that at first I felt he had to be pretending not to understand. But finally I recognized that

Terrans have not evolved the basic concept, and suggested that Leone resort to inner-withdrawal to discover it for himself.

"Meditation, I guess you mean," he said. "I've tried it, one way and another. I always seem to end up biting the back of my own neck." Since it is as impossible for a Terran to do such a thing as for a Gelban, I knew that Leone was indulging in the Terran habit of saying that which he does not mean, for some strange form of personal enjoyment that is of no injury to the listener. It seemed a sign to cease discussion of the Wholeness for that time; we talked of other things.

Leone had a mate on Terra, a permanent mate, though that concept is difficult to accept. She was called Margaret. He showed me a representation of her and asked me, did I not think her beautiful? To him she had beauty, so I spoke as though I saw it also.

He was to be separated from her for five Terran years, a period nearly equivalent to three Gelban. He wanted to be with her, and at all times, though he did not know or could not tell me if it were the time for him to produce a child.

Soon of course it became that time for me, so that Leone could no longer reside in the central chamber of my home. I and a few friends arranged to help him build a home for his own residence, not uncivilly close to mine but near enough for convenient interchange of meeting.

I felt that Leone was shocked when my mate of that time, Inarre, began to show the child, growing in the translucent pod outside the lower front of her body trunk.

"Your children grow *outside* the body before being born? Before being separated from the mother?"

"We have so evolved, yes. Yours grow inside the body, I assume," I said. "The comparative size of Gelban head and body would make that impossible for us, you must see."

"I see it," he said. "I just don't believe it." Another instance of saying the unmeant, accompanied as usually by a lip-grimace.

Leone was also startled when Inarre's nourishment gland began to appear and enlarge from its matrix at the center of her chest. But he did not say a great deal about it; he merely drew a picture of the Terran equivalent function which is once-redundant and explained that these glands are present in Terran females at all times, even when not needed. I had deduced or surmised as much from the fact that Leone himself was burdened by external sex organs at a time when he could have no possible use for them. And I am sure that he was puzzled because I and other Gelbans have no such handicap. But he did not ask, so I did not tell him. Imposing unwanted information on others is not truly civil.

So time went on, and although Leone never grasped the Wholeness as we know it, his speech and actions were those of one who is Whole. Perhaps Terrans interact with All That Is in a fashion that does not involve conscious speech levels. It may not be necessary for them to see the Wholeness as directly as we do, to be a true part of it.

In a manner without doubt, Leone the Terran became truly my friend. You may not understand without having experienced such a thing yourself.

And so for a time Tom Leone lived at my home when I was alone, and away in his own when it was the time for me to have a mate to reside here. It was a good time. I did not like to think of his absence, which must happen so that he could return to Terra and to—strange concept—his permanent mate.

There is a Terran thought that I do not fully understand but I think it must bear on what occurred. It is called irony; I believe it means that which is irrelevant while still causing effects.

It was when Abris of the Hills was near to shedding our child and its protections. A woman preparing to shed child must have all her energies reserved for that purpose, just as must a man or woman contemplating the Wholeness. And on that day I was in full contemplation atop the little hill at the side of my home, preparing to help Abris project the Wholeness to our child as soon as it was free, so that its life would be Whole in our Gelban fashion. As I contemplated, I watched Abris sitting on the mat she had unrolled in the open space before my home.

Either I had been careless or the Leaper had been shell-encased and undetectable, which is a rare thing at that time of the year but not unknown. It appeared suddenly from behind a tumble of boulders, directly in line with Abris from where I sat and over twice as far from her. Yet I knew it could reach her before I could; they are swift, swift, when they wish to be. But for the moment it moved slowly.

I strove to wrench myself out of contemplation, heedless of mind-risk and the danger to Wholeness, hoping to free enough

energies to project and repel the Leaper. But I had trained
myself too well; my mind would not leave contemplation
except in the slow whole way it had always known. Nor
could I move, save slowly and clumsily; contemplation is an
act of mind and body as well as spirit.

I saw Abris look up to the Leaper, and I knew she could act
with mind or body no more than I. Divert her energies at
child-shedding time? Impossible. She looked to me; I could
not hear her saying but I knew and whispered it back to her
own knowing mind. Then she bowed her head, placed both
hands on the child's protective cover, and began to sway
gently back and forth, consigning herself and our child to the
Wholeness as she waited for the death. I followed her movements with my own; nothing more could I do.

Then Leone the Terran appeared, coming by the low path
beside the water, carrying a spray of colorful leaves and
blossoms of the kinds most enjoyed by Abris. I ceased my
swaying and flailed my arms to draw his attention, then
pointed to the Leaper. For a moment I thought all was to be
well, but when Leone reached for his weapon it was not
there; he had lost the habit of carrying it in the usual peace
and safety of our homes.

Terrans cannot project from mind, and so I did not know
what he might think to do. He dropped the spray of color and
ran to Abris, faster than any Gelban but not so fast as a
Leaper. The Leaper still came on slowly, darting its great
toothed head from side to side as if puzzling about the two of
us who did not move and the one who did.

Leone took one of Abris' hands in both of his. For a time
he did not say or move. He shouted something to me but I
could not hear it clearly and spread my arms wide to show the
lack. He nodded and spoke to Abris, then turned to face the
Leaper.

Directly toward the Leaper he ran. It had begun its charge
but now paused. Just short of it, the Terran paused also. He
clenched and raised both hands, and shouted something upward. Not to me, not to Abris, not even to the Leaper, but to
the sky. Again, I could not hear his words. Then Tom Leone
and the Leaper ran toward each other. And met.

He had told me of a thing Terrans do which is called
combat, but I had not imagined how it could be. Now I saw
it. The Leaper was half again as big as the Terran, but Leone
went to it as though he were the Leaper and it the victim. He

jumped and drove both his feet hard against its head. He caught one of its forelimbs and broke it away. At every move he gave a great wordless shout. He clambered astride its upper body and twisted its neck from behind, but that great neck was too strong. He tried to pull its jaw apart, but again the Leaper's vicious strength prevailed; he lost fingers and fell to the ground. The next instant, the Leaper's jaws closed on his head. Then, though my eyes still looked, my mind refused to see. Until I came slowly out of contemplation and could move again. I walked down the hill.

Abris was in need, so I could only look quickly at the bones and at the still form of the fed Leaper. I could not kill it now and break the Wholeness needed for Abris and our child, but it would not move for hours; there would be time enough.

I went to Abris and stroked her gently; the time was near and we must be at peace. "Tell me quickly," I said. "You must finish with it."

"His hands that held this one of mine were cold. When you could not hear his shout he spoke to me: 'Say to Fairn good parting and that Leone never leaves a balance unrestored.' Then he ungrasped my hand and with no word went to the Leaper."

"Yes. Yes. But when he shouted to the sky. Could you hear his words?"

"I heard: 'Forgive me, Margaret! God knows I love you, but you are there, and they are here!' Then he met the Leaper."

I stroked her, here and there and over the child. "There was a Wholeness to Tom Leone, Abris, that I do not fully understand. Come, we must take the peace he gave us." And soon, in peace with the Whole, Abris and I shed her of our child and infilled it with the Wholeness. After a time, as always, Abris went with our child to the Hills, to her people.

I feel the pain of her going, as with any exceptional mate. But I know I will have other mates: perhaps Abris herself again, or another as nearly whole and fitting.

But never will there be another Terran Tom Leone. And his absence is painful.

I am here and he is not.

Proof

"SO THAT'S YOUR time machine," said Jackson. "Shades of
H. G. Wells." The Time Chamber, with its loose hanging
power cables and confused-looking control panel, didn't look
much like Mr. Wells' crystal bicycle.

"Oh, not mine, not mine at all," Dr. Gerard said. "Durrell in England provided the math; Bell Labs' computer study
translated it into hardware. My part is to plan and conduct the
testing program; nothing more." He smiled. "I wouldn't
want to see you spoil your record for accurate reporting."

Jackson's pudgy frame shook with half-suppressed laugh-
ter. "According to my boss," he said, grinning up at Gerard's lean face, "the last time I got anything right was my
birth certificate. But thanks, anyway. Now, can you give
me—hey, wait a minute!" Jackson stiffened, looking at the
corner of the room behind the Time Chamber, where the grey
wall expanded in an unusual convex arc, a quarter-circle. He
knew this room. After twenty years he still recognized it. It
had been blue, before.

"Is something the matter, Mr. Jackson?"

"Yeh. Isn't this building—this room—where Senator Burton was assassinated? I was just a kid, but . . ." The room
had been shown on TV over and over, with various dignitar-
ies giving the official version of the tragedy. Public doubt—
there had been too many killings, each too well explained—had
abruptly reversed the expected outcome of that year's presi-
dential election. Vividly, Jackson remembered the shock.
"Well?" he said.

"Why, yes; it happened here. I'd forgotten; it's been so
long. Afterward the building was used for storage for several

years; then it was remodeled and the Department got it for lab space. I had really forgotten.''

Jackson shook his head. ''No matter; it just jarred me for a minute.'' He scowled; this was no time to discuss his twenty-year obsession with the mystery. ''Let's get on with it, doctor. Can you give me a quick rundown on what this machine does and how it does it? Layman's language? So I can boil it down to five hundred words for my lip-moving readers.''

Gerard tipped his head back, hunched his shoulders. Jackson recognized the movement, could almost hear the tensions popping loose in the doctor's neck. Pushing himself too hard, he thought.

''Layman's language, eh? Let's see, now. Start with Durrell's formulation: the past is a solid compressed sphere with the Big Bang at its center and the present moment as its surface. All right so far?''

''Got it.'' Jackson scribbled pothooks in his notebook. ''You just cut us to four hundred words, though. I'll need room for a cartoon.'' He nodded a go-ahead to the taller man.

''Luckily, Durrell's hypothetical sphere is not impenetrable. Near the surface, at least. In theory this device—machine is hardly the proper term—will force an opening into it, so that we may insert test objects.''

''Into the past? How about the future?''

''Into the past, yes. By definition, the future is non-existent.''

''Hmmm. Doctor, how can the past have room for anything that wasn't there to begin with? You say it's solid, and that fits—we haven't been living in a world with holes in it, that I ever noticed. But two things can't be in the same place at the same time. How do you explain that?''

Gerard paused. He walked across the room, Jackson following, to the Time Chamber at the far side. Under the control console, against the convex arc of wall that had triggered Jackson's memory, lay a hammer, Gerard picked it up, held it out for Jackson to see.

''One of the workmen must have left this here,'' he said. ''The installation is complete and operable but the men still have some tidying up to do.'' He gestured toward the loose cables. ''As to inserting something into the past: I want you to look closely at the head of this hammer, where the end of the handle is exposed.''

Jackson looked. ''What am I supposed to see?''

"The wedges; see them? They are driven into the handle to expand it, so that it can't slip out." Jackson's brows climbed his forehead.

"The point is that the wedges don't occupy the same space as the wood. They displace the wood fibers, compress them, slip between them. To make a very rough analogy, Durrell's theory indicates that this device"—he nodded toward it—"will insert subjects into the past in much the same fashion, except that the insertion will not be perceptible from any past viewpoint."

Jackson snorted. "I'm afraid that doesn't sound very credible to me, doctor."

"I suppose not." Gerard smiled apologetically. "Perhaps the analogy was a mistake—all analogies fail if carried past their limits. The concepts can be stated accurately only in mathematical terms, and Durrell's math appears to be quite sound. Of course the proof of the pudding . . . Well, we'll test the effects thoroughly, one step at a time."

"Right. And what are those steps? That's the kind of thing the readers want."

"In brief, I shall start with inanimate objects such as this hammer, that paperweight, whatever else might be handy. Measuring their properties before and after insertion into and withdrawal from the past. Next, instrument packages, which can tell us a great deal more. Then living subjects, the traditional mice and guinea pigs. And finally, if indicated, the ultimate test."

"A human being," said Jackson in a flat voice. "You have a volunteer?"

"Oh yes, of course. Myself, actually. Who else could I risk? But the risk will be small. Preliminary experiments will tell the tale, and I have considerable faith in Durrell's hypotheses."

"I'm sure, doctor." Jackson needed something more. "Now how about a quick outline of your operating procedure? I mean, turn Knob A to Line B and push Button C? The public likes to think it knows how things work."

"Yes, I suppose so." Gerard gestured toward the control panel. "This looks complicated, all those knobs and switches. It's the prototype model, and believe me it *was* complicated at first. But you can forget about all the controls except the four that have been marked with red paint; the rest have been put on a computerized feedback circuit.

"The red handle on the left overrides the computer; I don't expect that we'll ever have to use it. The red knob under the 0-to-100,000 dial sets the number of years of penetration into the past; I'm told the calibration is accurate in theory but naturally I'll check it thoroughly. The 'Depart-Return' switch is self-explanatory, wouldn't you say? And to its right, the final red knob and its instrument dial are the timing control. A small bonus from the Labs."

"Yes?" Jackson was hearing more than he really needed to know, to make up his 400 words. But he had to play along. "What's the bonus?"

"Automatic return of the test subject, after a pre-set period of exposure to the past environment. Much more efficient than having to sit, watch the clock and push the Return switch personally. Or when I take the plunge myself, which seems to be a reasonable probability, I can pre-set the timing with no need for anyone else to sit on watch and and bring me back. A nice touch, isn't it?"

"Yes," said Jackson, "I'd think so. Now just one more thing—"

The picturephone, on a desk to one side, chimed. Doctor Gerard answered it, spoke softly, then shut it off. "Mr. Jackson, please excuse me for a few minutes. I'll be back as soon as possible."

Left alone, Jackson prowled the room restlessly. The device, the Time Chamber, violated his personal view of how things worked in this universe. But he had to accept what he had been told, didn't he?

Or did he? From what Gerard had told him, he could check it out for himself!

No, that was insane. The thing hadn't been tested. Try it with the hammer first. Was there time for that? Jackson's will divided against itself. Durrell was a big gun in theoretical physics, wasn't he? And Gerard swore by him.

Senator Burton: who had killed him, here in this room? Jackson had gnawed that bone for twenty years. Slowly he turned to the Time Chamber and its controls.

The Chamber didn't look like much, an overgrown phone booth without the phone, dimly-lit in an off-violet like a failing sunlamp. The controls were more intimidating. Push the button: Zap! You're extinct! Jackson shook his head, looked closer. How did it go, again? Under him, his legs were shaking. Funny; he hadn't noticed when the shaking had begun. He squared his shoulders, took a deep breath.

All right; he set the Years dial, hoping he had the mental arithmetic right for the date of Burton's killing. Timing? Five minutes should be enough for a first look; he had to be back here before Gerard.

Hell and damn! It wouldn't work; the Depart switch was out of reach from the booth. But surely Gerard must have thought of that hangup. Try everything. Ah! The timing dial pushed in, as well as turning. It latched; illuminated numbers began a thirty-second countdown. Yes, that should do it.

Years about twenty, timing five minutes; push the switch and sit in the booth. Waiting.

The world dropped out from under Jackson; before him was a senseless photomontage as twenty years of happenings in one room flashed past, each moment as distinct from the next as titles on a bookshelf.

He closed his eyes but couldn't close his mind; the overpowering input was still there. Unable to resist, he surrendered to it. At that instant it stopped, like crashing full-tilt into a solid wall. Jackson saw.

He saw one picture, one moment out of the history of that room. It was not at all what he had looked for. There was a girl, a typist, frozen in her expression of irritation or petulance, one hand scratching her leg just below her short skirt, the other resting on the keyboard of her typewriter. Her hair, bleached nearly white, was twisted into short corkscrews. Her mouth was painted a shape as improbable as its color. She looked uncomfortable. Recalling the fashions of the time, Jackson decided that she probably was.

To him, the five minutes frozen into the timing dial seemed to be forever. When the picture began to shift, to return him, he felt a vast relief.

The moments began to unroll again. But not as a coming and going. He had gone to the past and stopped at one instant. He expected the same thing, the same bookshelf-title confusion, to happen in reverse. It didn't.

The moments came and stayed all of them. He saw Time from a sidewise view, a spectator at the side of a race-course rather than a participant running along it. There was the bleached blonde at one end and himself pushing buttons and turning knobs at the other. If there had been any ends to it. There weren't.

He saw Burton killed, saw the killer clearly. It wasn't anyone he knew. He became tired of seeing it, seeing the police fumble and let the man escape back into his own irrelevant paranoia.

All in still pictures, fixed scene by fixed scene, an infinite number. All at the same time and yet also in sequence. And it wouldn't stop; it would never stop.

There was Doctor Gerard showing him a hammer, with wedges driven into the top of the handle. ''The proof of the pudding . . .'' The past isn't rigidly solid, Gerard was telling him. You can drive a wedge into it, displace it.

Yes. Jackson thought. *But have you ever tried to pull one out again?*

The Real World

"I AM MOST impressed by your improvement, Crawford," the doctor said, "and very pleased." He smiled again. Hercules, the muscular attendant, smiled too. Maybe it was Ajax, the other attendant. They're not different enough to matter, including their real names.

My name is not Crawford. It used to be but it isn't any more. I don't know what my name is now. I haven't decided.

"Two weeks ago you were catatonic," Doctor Baumer continued. "Just two weeks, and now here you sit talking to me, feeding and dressing yourself every day, with only a few minor behavior problems to overcome." He beamed. Beaming was one of his specialties; he did it well. Sometimes he almost convinced me.

I have more than minor behavior problems to overcome. I've seen too much. I've seen the underside of the universe—the one they don't tell you about. And the world doesn't want to let me forget the sight.

I suppose it began when my new roommate moved in last quarter. Before, I'd probably been no more miserable than anyone else.

"Soon you'll be going home, Crawford."

I nodded.

"And this time you'll know enough to stay away from the drugs that put you here."

Of course, Doctor.

My new roommate's name was Frankel. He was a Ph.D. candidate in organic chemistry, and an acid-head. I dropped a little myself sometimes but not the way Frankel did. Frankel cooked up new variations in the lab and tried them out on himself and on his friends. Frankel gave me some beautiful trips, very educational. Nothing compared to the one I gave him, I suppose, but mostly well and good.

"I'm glad to see you participating in the exercise program," the doctor said. "Nothing like a sound mind in a sound body; right?"

"Nothing at all," I said. "I wouldn't have it any other way." I lie a lot. Crawford never lied.

Acid and similar substances cut you free from the limited ways you've always looked at the world. They let you see it in new perspectives, some of which are possibly true. They may even let you see God, or His absence, or the footprints He left when last He passed this way. Acid itself never did quite that for me.

Doctor Baumer kept telling me how nice it was that I was so much better. I looked beyond him to pastel pictures of seagulls against the pale green wall. I wanted to look out the window behind me to see what the world was up to, but that would not have been polite, so I didn't.

"Would you like to learn to play handball, Crawford?" the doctor asked. "I work out solo every day; I'd be glad to teach you."

Yes. I nodded again. The handball court is small, indoors, in the basement. I'd been there but I didn't remember exactly, because I wasn't noticing.

"Handball is a lot of fun. Really gets the kinks out of your muscles."

I wonder if anyone will ever rediscover the drug Frankel brought home from the lab one Friday afternoon. It wasn't derived from lysergic acid; I never knew its pedigree. Frankel always talked in Chemical and I don't speak that language very well. Whatever it was, there was only enough for the two of us; we dropped it early one Saturday morning.

In the middle of the afternoon or perhaps six years later I saw where God had been and why He left. I couldn't really blame Him. Frankel saw it too; it showed in his face. I liked Frankel. Using my karate training I was able to kill his body with one abrupt chop, to spare him any more of the seeing. Then I curled up on my bunk and killed Crawford's mind. That took longer, but at last I was no longer Crawford.

"We'll have to wait until tomorrow morning, though, Crawford."

"That's all right."

"And tomorrow afternoon I have a surprise for you."

I raised my eyebrows.

"Nothing to worry about. Just a little injection to correct the metabolic flaw that made you so vulnerable to breakdown under stress. When you leave here you'll never have to worry again about losing touch with the real world."

"But we can play handball in the morning?"

"Really interested, are you, Crawford? Certainly we can. My promise on it." Doctor Baumer was very meticulous about keeping promises to his patients, to gain and keep their trust. I appreciated that.

"Aren't you interested in the new injection treatment, though?"

I nodded.

He opened the combination-lock of his office refrigerator and showed me a vial of purple fluid. "I'm the only one here who uses it," he said, "but they've had fantastic results in England. Zero relapse rate. It's going to open up a whole new era in mental health."

"That's wonderful," I said. There is only one door to the handball court.

"Well, it's been a rewarding interview, Crawford." The doctor rose and extended his hand for me to shake. "I suppose you'd like to go out and take advantage of Grounds Privileges for awhile before dinner now, wouldn't you? The gardens are becoming rather lovely, aren't they?"

"Yes, I would. Yes, they are." I suppose I'd better, since he thought I should want to. We were still shaking hands but finally we stopped.

I went out into the grounds escorted by Hercules. He left me alone outdoors; that was a first. The world was still there, as I had expected. Well, I shouldn't complain; it can't help it. Certainly it didn't ask me to trip with Frankel. Actually the world fakes it pretty well, for the most part.

There was a light warm breeze; over the scent of flowers I noticed that one of the attendants was smoking dope behind a thick green hedge. I envied him. Grass is better than nothing, even though it's not enough. Even though nothing is.

Eventually I went in to dinner. I enjoyed my status as the Improved Patient, with all the smiles and encouraging hellos. I enjoyed the flavors of those foods I allowed myself to taste;

I am rather particular, of late, as to what I allow myself to experience. When I have the choice.

I enjoyed lying in my room with the door open. I thought I'd better, because it hadn't been that way for long and wouldn't be for much longer. Ajax or possibly Hercules gave me my sleepy pill and watched to see that I swallowed it. After he left I thought of what I would do in the handball court this morning. Then I escaped from the world, thankfully into sleep.

I was wrong, of course; I didn't do anything in the handball court except play a lot of very clumsy handball, because Ajax and Hercules were there, each standing in a corner pretending not to exist. Doctor Baumer pretended they weren't there, too. But of course they were; for their benefit I played handball, quite badly. Doctor Baumer said I was doing just great; I'm not the only one who lies a lot. The world is the best liar of all. It pretends to be bearable, until you catch it out. Then it won't pretend any more, at all.

At lunch I tasted a veal cutlet, because for the first time I was allowed to cut my meat for myself. I ate but did not taste the zucchini; I loathe zucchini.

After an hour or so of Grounds Privileges, Hercules or Ajax came to take me to Doctor Baumer's office. It is not small, but very crowded. That is why only Hercules or Ajax was there and not both.

I waited, smiling, until Doctor Baumer operated the combination lock and was opening the refrigerator door. Then I broke the neck of Ajax or Hercules to kill his body, and locked the office door.

"What are you doing, Crawford?" the doctor shouted. "And *why?*" I told him. Then I killed his body also.

There was the hypodermic needle and the vial of purple liquid. I injected myself with a few cc's of saline solution to mark my arm properly. Then I filled the needle from the vial, shot a dab of purple fluid onto the mark and washed the rest of it down the sink. Yes, it looked convincing. I smashed the purpled needle against the wall.

I unlocked the office door, for it was time to scream and shout, to beat my head and hands against the wall. I used no karate when Hercules or Ajax came, even though he hurt me. I said I couldn't remember anything after the injection. Ajax or Hercules frog-marched me to my room, strapped me down and gave me a sedative. As sleep pushed the world away, I thought how nice it was that none of them would be bothering me much, now.

I thought of my last words to Doctor Baumer.

"If you think you're going to stick *me* in your real world for the rest of my life, Doctor, you're the one who's crazy."

Tell Me All About Yourself

IT WAS CHARLIE'S idea. He and Vance and I were on the town celebrating our luck. It hadn't been easy, cutting close to the edges of a minor typhoon to bring the big hydrofoil freighter safely to Hong Kong on schedule. So we celebrated, high-wide-and-sideways on a mixture of drugs; none of us were users on the job but ashore was different. Some alcohol, of course, plus other things of our separate choices. I stayed with cannabis and one of the lesser mindbenders; I forget the brand name. Vance was tripping and far out; Charlie was so speeded-up that I kept expecting him to skid on the corners.

"Hey, Vance! Dale! Pop one of these, and let's go get some kicks." He was holding out some purple Sensies, which don't come cheap; sensory enhancement is worth money and the sellers know it.

"What kind of kicks, Chazz?" When Charlie gets loose, I get cautious.

"There's a Nec down this way a few blocks. You ever try that, Dale?"

"No." I'd never been to a Necro house; I wasn't sure I wanted to, either.

"Well, hell, then; come on. kid. You'll never learn any younger."

"What do you think, Vance?" I said. It was a waste of breath. Whatever Vance was thinking behind his blissful smile, he wouldn't be able, from where he was, to find words for it. He nodded, after a while. Very deliberately. Another country heard from, in shorthand.

"OK then; what say, gang?" Charlie held a pill out to Vance, then one to me, and took one himself. Vance swallowed his. I hesitated, then popped mine too. Hell, I didn't have to follow through with the rest of it if I didn't want to. But we began walking along toward the Nec, Charlie leading.

"Have you done this stuff much, Charlie? The Necs, I mean?"

"A few times, Dale."

"What's the hook? I don't get it. I mean, the broads are dead and so what?"

Charlie shrugged. "It's just different, is all. Well, OK: one time in a regular seaport fuckery, Marseilles I think, I got a deaf-mute ginch. It was—restful, sort of; you don't have to talk. Wouldn't do you any good if you did. And at the Necs it's even more like that, 'cause they don't move. And you kind of wonder about them, what they'd say if they could, and all. I dunno, Dale; you have to *be* there, I guess."

Vance said, "What they don't say is the most important." I hadn't known that Vance was a Necro; Charlie, of course, is everything that doesn't kill him. And sometimes I think he crowds *that* a little.

Before I could decide anything one way or the other, we were there. At the door and then inside. A woman greeted us; somehow I hadn't expected that. She was small, Eurasian, slim in stretch skintights. I wished it were a live house; the Sensy was taking hold and I wanted her. I missed hearing Charlie's first questions.

"We have a good selection tonight in the A rooms," she said. "I trust that you gentlemen are interested in the A category?" I knew what that meant: after certain physical changes, the category reverts to B. I've heard of places where there's a C category but I don't like to think about that.

We all nodded, even Vance. A was the category of our choice; yes.

"Then I will show you the pictures of our A list," she said. She went behind a counter like a hotel registration desk and came back with two packets of eight-by-ten color prints. Each picture showed a woman nude, supine, arms and legs spread, eyes closed. Dead; they had to be, though it wasn't obvious.

She fanned the two sets of pictures out on a heavy teakwood table. "These," pointing, "are kept at body temperature. These others are at chill, for greater service life in the A category. Personal preferences differ."

Charlie and I looked only at the warm set: Vance smiled

brightly and sorted through both. I was, I found, very taken with the picture of a small dark woman, voluptuous in a compact way. Charlie took it out of my hand.

"Hey, that's for me," he said. I was about to argue, though it's futile to argue with Charlie, when the picture was taken from him in turn.

I hadn't seen the man come in. He was tall, thin-faced and pale, wearing a light-gray suit and walking with no sound. He looked at the picture.

"So she's attracting trade already," he said.

"Mr. Holmstrom," the woman said, "I have the bank draft for you. I trust everything is satisfactory? Mrs. Holmstrom's appearance, and so forth?"

"Quite." Once again behind the counter, she found an envelope, came back and gave it to Holmstrom. He put the picture back on the table, thanked her and turned to leave.

"Just a minute," said Charlie. "This here is your wife, maybe?"

"She was."

"Sorry; sorry. But could I ask you a little something?"

"Of course. If I choose, I'll answer." Charlie blinked.

"Well, then," he said, "what I want to know is, how was she when—I mean, like *before*?"

"I doubt that you'll notice much difference," the man said, wheeling to walk out. The door closed behind him while Charlie gaped.

Somehow I lost interest in the small dark woman; I leafed through the stack of warms. "I'll still take that one," Charlie said, and paid his money. The Eurasian woman handed him a numbered key. He took his direction from her pointing finger and walked away along a corridor to the right of the counter. I didn't notice whether Vance's choice was warm or chill, but he left by a different exit. I looked at the pictures, unable to choose, unable to consent.

The woman came to stand by me. "Perhaps we have nothing to interest you, sir, in this category? Perhaps the B category?"

God, NO! I shook my head violently, shuffling frantically through the pictures. Maybe that one? No. What the hell was I doing here, anyway?"

"Perhaps something a little special, sir. More expensive, of course. But if expense is not a problem . . . a girl, young, though developed. Death by sad accident. No obvious mutilation, no cosmetic corrections necessary. And very rare in our trade, a virgin. Let me show you her picture.''

The Sensy and the mindbender were fighting in my head and body. I waited while she brought the picture, then looked at it.

Virginity had never been important to me; it doesn't show visually, anyway. But I looked at this girl in glossy color and I liked her. She was someone I'd like to know. I decided to go about that now, the best I could.

Money paid, down a hall, key into the lock of numbered door, I entered and looked at her. At first I didn't understand the strangeness.

The way the best picture ever taken differs from a person is that the person is *there*; the depiction is not. Here, looking, I saw a halfway case. The girl was more than a picture but less than a person. I didn't figure the difference immediately; it took a while to sink in.

The pale-red hair was the same, longish and curling, spread out from her head. I wouldn't disarrange it; I didn't want to touch the tubes that pumped warm preservative fluid through her to maintain body temperature.

The slim strong limbs and body looked healthy enough to get up and walk. Her skin was warm, all right—a little dry, maybe. But it was the face that drew me: features strong but delicate. And I could not understand how she, or anyone, could smile so happily after she was gone. I wanted to ask her about that. I wanted to ask her about a lot of things.

The Sensy pill wanted more from me. There are things, I knew, that help a virgin girl. Though I'd had only two such, habit set me to those preparations. Then I realized, foolishly, that no stimulus could bring response, and that the house had prepared her as well as could be done. So I entered her.

Slow and easy, slow and easy, raising my head to see her smile. I had to speak. "Do you like that? This? You're beautiful; did you know?''

The smile flexed; I don't know how or why. But with that slight movement the beauty of her caught and held me. The intensity of the pull astonished me. I tried to lose myself in sensation—the augmented delights of the Sensy pill—but I couldn't. The smile wouldn't let me. And I ceased fighting what I felt.

"Why did you never know love?'' I asked. "You should have. You were made for it. I wish I—'' I wished I'd found her before. Because I knew, now, that always I had been looking for her.

And was this to be her only love? With care, with gentleness, I sought to make it worthy.

I had to know more. "Who are you?" Only her smile replied. "What did you want? What can I give you?"

My body answered that; I gave it. Not wanting to, begrudging the final ecstasy. I had so much more to say, to ask; I didn't want to leave her. But it was done; that is the rule, alive or dead.

I kissed her smooth forehead and released her, feeling empty, as though I should be the one lying there, not her. Numbly, I busied myself with my clothing.

Up and dressed, hand on the door, I looked back. Nothing had changed; she smiled as I had first seen her. In the picture, and here.

"But you haven't told me *anything*." No, and she would not. I said, "Goodbye. I'm sorry." And closed the door behind me. Opposite from the way I had come was an "Exit" sign. I went to that door, put my hand on the knob. And couldn't bring myself to turn it.

If I left, I would never see her again. I had to go back. My mind must have known all along; I found I still had the key.

She looked the same. Still the slim strong body, the hair, the smile. So lovely, and so alone. The silence.

I looked for a long time. Then I said goodbye again and turned away. But I couldn't go. I had remembered something.

Her picture. Now it would be in the warm stack of the A category, for Charlie and Vance and everybody. And she was defenseless.

I thought of Charlie with her. Charlie's all right; I like him, mostly. But sometimes, afterward, he says things I don't like to hear. I could not bear the thought.

And Charlie's not the worst. There are men who would hurt her.

No. They weren't going to have her. No one was going to to have her. She was mine now.

Gently I disarranged her hair to expose the brown plastic tubes pumping fluid to and from the nape of her neck. The connections were self-sealing; only a few drops of colorless fluid escaped as I set the tubes aside.

A robe hung on a hook beside the door. It was bizarre; a less gaudy pattern would have better suited her. But the robe was all there was.

I robed her, limp like a passed-out drunk, and carried her out of the room, out through the exit. I left most of my money in the room; it wasn't enough, I knew, but it would help me feel less like a thief.

Overcrowded Hong Kong still has the jinrikishaw; the man said, "Lady not feel good?"

"She'll be all right," I said, and took us to my hotel. After the first couple of times I don't book a room at the same hotel with Charlie and Vance, ashore.

The night clerk said, "Lady all right?" I smiled and nodded, carrying her.

In the room I arranged her beauty. "Is that all right? Would you like anything more?" Then again I loved her, and held her close in sleep against the threat of chill.

But in the morning there was no doubt. My head had cooled and so had she. Soon she would no longer be of the A category, or even B.

I couldn't let that happen to her. I couldn't let it happen to me, the seeing of what time would do.

I walked the crowded streets of Hong Kong, thinking, wondering. The drugs had worn off but the problem hadn't. Nowhere in the city could I bury her, even if I had wanted to. Burial at sea was out; I didn't want her moldering under earth *or* water. And the house would have the police pursuing me as relentlessly as Category B pursued her.

There is a waterfront area where tourists can rent motorboats; I went there and rented one, cruising until I found a derelict wharf for moorage. Rickshaws were sparse nearby but I found one and returned to the commercial district, where I purchased a life raft and a few other things, mostly on the black market. These I took to my boat. Then I went back to the hotel.

She was so cold, but still she smiled. I respected her withdrawal; it was her right. I told her my plans. "Am I doing right? Is this what you want?" Her smile did not change. I sat a long time, stroking her hair; nothing more. In the streaked wall mirror I saw a fool. I smiled, and the fool smiled back at me.

We sat until dark. She was so quiet, never answering my questions. Then it was time to go.

The rickshaw was slow; the man lost his way several times

more, I think, than his usual quota for tourists. But eventually we got to my rented boat, she and I.

Out into the water, out into the dark. Out into the middle of the bay where no one could interfere. I inflated the life raft and put it over the side. Then it was time to take her robe from her and spread it in the raft. At last, with the swells of the bay hampering me, I put her on the robe in the best beauty I could manage. Then I arranged the other things around her, that she needed, before I moved the boat away and threw the torch.

The first blaze showed her smile unchanged. Her hair vanished in a glorious crown of flame. I wanted, needed to look away, but I couldn't. I saw her smile widen into a look of ecstasy before a curtain of fire concealed everything. I'm so grateful that it did. Then the thermite went, that I'd placed around her. A searing blast of heat, a cloud of steam, and she and the raft were gone.

I took the boat back where it belonged.

Next day, back at the ship, Charlie talked a lot about his Nec piece. It sounded more like the B category but I didn't say so. Vance didn't say much; he just grinned. I think he was still up, though with Vance it's hard to tell for sure. He does his job.

I couldn't talk about it. Not to Charlie, not even to Vance. It's hard to think about.

I wanted so much for her to answer me, and she wouldn't.

Once Upon a Unicorn

SEVENTEEN YEARS OLD and washed up. I still can't believe it. It's a bitch, that's what; a bull bitch on wheels.

Rillo used to tell me, "Don't talk so rough. You'll ruin your God-damned image." He's washed up too; the hell with him. It wasn't all my fault.

That's right: Rillo Furillo, my husband the star. You know him, all right, with his big beautiful bod and male-chauvinist-pig smile. What you don't know is, he's playing with a thirty-eight-card deck.

You know me, too—sweet little Wendine Thorise, veteran Child Star, with the big blue eyes and long blonde hair down to keep your hands to yourself. Sweet sixteen and never been kissed. Well, there has to be *some* place I'd never been kissed; the tonsils maybe? Though some have tried.

Last fall we'd just wrapped up the third made-for-TV movie starring sweet little me. I was in big. I was also in bed with Arnie Karaznek, being produced just like his movies, with pauses for commercials. About when you'd expect, the phone rang. I said, "Oh, balls!" for what that was worth; he answered it anyway.

"Hello? Oh; Phil. Yeh, yeh, go ahead. I'm not busy."

"You're sure not, you bastard. Phil who?"

"Shut up, Not you, Phil. Phil Sparger, you dumbdumb. No, not you, Phil! Dammit Wendine, shut up or I'll belt you one. Forget you heard that, Phil. OK?"

"All right, Phil, what is it? . . . No. Oh God, no! In the showers? at a *Junior* High School? All right, Phil; all right. Now here's what you do . . ."

That's when I quit listening, because Arnie was always

good for maybe an hour on "now here's what you do." I
wiggled the rest of the way loose and went to the toity and
read Cleveland Amory in *TV Guide* some more. I was pretty
sure he liked my series "The Wendings of Wendine," but
he's sneaky.

I was into my third reading when Arnie banged at the door.
"Come on out of there, willya? You'll wear out the batteries
in that vibrator." Dumb Arnie. The batteries were already
dead from the last time he'd answered the phone in the
middle. But I came out, anyway.

"I don't have to ask about *your* batteries, though; do I,
Arnie? Already plugged back into the studio, solid. I wish to
hell you'd just once . . ."

"Come on, can it, Wendine. This is serious."

"Yeh? So am I. Oh well, go ahead; who blew it this
time?"

"Rillo. Only thank God he didn't, really. They just thought
he would."

I didn't say anything; what was there to say about Rillo? I
poured myself a short shot and lit a smoke, waiting for Arnie
to get it off his mind. Maybe there was hope yet.

"I told Phil how to fix it this time, but we've got to do
something permanent about Rillo's problem. I think I've got
it figured. I can count on you, now, can't I, Wendine?"

I didn't like it already but I had to ask. "Such as for
what?"

"It's the romance of the century!"

"What is?" I knew all right but I had to hear it to believe
it.

"You and Rillo. What did you think?"

I threw the shot glass but Arnie ducks better than I throw.
All I broke was one of his dumb ceramics over the fireplace.
It was better than nothing.

"I am not marrying any goddamned queer!"

"Look, chickie; Rillo isn't queer. He's just curious, is
all."

"*Damn* curious. The answer is still go shove it, Arnie."

It was a beautiful wedding in all the magazines. I cannot
convey, I really can't, the depth of my girlish emotions when
Rillo and I were at last alone with our great love, I said for
publication. There we were, all right, he with his great bod,

his manly smile, his limpid eyes and passionate voice. I was there too, sort of.

We really were a top news sensation; for three straight months I didn't see Jackie on a magazine cover. The climax, if you'll pardon the expression, came when Rillo and I made our movie together—a real live honest not-for-TV movie, with no commercials.

We made it damn fast, as a matter of fact, because I was expecting what they still call a blessed event in spite of population pollution. It had to be Arnie; the timing was wrong for that cute cameraman. Probably the week Arnie's phone was out of order. So in a way it was lucky Rillo and I got married when we did.

It's too bad that the movie is down the flush now. It was a horn of corn but kind of cute, a fantasy fairytale thing. Semi-adult Disney. Actually it was all Arnie's boss's idea, including keeping the whole production under wraps until he could spring the story on TV for crash effect.

Arnie Karaznek's boss goes by his initials, only, ever since he read a Harold Robbins book. The initials sound a little suggestive but he doesn't seem to mind. Would you believe Franklin Ulysses? Anyway, old F.U. ran into a scientific thing in the papers, and halfway understood it for once.

I'm not stupid, you know; just dumb. I catch a lot that goes on; sometimes I don't use it right, is all. I'll bet I understood as much as Arnie's boss did, about how some zoo groups were breeding present-type animals back to earlier forms that went extinct. Like you could take a cage of lizards and go for dinosaurs. Well, maybe not quite that—but West Berlin does have a corral full of Stone Age supercows. Aurochs, they call them.

Arnie's boss read where somebody in Africa had bred back to unicorns. You've heard of unicorns; there weren't any, really—not one-horned horses, anyway. There isn't any such thing as a one-horned animal: rhinoceroses have a mustache with a permanent hard-on and narwhals are freak porpoises with one long tooth each. I remember that from high school before I dropped out, to put the best face on that change in my life-style. But it seems there used to be an antelope with its horns twisted together so tight in front that it looked like one horn. And this African outfit had bred antelopes back to that model.

Arnie's boss wanted to cash in, some way. The movie was

called "The Lure of the Unicorn." Old F.U. paid a real bundle to get us an antelope in a hurry.

Too bad it won't go, now. The antelope was dumb and had a face like a camel's understudy, but it was *nice*-dumb, even if it didn't learn tricks too well. Gee, when I saw on the screen, the shot where it came and laid its head in my lap, I forgot about the lump of sugar it was really after, and cried all over hell. For a minute there, I almost thought that unicorn was right.

We got all the film in the can before I began to show much. Rillo and I did a good job, we thought; so did Arnie and even Franklin Ulysses. I figured we had it all on ice. Then F.U. got another one of his great ideas.

"A TV show, a Special, *live*! That's how we'll flack this flick," he said. "How can it miss?" By this time I was getting a little big in the gut, but everyone said it wouldn't matter.

"The added touch of your pregnancy will make the situation all that much more piquant," Arnie said at a P.R. meeting. Arnie has a lot of tact, around P.R. people. Without them he'd have said "Just do like I say, you dumb broad!" I wish to hell the kid were going to be the cameraman's.

At first reading the TV script didn't look too bad. After the taped lead-in somebody would lay the unicorn legend onto Mr. Nielsen's sheep, heavy on the whipped-cream. Rillo was supposed to do that bit but he was having a little problem with uppers and downers—nothing really serious. So Milan Banfield, the second lead, had to take it.

Then Rillo and I would do the part of our big scene where the unicorn did its trick. All I had to do was sit still and mug right, and all Rillo had to do was sit alongside me and not twitch too much while we spoke our lines. No big problem.

One thing bothered me. "Look, Arnie," I said one time, "Everybody knows I'm married; right? And some of the magazines are spilling it that I'm knocked-up, now. So we do this thing. What kind of klutz is going to believe that this freak antelope knows what the hell it's doing?"

"The kind of klutz that watches this kind of TV show and buys tickets for this kind of movie." I couldn't argue; sometimes Arnie does know his business.

So we went out and did it. It was pretty for the camera, sunshine on sparkling dew. The wet grass was freezing my butt. I kept smiling, though; it couldn't last forever. Rillo's smile must be a silicone-implant, I thought; I'd never seen anything shake it.

When it came our turn to help sell tickets, Rillo and I started through our lines; it all seemed to be working OK, until the camera was ready for the unicorn. It was too far back, out of the shot; somebody had blown the timing. I can ad-lib; I threw in a few lines to keep things moving. Rillo can't; half the time I had to answer myself.

Someone finally shoved the unicorn on-camera. About time. And then it all went absolutely to hell in a bucket.

The damn beast cut me dead. Up front of about ten million people who had just had the unicorn story laid on them with a double scoop, that goddamned creature ambled up, sniffed, and laid its head in *Rillo's* lap.

I guess even a freak antelope has to be right once in a while.

Road Map

HE WOKE, HUNGRY. The waking was sudden, not like his usual gradual drift to consciousness; he was fully alert. He opened his eyes and saw blurred masses of bright color—he couldn't bring them into sharp focus. He tried to bring his hands up to rub the sleep away. He couldn't do it; he felt the texture of cloth under his hands and vaguely saw them move, but something was wrong with his control, his coordination.

For a moment he was close to panic. Then he thought, Whatever it is, it doesn't hurt—and I can feel and move; there's no paralysis or numbness. Searching for an explanation, he wondered if he'd had some sort of surgery, and was suffering aftereffects from the anesthetic.

He couldn't recall planning or needing any operation, but temporary amnesia might be another side-effect. The thought encouraged him—rather, the realization that his mind was working well enough to think of it. Deliberately, he began to test his memory of the basic facts about himself: name, age, marital status, state of health—the lot.

Ralph Ascione, age fifty-eight, two years a widower—he paused to weather one of his still-frequent bursts of missing Elizabeth, and caught it short of seeing her death again. Health good, so long as he took care of his heart. Thought of that organ also gave him pause, but he decided his symptoms were nothing like those of his one serious attack. The mental recitation continued; the facts were all there: height, weight, home address, date of his son's imminent wedding, and all the numbers that specified the life of Ralph Ascione. His memories were sharply defined and readily accessible. The only thing that eluded him was any explanation of his condition.

What more could he learn of it? He listened, but heard only vague sounds that told him nothing. His mutinous hands brushed nothing but cloth. His tongue touched bare gums; where were his dentures? The air smelled of hospital; that part of his guess was probably right.

He squinted and tried to focus his eyes. If he were seeing at all correctly, his bed was a cage, at least five or six feet high—but open at the top. He considered the possibility of insanity but rejected it; the discrepancies that disturbed him were physical. And he didn't *feel* sick. . . .

Below his middle was warm wetness; whatever his ailment, it included incontinence. He felt depression; maybe his state was worse than he had thought.

A new sound came; in the blurred distances, something moved. Vaguely seen, a huge face looked over him and made soft, deep clucking noises. Then he understood.

Reincarnation, by God! They'd always said you don't remember; well, somebody was wrong. Either he was the exception—some kind of fluke—or else all babies remembered at first and lost the recall later. He didn't want to lose his. He ran a few facts through his mind again; no, they weren't fading. . . .

He was surprised at the way he absorbed the shock so easily. Before he could flinch at the loss of his lifelong identity, something inside him grasped eagerly at the prospect—a whole new lifetime:!

But his thoughts rioted in confusion, so that he hardly noticed the way his mouth sucked instinctively at the bottle or the warmth and gentleness with which his bottom was washed, dried and rewrapped. The cuddling and petting calmed him; first his body relaxed, then his taut awareness. He could think again.

The question of age puzzled him. Remembering his son's earliest days, he was almost certain he was at least a week past the newborn state. Perhaps, he theorized, consciousness could not emerge until the effects of birth trauma subsided. It didn't matter, but still he wondered. He'd like to know his birthday, he thought, and the year.

The year! He'd always been curious about the future, wanting to live to see as much of it as he could. Well, sooner or later he'd learn what part of it was now his lot.

The nurse talked to him and made crooning sounds, but at

first he couldn't force his ears and brain to shape the sounds into intelligible words. Then slowly, like becoming accustomed to a thick dialect or accent, he began to understand. And then he received his second shock.

"Sweet baby," said the nurse. "Oh, she's a sweet, sweet baby!"

His mind froze, his self-image fighting to keep its place as the nurse returned him to the crib and left the room. He recognized what was happening within him, he dove deep and found the concept of himself as a person first and everything else second, and the struggle eased. Well, came the thought, that's fair. See how the other half lives.

He could not think of himself as a she; he sought but could not find any feeling of *she*ness. His bodily sensations were too diffuse to tell him anything; from the internal feelings at his crotch he could have been male, female, hermaphrodite or completely sexless. His hands were no help; even if he could have controlled them, he was too well swaddled.

Intellectually there was no need to confirm the nurse's words; surely she knew and said the truth. And certainly it hardly mattered at the moment, and wouldn't, in a sense, for some years to come. But inside him was something that clung stubbornly to the concept of maleness and refused, without proof, to give it up. Inside him, against his will, raged conflict.

He'd have to wait and see, he decided. Either his inner attitudes would shift naturally, guided by glandular balance, or he'd have to work at adjusting to the new, the totally unexpected situation. He was pleased to find that he was not consciously resisting the inevitable; he had no desire to begin his new life with a built-in basis for neurosis.

Sensation brought his self-congratulation to a halt. He had wet himself again, and more than that. Without conscious intent, he began to cry, loudly. The noise he made was out of proportion to the mild protest he felt; he wanted to laugh at the incongruity. But what the hell, he thought; it's the only game in town. And eventually the nurse came and changed him again. He concentrated on the way it felt to be laved and patted dry, and was fairly certain that the warm washcloth encountered no protrusions. The nurse had not lied to him.

*   *   *

What would it be like, then? He thought of the women he knew well, of what he understood them to be like. He wondered if he understood them at all, or they him.

Elizabeth understood him, of course, sometimes better than he knew himself, and from the start—their agreement to marry came quickly and with few words. Elizabeth Wilson was so young as to need parental consent for marriage, but she was free of the gaucheries he expected from such youth. She seemed so much a part of him that when, rarely, she became truly angry in a disagreement, he acceded to her wishes almost automatically, out of sheer surprise. One time: "No! We will not take the morning flight. I can't be ready until afternoon." When the morning flight crashed without them, half-joking he accused her of precognition. "If I could see the future, Ralph, I wouldn't have led clubs into dummy last night, and cost us the rubber."

A part of him, and he a part of her. No wonder he missed her so much.

He thought of his mother, widowed when he was twelve—of how her warm love became overly protective for a time. ". . . wear your galoshes; it might snow . . . shouldn't you wear a sweater under that light jacket? . . . I'm not trying to choose your friends, but there's a lot of talk about that girl . . . Of course you can live on campus if you wish, but I'd feel much better if you stayed here and drove to classes . . ." Her touch on the reins was light but ever-present. Then one day, after much thought over a long period, he told her it was time he began making his own mistakes—the storm was less than he had feared, and afterward they could be friends. But as a woman, he realized, he knew very little of her.

His sister Cheryl? Happy child, then spiteful brat and runaway hellion. With Cheryl, the breakaway drew blood, and the later reunion was equally painful. Then, her life stabilized, she was a good friend to him and Elizabeth.

He could put little importance to the other women who crossed his life. No great loves, and after adolescence, no great hurts.

His thumb found its way to his mouth; the sucking pads in his cheeks worked diligently, but nothing came to swallowing but his own saliva. The crying reflex blurred his thought; he held it back for a moment, thinking: Elizabeth is really all I know of women.

He visualized her; the picture in his mind changed from

scene to scene, from time to time. And then, crashing through the defenses he'd neglected, came the bloody, mangled thing that had died in his arms.

It was good to cry, mindlessly, for nothing more than nourishment; he purged himself as he fed, and then slept.

Time was strangely extended; his experienced mind knew he'd begun consciousness only a few days ago, but his body emotions insisted the period was much longer.

He still found it difficult to accept the reality of his tiny female body; its size was also a dual, contradictory thing to him. And perhaps, he thought, when I can make my mouth and tongue say words, I can get the feedback to become "she." Meanwhile, he waited and learned, and wondered.

His vision improved, and the movements of arms and legs. He could see and sometimes touch the plastic toys that hung close to his face, and make them rattle. Once he stuck a thumb in his eye. It hurt, but the motion had been slight and random, and did no damage. Usually he could bring thumb's comfort to mouth at first or second attempt.

Governed by his body's needs, he slept much of the time.

Bowels and bladder were a minor outrage, out of his control. They voided, and his will had no effect. The boy began to handle it in about a year, he thought. Without much prodding. I wonder how old I am.

He thought more about his son Carl, regretting that he hadn't lived to see the boy remarried. But perhaps Carl was still alive at the start of this new life, and someday he could see him again. What a strange meeting that would be! And what a thing it was, to have fathered a genius. As a child, his son seemed to learn by instinct. Later he had no need of adolescent rebellion; he was always amenable but never subservient. Quite a boy, and quite a man . . .

Thought of fatherhood gave way to pangs of hunger. He cried and was answered.

He was fed by breast as well as by bottle. Bottle was more efficient but breast comforted him warmly; instinct did not always make him sleep after bottle. He wondered who his mother might be, and where he was, and when; he liked the blurred glimpses he'd had, of her smile. He was fairly certain that he was in the United States and near his own time; the language hadn't changed, the little he'd heard of it. And he knew he was Caucasian and of a relatively affluent family,

for he could see his skin and knew the cost of private accom-
modations. And where, he wondered, was his own father?

Nothing was said in his hearing to answer the questions
that still plagued him. Very well, he would wait. In him,
content and patience grew, but not at the expense of memory
or purpose.

One day, feeding at breast, he heard a new male voice.
"Hello, dear, I couldn't get back any sooner. You're all
right, I see?"

"Oh, yes!" He heard the sounds as much through his
mother's chest, one ear close to it, as through the air. He
strained to hear what was said, but sleep was upon him, and a
thought: That's my father; I wonder what he looks like.

He woke, being lifted and laid into a smaller resting place.
Then he was jounced in walking-rhythm, felt cold air on his
face—then he was set down. Doors closed, ear-hurting; he
was in a confined space of dead air. Noise came, and bad
smells, a pattern of harsh movement. His memory knew the
bounce of city streets and the stench of vehicle exhausts. His
young body knew only fright and discomfort.

Lifted again at the end of it, his place-of-lying moved and
swung in strides—more cold air, and then warm—until it was
again set to rest. The light was dim, but he could see, leaning
over him, the faces that were now his mother and father. His
memory prickled but did not speak.

"Well, now," said the father-face. "Welcome to our home,
Betsy Wilson."

Unease tugged at his gut; he strained to see more closely.
The faces were so big to him, and strange. Both were smiling; suddenly an old picture superimposed on what he saw
. . . and then he knew.

He was not in the future; he was more than fifty years deep
into his own past. These were Elizabeth's parents. He was
Betsy Wilson, who one day would become Elizabeth Ascione.

He thought—when he could think again—no wonder she
knew me so well!

If only I can remember as well as she had.

But of course she would, for she was herself; there had
never been any other. Ralph was the earlier segment of her
conscious life and she the later—though the two ran, had run,
would run, parallel through the years he had lived and she

was now to have. And with knowledge of her personal identity came acceptance of her sex.

What will it be like, she wondered, to meet him—see him—and *know*? He had never known; there had been no hint. What if she told him? She hadn't; could she? Probably not; he wouldn't believe it. Only after her death had his hardheaded materialistic view of the universe began to broaden.

Her death! She had forgotten that there are drawbacks to living in known time. The freeway horror that lay two years back in her memory also waited for her, fifty-two years ahead. Oh, God! If only I hadn't outlived myself. Then I wouldn't know. I wouldn't know . . .

But was the future predetermined in such detail? Did it run on tracks, or could it be changed? She had to find out. She had no way to do it now, and wouldn't for years; she simply didn't know enough details of her early life. Oh, a few things, from mutual reminiscences, but nothing she could think to use as a test. For the present she could only wait and think, and learn.

The fierce vitality of her young body would not allow depression to hold her for long. Time enough later, she thought, to try to rattle the bars of time, and evade or accept a death more than half a century away.

Then she realized—it would be her second death in that remote decade. And she couldn't even remember Ralph's. . . .

"Look, dear," said her mother. "I think she's trying to laugh."

Learning and achieving seemed slow to her, but instinct combined with mature knowledge and purpose to make her development precocious; her parents occasionally remarked on it.

First she needed to communicate. Not by speech—that was months away, and she shouldn't introduce it too soon, for fear of being considered a freak or prodigy. She used crying and movement; deliberately she cultivated different tones and cadences to ask for food, to be changed, to be held and cuddled. For the latter she also worked to make her arms reach out when her mother or father came near. She found that snuggling *was* essential to well-being—the psychologists were right—the contact, the warmth, the rocking and soft-voiced crooning had a definite physical effect, and for best vitality she needed it. Luckily, her mother seemed to feel the complementary need, and satisfied it often.

The infant Elizabeth grew, became a toddler. Overt sexual development was years ahead, but she began to notice that it *felt* differently, to be a girl. She couldn't remember male infancy; those recalls were buried nearly six decades deep. But being Elizabeth did not feel the same as being Ralph. She had no words to describe the difference, and she knew why; words derive from shared experience. She decided the distinction was something like that of being right- or left-handed: no "better" or "worse," but merely two states of being.

When the time came for speech, she was ready; she practiced, when she was alone, to train her tongue and lips. She knew better than to go too fast or use adult vocabulary, but she would not stoop to babytalk. Her camouflage was not perfect; occasionally she caught puzzled looks on her parents' faces.

And once her father said, "I know what it is, honey. Betsy always has just the right word. She seldom makes mistakes." After that she took pains to err more often. But not too often; she had her pride.

The one thing she did hurry, camouflage or no camouflage, was toilet training.

Early along, she worried about the problem of adapting fifty-eight years of male experience and habit to a pattern of acceptable female behavior. The worry was waste; she found as she came to walk and speak that her parents gave a constant flow of clues, with and without words, to what was expected of her. The less she relied on deliberate thought, the more she relaxed and responded naturally to them, the easier she found it to be a convincing Elizabeth. Yet she did not lose herself in the role; her memories were intact, with their commentaries on the ways of her life.

Now, she thought, I see what Women's Lib was complaining about. Role-training? Every minute, and in ways they don't even realize, consciously. But she herself had no complaint; the role was necessary to the years and the life she would have. And so far as she knew, Ralph hadn't tried to press her into any mold. She'd had many activities, anything she said she wanted, outside the homemaker's sphere. Of course it might look different from this side, when the time came. Wait and see.

Ralph had not much enjoyed the jungle-law years of small-boyhood; Elizabeth was glad to be spared a rerun of the experience. She found the world of small girls utterly new: sometimes delightful, sometimes appalling, but generally fascinating. Staying in character became more difficult; slips of knowledge that her parents would not notice were grossly apparent against the bright clear light of misinformation firmly shared by her playmates. When in doubt or in no doubt at all, she learned to stay out of the line of fire. As when Sharon-down-the-block, three years older, explained the facts of life to Betsy and a group of her agemates . . .

"You get married and the minister does something, and a baby comes out your bellybutton."

"Right in church?" "I bet it hurts a lot." "*Does* it hurt, Sharon?"

"I dunno," said Sharon. "Kathy didn't say. But anyway, we don't *have* to."

Maybe you don't, thought Elizabeth. But I think I do. . . .

Except for occasional rediscovery of something long forgotten in the times she was reliving, school became a dull and boring ache. The prison of childhood stretched ahead, interminably. She had forgotten the way childhood's thought and speech can remain the same for so very long. Sitting through hours of repetition, varied only by the wrong answers that led to still more repetition, she longed to come to grips with a future she could put to test.

She had put in abeyance her need to try the future, to attempt to change it; she'd kept busy learning and practicing her role. Now she looked for a checkpoint of some kind, for a handle she could turn. Occasionally she tried to do something she was fairly certain Ralph's wife could not have done as a child, but the results were never conclusive. There seemed to be an inertia, along with her own trained wish and habit, that kept her from doing anything that might make her seem unusual, or shock or hurt her parents. So when she was ten, she watched thirteen-year-old Sharon pass for twenty-one and acquire a small arm-tattoo in the carnival tent, the drunken man's hand so steady, as his mouth was not. But she could not bring herself to follow suit, even if the man had allowed it.

Impatiently, she awaited the onset of adolescence; she was in no hurry for sexual development as such, but she felt prisoner of the static ways of childish glands, in herself and in her associates. The world of little girls had lost its charm for her; changes in minds and personalities would be welcome. She knew how banal the teenage mind could be, but at least it would be a different banality, and could interest her for a time.

Still, menarche at eleven caught her unprepared; signs at chest and pubis had not seemed so far advanced. But one day at school her skirt was wet where she sat. Her role-playing body panicked. Drawing upon earlier knowledge, she excused herself and walked home. Well, it was time for that talk, the one her mother had begun several times but never completed. She entered her home.

"Mother?"

"Yes, Betsy." Elizabeth, like all her friends, changed her nicknames frequently; nonetheless, her mother always called her Betsy. "I'm in the kitchen here."

Sitting on a high stool, Mrs. Wilson peeled potatoes at the kitchen sink. She weighed more than she had earlier or would a few years later, more than her daughter would ever weigh. Her hair, bleached lighter than the brown of Elizabeth's, was piled in a loose upsweep that drooped alarmingly on the left side. "Yes, dear?" she said.

"I've started, Mother." Elizabeth turned to show her stained skirt. "I'll rinse it with cold water. But you'd better show me how those things work, the ones you use."

She knew her mother would cry and embrace her, and she did. Then, the skirt rinsed and the flow controlled, the two women sat in the kitchen, the older with coffee and the younger, bathrobed, sipping milk.

"Betsy, I've never got around to tell you much. I should have, but . . . well, what do you know already? I mean . . ."

From sounds heard clearly, late at night, Elizabeth knew her mother enjoyed sex well enough; she simply couldn't talk about it. The problem was, how to make things easy.

"I know how not to get in trouble like Sheila across the street last year. I mean, I know what it is they do." No point in discussing the ovulation cycle—she wasn't sure her mother knew how it worked. And contraceptives? Forget it.

"That's good," said her mother. "I'm so glad we had this nice talk, Betsy." Another embrace; Mrs. Wilson wiped her eyes.

"Yes, Mother. So am I." She went to her room; it was time for homework.

Her mother wasn't stupid, she thought, nor ignorant. She was merely a product of her times. Elizabeth opened her notebook, then closed it, lost in thought. . . .

Unless she had lied to Ralph, she came to him virgin. And she wouldn't have to lie; she knew him too well. So what if—was this her chance to test her future?

She thought about it. There was no hurry; she would wait for her body to ready itself more fully. There was still nearly half a decade, before Ralph.

She had chances to do things she *hadn't* done—*knew* she hadn't done—but she didn't, somehow. Once she watched Sharon and two other girls, giggling over a newspaper picture of a fashion model, cut each other's hair into an imitation of the scalplock worn by the girl in the picture—but she went away with her own hair intact. The three were suspended from school and pictured in the local press, but not she. Now why, she thought, didn't I? It would have been harmless enough. . . .

At fourteen, crushed under sixteen-year-old Ricky Charlton in the back seat of his car, she wished she'd chosen an easier way. "Please, Beth!" In the heat, sweat trickled down her sides. She'd guessed Ricky to be a good choice for her gambit, but his hand on her labia was clumsy and downright painful. She'd have to be the one to make sure the condom was worn properly; Ralph had used them, sometimes.

And from Ralph's experience she knew she couldn't acquiesce too soon; Ricky had to believe he alone had won, could have won the goal. That was the way boys thought, at his age in this time. She had her reputation to think of, at school.

Too soon or not, neither of them could take much more of this. Silently she consented, and helped him fit the necessary appliance. Against his heedless urgency, she tried to arrange them both for better comfort.

Alongside the car, a series of explosions; someone had thrown a string of firecrackers. When it was done, she waited, "Ricky?"

"I don't know—it won't—it's your fault! Why did you make me *wait?*"

Oh, the hell with it.

*   *   *

She met Ralph when she was sixteen, he was twenty. As the time neared she thought of those days, over fifty years past on the one hand and rapidly approaching on the other. At times she found herself remembering scenes between them from her own viewpoint; the phenomenon worried her—was she losing her firsthand memory of Ralph's lifetime? Then she realized that her mind was composing the events from a mixture of memory, empathy and extrapolation. As well as anticipation . . .

Tom Gilchrist, a stocky goodhumored boy of her own age, escorted her to the "social" at the neighborhood dance hall. It was their third date—and, as she recalled, their last; their friendship was only lightly tinged with romance. At the entrance they paid admission—Dutch treat—and were given nametags.

They danced, talked, sipped sweet insipid punch. Constantly she looked to find Ralph Ascione; if she could remember where in the large hall she first met him, she would find the spot and stay there. And when she saw him she did not recognize him.

She saw the nametag, yes. But he so young, ears leaping out from the thin face, hair cut and slicked in a fashion she'd long forgotten seeing above that face, was almost a total stranger.

How had it gone, before? Seeing the person she had been, she could not remember. How old? Twenty? But he was turning away, she had to make her move.

"I think I know him, Tom." Pointing. "I should say hello."

Young Gilchrist obliged; he touched Ralph's shoulder, turned him and brought him to her, and read the nametag as he saw it. "Ralph Askeony."

"No," she said, "it's Ash-*own*." Yes, she thought, that's exactly what she said to me.

Ralph smiled as he took her hand. "How did you know that?"

Constantly, within the limitations of her school and his work, they were together. To be with my earlier self, she thought—and I know, and he doesn't. I wish I could tell him; that would break the pattern, that ends with me lying in my blood as a baby lies in its wet—only, so much more of it. . . .

But he couldn't possibly believe; I know. And there will be other ways. There is time; my world can't outwit me forever.

And one day he will know. This day, when he is me. But that is *now*. No, it's all too complex. . . .

She gave herself to the situation and found it charming, trying to recall events from his viewpoint so long-ago to her, watching his reaction from outside him and remembering what he felt, seeing her as she was now. She knew her own beauty both from inside and outside.

The years between dimmed but never vanished. As before, she was not certain as to how the decision of marriage was reached so quickly. Her parents were startled, but agreed with surprising readiness.

Had ever such a marriage been? She knew him, and as if in reflection he seemed to know her as well. She had indeed come virgin to him, but from his period of their life she drew comparisons that confirmed the joy she found in their sex together.

She could share his hobbies—spelunking, rockhounding, ham radio—she knew them from his life. And the companionship, the talking—I talk to myself, she thought—yes, but I love that self and its answers.

She found she had to be careful not to answer questions before he asked them. It was not that her memories over fifty-plus years were so detailed, but that empathy built upon her recalls, almost to a semblance of precognition.

Absorbed in her present, she forgot to expect pregnancy. And she realized that since meeting Ralph she'd also forgotten to look for ways to test the shape of the future. How many chances she'd wasted, she couldn't know. Well, there was time enough yet, and now was no time to take risks with a small life for the later sake of her own. No, not now.

Tiny events, she thought, are less certain. What if I have conceived a daughter? Then—God, no! I can't give up Carl. We both loved him so much.

That night and several more, her sleep was troubled.

Pregnancy was more difficult than she expected, but she didn't complain. One day she realized that her reticence, seen by Ralph as sign that all was well with her, had misled her into expecting an easier time. She could almost laugh, but came to dread the birth itself.

It was neither as easy as she hoped nor as bad as she feared. At the last moment she was put under by the anesthetist; she could not recall clearly the moment she saw the baby and felt it laid onto her collapsed belly. Relaxed, still to a great extent under the effects of the drug, she heard Ralph's congratulations and reassurances from a far distance. There was something . . . why couldn't she remember?

She had complications, dangerous and painful. The sedatives did not allow her mind to clear. Dazed, she came partially awake at intervals, to be allowed to cuddle her baby. Was it Carl? She could not summon energy to ask.

One day she awoke almost fully, knowing, somehow, that now she would live. The baby was brought to her. "You can nurse the little one now, Mrs. Ascione." What a sweet ache it was!

Then the baby lay at her side, her arm around it and its hand tightly gripping her finger, then relaxing, rhythmically. No, not quite rhythmically. In fact, not rhythmically at all.

Squeeze, squeeze. *Squeeeeze, squeeeeze, squeeeeze. Squeeeeze.* Pause. *Squeeeeze*, squeeze, squeeze. Squeeze, squeeze. Squeeze. Pause. . . .

Something . . . old memories surfaced. Squeeze, *squeeeeze*. Dot-dash. Morse code! The sedatives had given her strange thoughts before this. . . .

The patterns resonated with Ralph's memories. Letters, words, came to her.

. . . not die . . . freeway . . . more years . . . I know . . . as you will . . . hello myself . . .

Elizabeth hugged herself to her, still wondering if it were daughter or son she held.

But either way, she thought, I know where I'm going.

If This is Winnetka,
You Must Be Judy

THE CEILING WAS the wrong color—gray-green, not beige. Alert, well-rested but still unmoving after sleep, Larry Garth thought: It could be the Boston apartment, or possibly the one in Winnetka—or, of course, someplace new. Throwing off the covers and rolling over, he put his feet over the side of the bed and sat up. His back did not protest; cancel Boston.

The walls were gray-green also, the furniture stained walnut. Yes, Winnetka. As a final check before going into the bathroom, he raised the window shade and looked out. It had been a long time, but he recognized the details. Winnetka for sure, and he was thirty-five or thirty-six; there were only about two years of Winnetka. One question of importance remained: Judy, or Darlene?

The bathroom mirror agreed with him; he was at the time of the small mustache; he'd seen the thing in pictures. He didn't like it much, but spared it when he shaved; it was bad policy, at beginnings, to introduce unnecessary change.

He went back to the bedroom and got his cigarettes and lighter from the bedside stand, hearing pans rattle in the kitchen. Judy, or Darlene? Either way, he'd better get out there soon. As soon as he checked his wallet—first things first.

He lit a cigarette and leafed through the cards and minutiae that constituted his identity in the outside world. Well . . . knowing himself, his driver's permit would be up-to-date and all credit cards unexpired. The year was 1970. Another look outside: autumn. So he was thirty-five, and the pans clattered at the hands of Judy.

Just as well, he thought. He hadn't had the breakup with Darlene, but he knew it was, had to be, hectic and bitter.

He'd have to have it sometime, but "sufficient unto the day
. . ." Now, his wedding with Judy was only days or weeks
distant—but he didn't know which way. The trees across the
street were no help; he couldn't remember when the leaves
turned color here, or began to fall. Well, he'd listen; she'd let
him know . . .

In a plastic cover he found an unfamiliar card, with a key
taped to one side. He drew it out; the other side was more than
half-filled with his own small neat printing, mostly numbers.
The first line read: "1935–54, small misc. See chart. 8/75–3/76.
2/62–9/63. 10/56–12/56." There was much more: wonder
rose in him. And then excitement, for suddenly the numbers
made sense. Months and years—he was looking at a listing of
the times of his life, in the order he had lived them. And
would live them, for the list went far past his own experience.
"9/70– 1/70" caught his eye—that was *now*, so he wasn't
married to Judy yet, but would be before his time ended. And
the crudely dated record listed six more life-segments between this one he was beginning and the one that had ended
yesterday! He scanned it, scowling with concentration. Automatically he took a ball-point from the stand and completed
the final entry, so that it read: "12/68–9/70."

He'd never kept records before, except in his head. But it
was a good idea; now that his later self had thought of it, he'd
continue it. No, he'd *begin* it. He laughed, and then he didn't
laugh. He'd begin it because he'd found it; when and how
was the actual beginning? He grappled with the idea of
circular causation, then shrugged and accepted what he couldn't
fully understand—like it or not, it was there. He looked again
at the card, at the signposts on his zigzag trail.

A short time, this one, ending a few days after the wedding. Then about seven months of being twenty and back in
college; probably it would be when he found the sense to
quit that farcical situation, in which he knew more of many
things than his instructors did, but very little of what his
exams would cover. He looked forward to seeing his parents
again, not only alive but in good health. They'd nag him for
quitting school, but he could jolly them out of that.

And next—no, he'd look at it again later; Judy would be
getting impatient. A quick look at the other side. Below the
key was printed *First Mutual Savings* and the bank's address.
The key was numbered: 1028. So there was more information
in a safety-deposit box. He'd look at it, first chance he got.

He put on a robe and slippers; the last time with Judy, in 1972–73, her freedom from the nudity taboo was still new and strange to her. Shuffling along the hall toward breakfast, he wondered how the record he'd just seen was lost, wiped out, between now and that time. Did he later, in some time between, change his mind—decide the knowledge was more harm than help? He came to the kitchen and to Judy, with whom he'd lived twice as husband, but never met.

"Morning, honey." He moved to kiss her. The kiss was brief; she stepped back.

"Your eggs are getting cold. I put them on when I heard the water stop running. There's a cover on them, but still . . . what took you so long, Larry?"

"It took awhile to think myself awake, I guess." Looking at her, he ate with little heed to temperature or flavor. She hadn't changed much, going the other way. Red-gold hair was pinned up loosely into a swaying, curly mass instead of hanging straight, and of course she was bundled in a bulky robe rather than moving lithely unencumbered. But she had the same face, the same ways, so different from his first time with her. That was in the late, quarreling stages, five years away, when she drank heavily and was fat, and divorce was not far off. He did not know what went so wrong in so short a time between. Now at the start, or close to it, he wished he could somehow rescue the fat drunk.

"More coffee, Larry? And you haven't even looked at the paper."

"Yes. Thanks. I will, now." Damn! He had to get on track better, and fast. "Well . . . what's new today?"

He didn't care, really. He couldn't; he knew, in large, how the crises and calamities of 1970 looked in diminishing perspective. The paper's only use was to orient him—to tell him where in the middle of the movie he was, what he should and should not know. And today, as on the first day of any time, he looked first for the exact date. September 16, 1970. His wedding was six weeks and three days ahead of him, on Halloween. And this day was Wednesday; the bank would be open.

As if on cue, she asked, "Anything special you need to do today?"

"Not much. I want to drop in at the bank, though. Something I want to check on." That was safe; she'd know about the bank. He kept only essential secrets. "Anything you'd like me to pick up at the groshry?'' He remembered to use their joke pronunciation.

"I'll look. I have a couple of things on the list, but they're not urgent."

"Okay. Come here a minute first, though." Short and still slim, she fit well on his lap, as she had two years later. The kisses became longer.

Then she pulled back. "Larry. Are you sure?"

"Sure of what?" He tried to bring her to him but she resisted, so he relaxed his grip. "Something on your mind, Judy?"

"Yes. Are you sure you want to get married again, so soon after . . . ?"

"Darlene?"

"I know you had a hideous time, Larry, and—well, don't get on that horse again just to prove you're not afraid to."

He laughed and tightened his hold; this time she came close to him. "Proving things isn't my bag, Judy. To myself, or to anybody."

"Then why do you want to marry me, when you have me already? You don't have to—all you have to do is not change, stay the same for me. So why, Larry?"

"Just old-fashioned, I guess." It was hard to kiss and laugh at the same time, carrying her to the bedroom. But he managed, and so did she, her part.

She got up first; the "groshry" list was ready when he was dressed to leave. Their goodbye kiss was soft.

Downstairs, he recognized the car with pleasure—a year-old Volvo he knew from two and five years later; it was even more agile and responsive now.

The drive to the bank gave him time to think.

In his early time-years the skips were small, a day or two, and his young consciousness took them for bad dreams—to wake with familiar sensations, body changed and everything out of size. Much later, waking in a hospital, he learned they were real.

"Do you use drugs, Mr. Garth?"

"No, I don't." A little grass now and then wasn't "drugs." "I'd like to know why I'm here."

"So would we. You were found lying helpless, unable to talk or coordinate your movements. Like a baby, Mr. Garth. Do you have any explanation, any pertinent medical history?"

So this is where I was, he thought. "No, I've been under a lot of pressure." That was probably safe to say, though he didn't know his body-age or circumstances. But in some thirty consciousness-years he'd learned to keep cover while he got his bearings in a new time. And eventually, as he hoped and expected, they told him most of what he needed to know about himself, and let him go. As sometimes happened, his research into the parameters of now was largely wasted; the time lasted only a dozen or so days. But the waste was not total, for when the following time came to him, he would still remember.

Once as a four-year-old he woke to middle age and panicked, screaming for his mother. He remembered being taken to the hospital that time, and did not look forward with pleasure to waking in it. But what had been would be. And he was certain there was at least one more infancy skip to be lived down someday.

At first he did not talk of these things in "home" time because he had no speech. Then he remained silent because he thought it was the same for everyone. And finally he kept his counsel because he realized no one could help or understand, or even believe.

Once in his seventh consciousness-year he woke with a throbbing joy at his groin; the woman beside him overrode his bewilderment and fulfilled his unrealized need. It was a time of a single day, and he hadn't seen her again. He didn't know the time-year or where he was, but he knew enough to say very little. He kept the situation as simple as possible by saying he was tired and didn't feel well, remembering just in time that grownups say they're not going to *work* today—he almost said *school*. He got away with it, and his confidence improved.

There were other dislocations from his early time-years, but none major until he went to sleep aged nineteen and woke to spend seven months as a forty-year-old man, twice-divorced. He wondered what was wrong, that twice he had failed in marriage. His unattached state simplified his adjustment, but after a time he became convinced that he'd lost twenty years and was cheated. But the next skip was to an earlier time, and then he began to know the way of his life.

The changes came always during sleep, except for the one that came at death. He didn't know how old he died; his brain's constricted arteries would not maintain an attention-

span of any useful length. Inside him, his brief thoughts were
lucid, but still the effect was of senility. How old, though?
Well, he'd once had a year that included his seventieth birthday and golf, an operation for cataracts, a lawsuit success-
fully defended and a reasonably satisfying state of potency.
So when he came to the last, he knew he was *damned* old.

Having died, he still feared death. It would be merely a
different way of ending. For he had no clear idea how much
of his life had been lived, back and forth in bits and pieces.
One day he would use up the last unlived segment, and then
. . . he supposed he simply wouldn't wake up. At his best
estimate, he had lived something less than half his allotted
time-years. He couldn't be sure, for much of his earlier
conscious time was unmeasured.

Dying itself was not terrible, even his senile brain knew he
had not yet filled all the blank spaces of his life. The pain was
bad, as his heart fought and for a time would neither function
nor gracefully succumb, but he had felt worse pain. His mind
lost focus and came clear only for a few seconds at the end.
He died curious, wondering what might come next.

It was the other book end; the circle closed. He was
trapped, constricted, pushed. Pressured and convulsed, slowly
and painfully. Finally cold air reached his head and bright
light stabbed at his eyes; at the consciousness-age of perhaps
thirty, he was born. Except for the forgotten instinctive rap-
ture of feeding, he found the newborn state unpleasant.

Filling early skips involuntarily, he dipped twice again into
infancy. The first time bored him almost to apathy; he could
neither see clearly nor move well. The second time, better-
learned, he concentrated on his wide-open senses, trying to
understand the infant condition. He found the experience
instructive, but still was glad when next he woke adult.

Relationships with others were ever difficult; always he
came in at the middle of the second feature, unsure of what
had gone before and of correct responses to people he was
supposed to know. He learned to simulate a passive streak that
was not his by nature, so that his friends would accept the
quiet necessary to each new learning period. He cheated no
one by this small deceit; it was as much for their benefit as
his. And while he stayed in one time, at rest between zigzag
flights, his friends and lovers—and their feelings—were real
to him, of genuine concern. When he met them again, before

or afterward, it pained him that they could not also know and rejoice in the reunion.

Early in his experience he sometimes fumbled such reunions. Now he knew how to place the time and adjust his mental files to produce only acceptable knowledge for the year.

There was no way he could pursue a conventional career with organizational status and seniority, and at the end of it a pension. Hell, he couldn't even finish college. Luckily, at his first major change, when he skipped from nineteen to forty, he found himself a published author of fiction. He read several of his works and enjoyed them. In later times, half-remembering, he wrote them, and then others that he had not read. His writings never hinted at the way of his own life, but a reviewer said of them: "Garth presents a unique viewpoint, as though he saw life from a different angle."

It was a strange life, he thought. How did they manage it? Living and seeing solely from one view that plodded along a line and saw only one consecutive past.

So that they could never, ever understand him. Or he, them.

He had attuned so easily to the car and the locality, hands and feet automatically adjusting to four-on-the-floor and quick brakes and steering, that, daydreaming, he nearly drove past the turnoff to First Mutual Savings. But from the right-hand lane, braking and signaling quickly, he made his turn without difficulty. He found a slot at the end of a parking row, well away from the adjacent car in case its driver was a door-crasher.

He didn't know the bank, so he walked in slowly and loitered, looking around with care. The safety-deposit counter was to his left; he approached it. On it, a marker read "Leta Travers"; behind the desk was a gray-haired woman, spectacularly coiffed, who wore marriage rings. He couldn't remember how people in this suburb in this time addressed each other in business dealings. Well, it couldn't be too important . . .

"Good morning, Mrs. Travers."

She came to the counter. "Mr. Garth. Going to change your will again?"

What the hell! No; she was smiling; it must be a "family joke." Damn, though; how had he later come to set up such a stupid thing? He knew better than that, *now*.

Well, go along with it. "Yep. Going to leave all my

millions to the home for retired tomcats.'' But he'd have to kill this for later, or else change banks. Or some next-time, off guard, it could bad. Maybe that's why he dropped the records . . . wait and see.

Leta Travers led him to the aseptic dungeon, where their two keys together opened Box 1028. Saying the usual polite things, she left him to its contents.

The envelope was on top. He didn't like the label: *This Is Your Life* with his signature below. That was showoff stuff. Or dumbhead drunk. He'd brought a pen; with it, he scribbled the designation into garble. He thought. Then wrote: *Superannuated; For Reference Only*. He repeated the phrase subvocally, to fix it in his mind.

He unfolded the envelope's contents and was impressed. There were two major parts, plus some side-trivia he could study later. The last looked interesting, but it had waited and could wait awhile longer.

First was an expanded version of the card in his wallet: a chronology of his consciousness, more exactly dated than he could verify from memory. Somehow, later, he'd checked these things more closely. He couldn't imagine how to do it. Or maybe, along with the dumbhead labeling, he had taken to putting exact dates to inexact recalls. He didn't like to think of his mind going so flyblown, and determined to watch against such tendencies.

He skimmed without going deeply into memory. The list seemed accurate; he'd have to look more closely later. The second paper described his life from a different aspect: by time-years it showed the parts he'd had and what he'd known and guessed of what had gone between. At the back was a summary in chart form.

Both parts went well past his own experience, as the card had done. He looked, at the first and read, after the college section: ''February 6, 1987, through March 4, 1992. Three years wonderful with Elaine and the others, then two so terrible as she died and afterward. She died November 10, 1990, and we are alone.''

He could not read any more; he couldn't make sense of it. Elaine—how could she die so soon? He was *counting* on her, someday, for a lot of good years: now and then, as it would happen. Suddenly he could see a reason for destroying records— he'd rather not know of the end of Elaine. But obviously he hadn't thought that way afterward, or the papers wouldn't be here before him. Something else must happen, later, to change his mind.

He knew Elaine from two times: first when their matured marriage was joined fully to that of Frank and Rhonda. Only two months then. And later, starting when they were six months married, he had the next year and a few months more. And she was the person he most wanted, most loved . . . and most missed.

He couldn't take any more of it, not yet. He needed to study and memorize the record, but not here, not now. Well, Judy wasn't nosy; he could take it home. He put the envelope in a pocket. Everything else went back in the lock-box; he pushed it in to click its assurance of security. All right; time to go.

At the counter he thanked Mrs. Travers. "And I've decided to leave my will alone from now on," he said. "The retired tomcats will just have to do the best they can."

She laughed, as he'd hoped she would. "Well, whatever you say, Mr. Garth."

"True," he said, "it's my nickel, isn't it? Well, then . . . see you again, Mrs. Travers, and thank you."

He walked toward the door.

The black-haired girl walked by as he came out to the sidewalk, and before he could think, he called to her. "Elaine!"

She turned; frantically he tried to think of a nonincriminating excuse. But her eyes went wide, and her arms; she ran to him and he could not resist her embrace. "Larry! Oh, Larry!"

"Uh—I guess I made a mistake," he said. His mind churned uselessly. "Perfectly natural. I guess I do look like a lot of other people."

She shook her head, scattering the tears that leaked onto her lashes. "No mistake, Larry." Her hands gripped his upper arms; he could feel the nails digging in. "Oh, think of it! You too, Larry! You too!"

His mind literally reeled; he felt dizzy. He breathed deeply, and again and a third time. "Yes," he said. "Look. Elaine— let's go someplace quiet and have coffee or a drink or something. We've got to talk."

"Oh, yes! We have to talk—more than any other two people in the world."

* * *

They found a small bar, quiet and dimly lit, and sat at a corner table. Three men occupied adjacent stools at the bar; across the room a couple talked quietly. The bartender, scowling in concentration, mixed something in a tall glass.

Larry looked at Elaine, ten years younger than he had ever seen her. She aged well, he thought; the little lines at the corners of her eyes hadn't advanced much by the time they were married. The gray eyes themselves did not change, and the line of her chin was durable. The black hair was longer than he'd seen it; the few threads of gray were yet to appear. He could close his eyes and see the slim body under her bright dress; he felt desire, but remotely. More important now were things of the mind—of both their minds.

The bartender was coming to their table. "Vermouth on the rocks?" Larry said. "You always like that."

"I do?" She laughed. "That's right; I do, later. Well, perhaps this is where I begin to acquire the taste. All right."

He ordered the same. Both were silent while the drinks were brought. He started to raise his glass in a toast, but she didn't wait.

"How much have you had, Larry? Of us?"

"I haven't met you. Except now, of course. I had the last half of our first year and most of our second." He showed her the envelope. "I have the dates here. And earlier I had a few weeks in the middle, in '85, when we were with Frank and Rhonda. I was pretty young; it really confused me at first."

She nodded. "I should have known then. I've had that part too, and suddenly you seemed withdrawn, you wouldn't talk. Then, gradually, you came out of it."

"How much have you had, Elaine? I mean—how much do we have left, together? Not too long from now I get the last—" Good Lord! What was he *saying?* "Elaine—have you had, uh, your death yet?"

She nodded. "Yes. It wasn't as bad as it probably seemed. I looked awful and smelled awful, toward the end, I know. And made noises, from the pain. But that was just my body. Inside, except for seeing how all of you hurt for me, I was pretty much at peace; the pain was out there someplace where I hardly felt it.

"Poor Larry! I gave you a bad time, didn't I?"

"I haven't had that time yet. I'll be having it pretty soon, though."

"You'll *what?* How can you know that?" Her face seemed to crumple. "Oh! We're not the same, after all?"

He took her hand. "Yes, we are. It's—I keep records, or I will. And I found them, written in the time just before now." He showed her the lists from the envelope. "Here—you can see what I've had, up to here, and what I'll be having up through the time that ended a couple of days ago."

She recovered quickly and studied his life-records with obvious fascination. "But this is marvelous! I never thought of doing it; I don't know why. It's obvious, when you think about it. Stupid me!"

"Stupid me too, Elaine," he said. He sipped his drink. The ice had melted; the taste was watery. "I didn't think of it either, until I saw it on paper."

"But that means you did it because you'd done it." She grasped the circularity of the process instantly—which was more than he had done.

"Larry, do you mind if I mark on this—the chart here—a little bit? In pencil? I want to see how much we have left together." Quickly she drew neat lines. "Both *knowing*; won't that be—what's a bigger word than 'wonderful'?"

"Whatever it is, it fits." Impatience gripped him. "Well, how does it look?"

"Better than I expected, but not as good as I'd like. Damn! I've met you and you haven't met me. Then here, late in 1980, we overlap; we've both had a couple of months there. And you've had most of 1981 and a little of '85, and I've had nearly all of '85 and all of the last three years. Oh, dammit! See here? Out of our ten years, one or the other of us has already had nearly six. Not knowing. Not *knowing*, Larry!" She wiped her eyes and gulped from her glass.

"Yes, Elaine; I feel the same way. But what's lived is lived; we can't change it."

"Can't we?" She raised her face to him, shaking back the hair that had fallen forward. "What if—what if the next time you've had and I haven't, I just *tell* you? Or the other way around? Why not, Larry? Why the hell not?"

He shook his head, not negating her but stalling. The idea had come to him too, and the implications rocked him. Not her, though—God, how he loved that bold mind! But he needed time to think.

"I'm not sure, Elaine. What would happen? We were there, you see, and we *didn't* tell, either of us, our selves who remembered sitting here right now. Why didn't we?'' He was still holding her hand; he squeezed it once and let go. ''Was it because of something we decided in the next few minutes? Or hours, or days? We've got to think, Elaine. We've got to think in ways no one's ever had to think before.''

She smiled. ''You're sure of that? There are two of us. Maybe there are others.''

''Maybe. I've watched, and never—what are the odds against recognition? If I hadn't been off guard, you know, I'd never have given myself way.''

''But I'm so glad you did. Aren't you?''

''Of course, Elaine. Christ, yes! I mean, even if it's only the four years . . .''

''But maybe we could have *more*. The overlap—you see? —the parts we've both had, where neither of us knows about the other—there's not much of it.''

''No, there isn't.'' He signaled the bartender, holding up a glass and extending two fingers of the hand that raised it. ''Elaine, we don't have to decide this right away. Put it on the back burner and let it simmer. Let's talk about us. For instance, how old are you?''

She laughed. ''I thought your memory was better than that. I'm two years and five days younger than you are.''

It was his turn to chuckle. ''I don't mean body-years. How old in consciousness-years?''

''Oh. I call them life-years. About twenty-four, I think, give or take a couple. And you?''

''Close to forty; I can't be exact about it either.''

The bartender brought filled glasses, collected his money and went back to the bar, all silently.

''Getting old and cautious, are you, Larry? No, I don't mean that. We learn to be cautious; we have to. It's just that *this*—not to be alone with the way I live—I'll take *any* risk. Any risk at all, Larry.'' She sipped vermouth; the ice clinked as her hand shook slightly. ''But yes, let's talk about us.

''You asked about my death,'' she said. ''Have you had yours? Or what's the oldest you've been?''

''I had it, and I don't know; I was senile. You're all right on the inside, but you can't keep track for very long. But I was damned old; I know that. Because I was seventy for a while once, and still in pretty good shape.''

''And I died at fifty-three. God *damn* it, Larry!''

"Elaine!" What could he say? "Sometimes quality counts more than quantity."

She made a disgusted grimace and a half-snort. "Some quality! Do you remember any of my life history? Well, I'm with my first husband, Joe Marshall, and he's just making a start on drinking himself to death. It takes him fifteen years, as I recall. Oh, I can't complain about my childhood, or college, or even the first five years of the marriage, what I've had of it. But I've also had four of the next eight, before the divorce. In three times, separated and out of sequence. No, Larry. When it comes to quality, it's all in the times with you. With you and our other two."

"Those were good times for me too," he said. "But you know something? I tried to feel alike to everybody, the way we were supposed to. And I was with all three of you *before* the time you and I were alone earlier, but I felt more yours than Rhonda's, anyway." He paused and drank. "I wonder if somehow the body gives feedback, under our conscious memory."

Her mind looked at him from somewhere far behind her eyes. "I don't know. Sometimes there are hunches . . . feelings . . ." She shook her head and smiled. "Larry, how is it with you now?"

"Mixed up, for one thing. I've probably told you, maybe in some time you've had and I haven't, about my first two marriages—what I knew of them. Well, you can see here on this diagram—I woke up today between wives."

"Today? You're just beginning a time today?"

"Yes. Judy's living with me; we get married in about six weeks."

"Judy? She's the lush, isn't she?"

"Not now, and not two years from now. Maybe I'd had only the bad end of it when I told you about her—yes, that's right. Someday I'll find out what happened, I expect. I just hope it isn't my fault. But it probably is . . ."

"You can't afford to think that. You didn't ask to be born zigzag, any more than I did. If we can take it, why can't they?"

"Can we take it, Elaine?"

"We're doing it, aren't we?" She looked at her watch. "Oh, I have to go! Joe—my husband—I'm an hour late! He'll be drunk again if I don't hurry."

"Yes. All right. When can we see each other?"

"I don't know yet, but we will. We have things to settle, you and I. You're in the phone book?" He nodded. "I'll call."

She stood, and he with her. She started to move away, but he took her arm. "Just a minute, Elaine. It's been a long time." They kissed long, before they moved apart and walked out.

"I go this way," she said. "It's only a few blocks. Don't come with me."

He stood looking after her, at the grace of her walk. After a few steps, she turned. "I'll call you tonight," she said. "We can meet tomorrow, if I'm still here. Still now, I mean."

"Well, you have to be, is all." They smiled and waved; then he turned and walked to the parking lot.

When he unlocked his apartment door, he almost knocked Judy off the ladder; she nearly dropped the picture she was hanging. "Oh, it's you!" she said. "Here, catch this." Off-balance, she leaned to hand him the picture. Her hair was hanging loose, brushed smooth, and her robe was open. She descended, and closed the robe before she turned to face him.

"Have you had lunch, Larry? I waited awhile, but then I got hungry and had mine. I'll do yours if you want, though why I should when you're so late . . ."

He started to say he wasn't hungry, then realized he was; he'd missed lunch. "Go ahead with what you're doing, Judy; I'll make a sandwich. My own fault; I got hung up." From the refrigerator he took bread, meat to slice, pickles and a jar of mustard. "When we're both done, let's have a beer and chat some."

She went back to her task, picture in one hand, hammer in the other and tacks silencing her mouth. Climbing a ladder, he thought, does a lot for a good round butt.

He knew what he wanted to talk about. A trip out of town, a fictitious assignment. A pre-honeymoon, by about ten years, with Elaine.

Keeping cover was one thing; he'd always had to do that. Lying was something else, he found; as he and Judy talked, sipping beer from bottles as though it were champagne from frosted goblets. The beer went well, after his sandwich.

"I'm not sure yet," he said, "but I may need to cut out for the last of this week and the weekend." He knew his slang had to be a little out of date, one way or the other, but always there was some leeway in speech patterns. "Let you know for sure, soon as I can."

"Sure, Larry. I wish I could go with you, but you know I'm tied this weekend."

"Sure." He hadn't known it, but it helped. "Next time, maybe."

She was vital and desirable, Judy. Mobile mouth, bright hair, lithe body carrying no more than five excess pounds, all nicely hidden. No genius, but a good mind and compatible nature. And in bed, like a mink with its tail on fire. So why could he not cleave to her? Because she was of the other species, the one that lived along a single line and knew nothing else.

And was that the reason she would become a fat, surly drunk? He wished he knew, and that it didn't have to happen.

Dinner wasn't much to brag about. "Leftovers Supreme," said Judy; her grin was wry. They were drinking coffee when the phone rang.

It was Elaine; he put her on hold. "Business stuff," he said to Judy. "I'll take it in the other room so you can read your book." Again, it hurt to lie; Judy didn't deserve lies.

On the bedroom extension: "Elaine?" The connection was noisy.

"Yes, Larry. I've been thinking."

"So have I. We need more time."

She laughed through the circuit noises. "Yes. We always do."

"I mean, time to ourselves. To think, and talk together." He paused, surprised to find himself embarrassed. "And to have each other, if you'd like that. I would."

She was silent for a moment. "What's the matter? Are you hard up? Has your lush gone dead?"

Anger! "You have no right to say that. You don't know her. And why—?"

Her voice came softly, almost drowned in the crackling sounds. "All right, Larry, so I'm jealous. Sorry about that. Shouldn't have said it. I'm a little drunk, boozing along with Kemo Sahib before he passed out a while ago. Leaving myself untouched, as usual. It does make me bitchy, when he spends all evening working up to nowhere. I wish I knew what he does with it."

"I wish I knew a lot of things," he said. "But never mind

that. What do you say—Elaine, let's just take off for a few days; the hell with everything. Okay?''

She waited longer than he liked. Then, ''I can get away with it if you can.'' Another pause. ''And we can talk? Everything?''

''That's what I was hoping.''

''All right, Larry. I'll be in that same bar tomorrow, about noon. Or a little later; I'm not much for being on time. But there. With my suitcase.''

''Yes. Yes, Elaine. And goodnight.''

''Cautious Larry. It's all right; I can wait for you to say the rest.'' The phone went dead, dial tone blurting at his ear. He listened as though there were meaning in the noise, then hung up and went back to Judy.

She was reading, TV on but the sound off; he'd never understood that habit, either time he'd known her. It's not so alone, was all she ever said.

''Like a beer or anything?'' he said. ''I think I'll have one or two, look at the paper a little. And then crap out early.''

''With or without?''

''Huh?''

''Me.''

''Oh. With.''

''Good. Yes, I'd like a beer with you, Larry.''

That part was good. Instead of reading, they talked. After a while, he told her about his ''assignment''—not what or where, but when. ''I'll be leaving tomorrow morning, not too early, and be back Monday. Maybe Sunday night.''

''Yes. Well, with luck I'll be too busy to miss you properly.''

He began to laugh, but stopped. For he didn't expect to be missing Judy.

He finished his beer and went to the refrigerator. ''Another, honey?''

''No, but you go ahead and have one while I shower.'' He did, then showered also.

Later, plunging together and close to all of it, he found his mind was with Elaine. Fantasy in sex was nothing new, but this reality deserved better. He almost failed to climax then; when he did, it was minor, a mere release. But he had good luck with Judy-the-unpredictable, she made it big and asked no questions. He was glad of that much.

*   *   *

Elaine, suitcase and all, arrived as the bartender set drinks on the table. "Am I late, Larry?" He shook his head; they kissed briefly.

"Where do you want to go?" he asked. "Anyplace special?"

"Yes, I think so, if you like the idea. If you don't think it's too far." She sipped the chilled vermouth. "There are some lakeside cabins a little north of Fond Du Lac. I was there once, with the great white bottle-hunter."

"Oh? Memories?"

She made a face. "He hated it; I loved it."

"Do you remember the name of the place? Maybe we should call first."

She shook her head. "It's past the season. School's started; all the little sunburns are back in their classrooms."

"Okay. I'll take the chance if you will."

They left their drinks unfinished.

The cabin was at the north end of the row, adjoining a grove of maples. The inside was unfinished, the studding exposed, but the bed was comfortable and the plumbing worked. They sunned beside the lake, swam a little, and dined on Colonel Sanders' fried chicken. Correct dinner attire was a towel to sit on.

"Tomorrow we'll go and eat fancy," he said, "but tonight we're at home."

"Yes, Larry. Just don't lick your fingers, or I'll swat you."

Indian summer cooled in twilight; they had waited for the heat to slacken. Now, he thought, comes our time together. It did, and not much later, again.

Then they sat side by side on the bed. He brought a wooden chair to hold cigarettes, ashtray and two bottles of cold beer. For a time they talked little, busy smoking, sipping beer, touching each other and smiling. It's just the way it was, he thought.

He touched the breast, small and delicately curved, that was nearest him.

"I was never much in that department, was I?" she said.

"Beauty comes in all sizes, Elaine."

"Yes, but you know, I felt so one-down, with Frank and Rhonda. She was so damned superbly—uh, endowed, it just killed me." She was smiling, but she stopped. "It did, you know. Literally."

He was running his hand through her hair, bringing it over to brush slowly across his cheek and then letting it fall, over and over. "I don't understand."

"Larry, I knew I had a lump. For more than a year, before you found out and made me see a doctor—what was his name? Greenlee."

"But why—?"

"I didn't have much, and I was afraid of losing what I had. So I tried to think it wasn't serious. And the worst—I don't know if I should even tell you . . ."

"Come on, Elaine. You and I can't afford secrets."

She butted her cigarette with firm straight thrusts. "All right. Greenlee told me, after the examination, that if I'd gone to him earlier I could have gotten by with a simple mastectomy at *worst*, and not too much of a scar. But I couldn't take the idea, Larry. So I put it off, and ended up with that ghastly double radical, all the muscles, all that goddamned radiation and—*you* know—and even that was too late." Her eyes were crying but she made no sound.

"Jesus, Elaine!" He had to hold her, because there was nothing else he could do. And besides, he had to hold her.

Finally he spoke. "You just made up my mind for me; you know that?"

"About what?"

"What you said. Next time we're together we tell each other, even though we didn't. If we can; I'm not sure. But if we can—look; the record says I'm with you again, right after this time and then a few months back in college. And first thing, I'm going to try to tell you. About how we're the same, and then about the cancer too."

"But I've lived that, Larry. And died of it."

He was up and pacing. He laughed shortly, without humor, and went to the refrigerator. He set two fresh beers on the chair and sat again.

"I've never tried to change anything before, Elaine. I guess I thought it couldn't be done. Or I was too busy keeping cover to think of making waves. I don't mean I followed any script; I didn't have one. But I went along with how things were, and it all seemed to fit. Now now, though." He gripped her shoulder and turned her to face him. "I don't want you to die as you did."

He was really too tired for sex, he thought. But he found he wasn't.

They planned to stay until Monday, but Sunday came gray, cold with wind and rain. So for breakfast, about ten o'clock, Larry scrambled all the remaining eggs, enough for four people. They had more toast than they could manage, and gave the rest to a hungry brood of half-grown mallards.

In the cabin, luggage packed. "I hate to leave, Larry."

"I know. Me too." He grinned. "We could stop at a motel for seconds if you like."

She shook her head. "No. It wouldn't be the way it is here." So they didn't. Except for a mid-afternoon snack break, he drove nonstop, and pulled up to let her off at her apartment house.

"It can't be as good, Elaine, but we've got to see each other anyway. I'm only here through November ninth."

"I don't know how long I am, of course. But, yes—I have to see you."

After the kiss she walked inside without looking back. He drove home, trying to put his mind in gear for Judy.

But Judy wasn't there, and neither were her possessions.

The letter was on the kitchen table:

I'm sorry Larry but I'm bugging out. I don't know what's wrong but I know something is, you aren't the same. It's not just you going off this weekend, I need people to be the same. I love you, you know that Larry, but you changed on me. The day you went to the bank you came up different. I need you to be the same to me, I need that. So I'm bugging out now. Don't worry, I'll call off all the wedding present stuff, you won't be bothered with it. I do love you when you were the same and I'll miss you a lot.

Judy

Well. She didn't say where she was going; it could be anywhere. The hell with unpacking; get a beer, sit down and think it out.

Two cigarettes later, the memory came—the time she told him about this.

"Remember when I ran out on you, Larry? I was really

spooked; I don't know why, now. And I never knew how you found me. You didn't even know I *had* a cousin Rena Purvis.'' He laughed and memorized the name, as he did all things concerning his future in someone else's past.

Rena Purvis' number was in the book. He dialed the first three digits, then thought a moment and hung up. He dialed Elaine instead.

A man's voice answered. "H'lo? Who' that?" Kemo Sahib had a good start.

How to play it? "Mr. Marshall? Mr. Garth here. I have the report Mrs. Marshall requested early last week."

"S'okay. I'take it, fella."

"I'm sorry—Mrs. Marshall's instructions . . . would you put her on the line, please?"

"I said I'take it. Or leave it. Take it or leave it. Get it?"

"Perhaps Mrs. Marshall could call me back? Mr. Garth?"

The slurred voice harshened. "Saaay—you' the bastard she was off with, right?"

The hell with it. "The very bastard, Joe; the very same. Your own stupid fault, Joe—waste not, want not. Now, are you going to put Elaine on the phone, or am I going to come over there and show you just how much of a bastard I can be if I put my mind to it?"

It took Marshall three slams to get his phone safely on the hook; the crashes hurt Larry's ears. That was dumb of me, he thought—or was it? Should he get over there in a hurry? No. Whatever else Elaine felt about her husband, she wasn't afraid of him . . . and the slob had sounded completely ineffectual. So, give it a few minutes . . .

It took twenty; then his phone rang. "Hello. Elaine?"

"Yes, Larry. Joe . . ."

"Any trouble? I can be there fast."

"Noise trouble, is all. As usual. He's settled down; he's telling his troubles to his glass teddybear. What in the world did you say to him?"

"Sorry. I tried to play it nice but he wouldn't. So I laid the truth on him. Maybe I shouldn't have?"

"No, that's all right. I'd already told him, and that he and I are through. We were talking about changing things, Larry? I'm doing it. I don't know if it will work; I lived through four years with him after this, so probably I get stupid and relent. But for now, I've had it." She paused. "But you're the one who called. What is it?"

He told her, reading Judy's letter aloud. ". . . and then I didn't call her. And maybe I shouldn't go bring her back, even though I did. Because I think I made her a lush, not being the same, not being able to be the same. What do you think?"

"I think you're not through talking yet, and I'm not done listening."

It wasn't easy, but he had to laugh. "Yes, Elaine. Will you come live here?"

"Where else?"

"Tomorrow?"

"I haven't unpacked my suitcase."

"Shall I come get you?"

"No. I'll take a cab."

"All right. You have the address?"

"Yes. And number 204, right?"

"I'll leave the door unlocked. Hell, I'll leave it open!"

Time, stolen from a programmed future, was sweet. Despite everything, he felt occasional guilt about Judy. But she didn't call, and neither did he. Joe Marshall called several times, more or less coherently. Larry always answered, gently, "Forget it, Joe." Elaine simply hung up at first recognition.

All too soon, like Judgment Day, came November ninth. They made a ceremony of it, with dinner in the apartment from none other than Colonel Sanders. Larry did not lick his fingers. Later in bed, they did everything slowly, to make it last until . . . whenever.

He woke. Elaine's face was close above his; her smile was wistful. "Hello, Larry. Do you *know*?"

To see, he had to push her soft hair aside; the ceiling was gray-green. "I *know*. But what's the date?"

"November tenth, 1970." Her voice was level, cautious.

He whooped. He kissed her with fierce joy, with elation; he kissed her out of breath. "Elaine! We changed it! I didn't skip!" Tears flowed down her cheeks, around her laughing mouth.

For the second part of their celebration he scrambled eggs in wine; it was messy, he thought, but festive.

"How much can we count on, Larry?"

"I don't know; we can't know." He held up the envelope with its carefully detailed records. "But this is useless now."

"Yes. Don't throw it away yet. I want to see where you've been, and talk about it together."

"All right. We can sort it out later."

It was a new life; he set out to live as though it would be endless. They couldn't marry, but Elaine filed for divorce. Joe Marshall filed a countersuit. It didn't matter; no law could force her to live away from Larry Garth.

New Year's Eve they drove to Chicago for dinner and night's lodging at the Blackhawk. The occasion was a thorough success.

The ceiling was silver, with fleeting iridescent sparkles. He came awake slowly, feeling minor aches one by one. Whatever this was, it was no part of college. For one thing, he hadn't often slept double there, and now a warm body pressed against him.

He turned to see. Only a brief spill of hair, salt-and-pepper, closely cut, showed between covers and pillows. He drew the cover away.

She *would* age well, he thought. Then Elaine opened her gray eyes.

He had to say it fast. "I'm new here, Elaine. Straight from 1970. Nothing in between."

"Nothing? Oh, Larry, there's so *much*. And I've had only a little of it myself. Back and forth—and it's all so different."

"From . . . before, you mean?" His fingers ruffled her hair, then smoothed it.

"Yes." Her eyes widened. "Why, you don't *know* yet, do you? Of course not; you can't."

"Know what, Elaine?"

"How much have you had after 1970? How many years?"

"How much have I used up? I don't know—twelve years? Fifteen, maybe. Why?"

"Because it's *not* used up; it's all new!" Her hand gripped his wrist tightly, to the edge of pain. "Larry, I came here from '75—from a time I'd had *before*, married to Joe. But this time I was with you. This time we're together all the way."

He couldn't speak and his laugh was shaky, but his mind flashed. I'll have to die again, he thought—or will I? And then: We've gained ten years together; could we make it twenty? I've never had the actual wedding to Darlene! What if . . .

But he said only, "There's a lot to tell, isn't there?" And so much he wanted to ask, when there was time for that.

"Yes." She turned her face upward, wriggled her head and neck hard into the pillow, then smiled. "I saw Judy once, in '74. She married a lawyer and had twins. And she wasn't a lush."

"I'm glad."

"I know. You were when I told you then, too."

He laughed. "What lives we lead, Elaine. What lives. . ."

Then he remembered. "But *you*. Are you—?" The bulky comforter hid her contours. Two breasts, one, or none? He told himself it didn't matter. She was alive, wasn't she?

"Oh, I'm fine, really," she said. "It worked. Of course the scar was horrid at first. To me—*you* never seemed to mind. But it's faded now; you can hardly see it."

"How long—?"

"It's been five years." She must have seen the question in his face; she shook her head. "No; I don't know how long I live—or you. This is the oldest I've been. And I haven't known a *you* who's been older."

"Elaine? How old are we now?"

She smiled, and then her mouth went soft and full. She pushed the cover back and turned to face him squarely. He looked and saw that she had lost nothing of herself, save for the tribute to the years. Part of him that had been prepared to comfort and reassure her took a deep breath and relaxed.

"How old?" she said. "Does it matter? We'll have time enough to be young."

One of them reached out, and the other responded.

Three Tinks on the House

FOUR O'CLOCK IN the morning! Why do you have to work such crazy hours?" Stuffing the thirty-hour week into three days cuts commuter traffic a lot, but it doesn't do much for my wife's disposition. "If I didn't have to ride in with you for this damned dentist's appointment . . ."

Normally, Linda's a good-looking woman—big green eyes, shiny black hair in a monkey-fur cut, skin holding up better than most. After eighteen years of marriage I still like to look at her, especially when she smiles. But when she's feeling hacked about something, she can look like a witch.

"More coffee?" I said, and poured for her. "Good breakfast, honey." I'd finished my egg, toast and juice, and was relaxing over coffee.

"Wouldn't be so bad, Johnny, if it didn't take so long to get to town."

"All right! Let's get out where there's room to breathe, you said. OK, here we are. Out of the high-rise jungle—no apartments over fourteen stories. Of course, they're *all* fourteen, but what the hell. Use of the pool Tuesday and Friday if we want. Our own parking slot in the secured area. So it takes a little longer to get to work; you win some, you lose some."

"I suppose. If I just had my own car again . . ." She stopped, and smiled a little. Not much, but a little. Breakfast was beginning to help. "Look—I know it's not practical—the double tax on second cars, and all. It's only that I had a lot more fun when I had my own job and my own car."

"Sure, I know, Linda." A computer took her job and the Eco Laws took her car. I was glad she hadn't rubbed my nose in one bet I'd lost; when the first big Eco crunch had hit, the color-coded routes and the Federal horsepower tax, I'd had to sell the one car to pay for propane conversion on the newer one. I'd thought propane was a safe bet, and only five dollars tax per horse instead of the twenty for Diesel or gas-hogs. Not to mention the saving on fuel tax . . .

So what happened? The Enumclaw Freeway, my best route to Seattle, had been coded yellow—*no* internal combustion. Commuterwise, I was up the creek. But to convert to an outside-burner I'd have had to put a second mortgage on the condo. Well, I'd taken the chance, and lost.

She made a grimace, a little one-sided grin. "Maybe Metro Transit really will run the Renton line down here, complete the loop to Kent. They keep promising. You know, with all the taxes we pay . . ."

"Yeah. The taxes." I sipped the dregs and stood. "Ready?"

"Un momento. Better safe than sorry." She went into the bathroom.

I had to smile, remembering her story of the last time she'd stopped at a service station to exchange the lefthand propane tank for a full one. First there was a guy in the john who stayed in a long time, and when he came out he let the door go locked. Any decent fellow would have held it for her, with the attendant not watching. Then it turned out she wasn't carrying the company's credit card, and the door scanner wasn't programmed to recognize her bank card. The station attendant couldn't be bothered to help.

"Unlock this goddamned door," she'd said, "or I'll piddle right here in front of it!"

But he'd told her, "Go ahead, lady. The fifty bucks for littering, you *can* put on your bank card." There wasn't any other place handy, so she'd had to hold it until she got home.

On second thought, it wasn't funny. Those things used to be free, part of the service—not a gimmick to promote a company's own credit cards.

Linda was ready to go. I cut the alarms, checked the hallway and motioned for her to come out. I made sure to thumb the ten-second reset button before closing the door behind us. The building hadn't had a successful break-in during the four years we'd lived there, and only one killing and two rapes in the halls. But still I think it pays to stick to the routine.

We showed ID to the guard by the elevators, to the one in

the elevator itself and at our parking sub-deck. The man on duty there handed me our car keys. As we walked away he was alerting the outside guard over the intercom.

The car was an '82 VW Matador, remodeled slightly for the propane. Even if I couldn't drive it on the yellow-coded freeway, I still liked it. For one thing, it covered only seventy-five square feet of ground space; the size kept my surcharge down to $225. The Matador started on the first try; I drove slowly through the well-lighted aisles.

The inner doors were open. I drove through them into the security pocket, waited for them to close behind me and then for the outer gates to open. We were on our way. The smog wasn't at all bad; I could see the sun.

Old Route 516 was still coded blue, barred only to gasoline and Diesel. It was slow, a four-lane back road crowded with freeway-rejects like myself, but it was the best route available.

"Do you know if Marise came home last night, Linda?"

"No. I mean she didn't. She and Sydni were going to stay with Ali and George." I felt relief—Marise and her girlfriend, at seventeen, were still satisfied with the young studs in our own safe building.

"Ali and George, again? She could do worse. Anything serious, do you think?" We were approaching the interchange to I-5 North; I switched lanes. By rights, I suppose, I-5 should be yellow. But it's the only good secondary route north into Seattle, so most of the time it stays blue. Luckily for me.

"Marise says she and Syd would like to try a four-marriage there for a while, if they could pry the two boys out of each others' arms long enough. Not for children, yet; you know Marise is in no hurry to make paternity choices."

I swung into the interchange and merged onto I-5 North. Not far ahead, I could see highrise country looming. But my mind was on our kids.

"Yes, she'll be all right," I said. "George doesn't have much in the way of brains, but those four aren't likely to hurt each other much. And since the abortion, Marise gets her implants renewed, right on schedule. But . . ."

"It's Les that bothers you, isn't it?"

I didn't answer immediately. I was trying to think it out— how I felt, and how much of what I felt was leftover from cultural conditioning.

We passed the first Sea-Tac exit. The old airport wouldn't handle anything bigger than a 747. But as long as the FAA still defined flight-paths in piston-engine terms, Sea-Tac held the highrises at bay.

"Yeh, Les," I said, finally. "I'm not arguing against adolescent bisexuality—for one thing, it holds down the abortion rate. But when a fifteen-year-old boy can't see a girl at all, for his boyfriend's ass, I think maybe the schools and the media are pushing it a little too much. When I was his age—"

Highrise country began, about where Boeing Field used to be. Not much diluted sunlight from there on—the tall boxes cut off all but an occasional shaft.

Linda laughed. "I know. When you were his age you were in love with the *Playboy* centerfold and got your sex in the bathroom with the door locked." She patted my thigh, high and inside; not expecting the touch, I jumped a little. "But didn't you ever—"

"A little. Playing around, experimenting, I guess. But not much."

Billy Jordal and I, maybe twelve. Excited as hell from talking about how it would be with a girl. Trying some things that were as close as we could think of to the real bit. Not doing too well at them. Then, when somebody else got caught, not us, learning what other people called what we'd done, and what they thought of it. After that, Billy and I weren't friends anymore. We stayed away from each other. At least, I thought, Les wasn't getting loaded down with all that guilt crap.

"Oh, Johnny—isn't that the tunnel exit? I'll look . . . no, no enforcement behind, that I can see."

The waterfront tunnel exit was a permanent gripe of mine. Naturally, the tunnel itself was coded red—*no* combustion cars. But the exit ramp went several hundred yards in open air to get to the tunnel, and halfway along it was a second exit that saved me twenty minutes of dumb stop-and-go traffic. Because some moron ran his red pencil further up his map than necessary, all the way to I-5, I was not supposed to use that shortcut.

I did, though, habitually—except when I spotted enforcement in position to see me. I'd caught three tickets in four years; I figured I was ahead of the game. But it still pissed me. I'd written a letter to the morning paper once. It wasn't printed.

I won again—no pursuing tweeter, no pullover, no citation. But it still frosted me, having to take that chance for no good reason.

The thing is, I have better things to do with any twenty minutes of my life than sit looking at red lights.

We drove west along the south edge of downtown. White-coded, to my right—no private vehicles at all. I let Linda off near a Transit station, about a dozen blocks from my parking area. We kissed. I was glad I'd married a woman who didn't forget how. "You want to wait and ride home with me," I said, "or go earlier?"

"No," she shook her head. "I'll take Transit to Renton and chances from there." I knew what she meant. The electric buses were regular, but we lived two miles from the nearest. The free lance jitneys were more flexible—if you could find one. Private cars would give rides sometimes, but a woman couldn't be too careful. Or a man, either, for that matter. Linda has a good instinct for safety, though. She'd had only one bad scare—a freak in a Rotarian suit; they'll fool you—and she'd gotten out of that one okay.

As soon as she entered the station, I drove on. The parking area at work handles eight or ten plants and hasn't enough security to plug your nosebleed. We get by because everybody knows there's nothing much to steal or mug in an industrial parking lot, outside of the Executive Section. There are a lot of rapes, though, mostly by employees. No security system can prevent all of those.

I got lucky, and parked only about half a mile from the plant. I decided the hell with the respirator; even down in industrial territory the smog was light. I brought it along, though; the afternoon could be different. The shuttle car wasn't in sight or hearing, but the walk was good exercise; I could use it.

I found the office shorthanded. That's par when it's not our regular workday, when we're shifted so that the high-pollution plants can operate on a low-smog day. It happens so irregularly that routine-bound types aren't braced for it and are apt to miss work.

Ten hours makes a long day; everyone gets irritable. Franzen over in Expediting tried to bend me once too often. I told him to freak out; it was time he knew I don't work for him. I came close to asking him to sign waivers with me and have it out: any limits he wanted, or none. He's big, all right, but not *that* big.

Being still chugged at Franzen was my only excuse, if any, for bumming Leda Robarge when she came around at the afternoon break. I knew her trick; everybody did, around there. Why she doesn't find a new hunting ground, I'll never know.

I have nothing against a little healthy seduction, or most forms of sexual freedom, in moderation. Linda and I will swing a little with good friends and don't begrudge each other an occasional night out. The time we tried a four-marriage, it broke up over such things as garlic and wet towels. But Leda's scene was not healthy.

She'd collected for help on two abortions—"my doctor has no *idea* how it could have happened"—before a third guy checked and found she'd drawn her Federal sterilization bonus when she was twenty.

My problem was that my skull was running at half-speed, same as the air conditioning. When she began to put it on me, fluttering her eyelids to emphasize the fashionable gold foil that covered them, I said, "Leda, I expect you're one hell of a good spread. But we have to think of the future."

"The future, Johnny? Why, I don't know what you mean."

"Well, if anything should go wrong—if you were to, say, get pregnant—don't worry about a thing, Leda. *I'll* have the baby for you."

She threw a mean coffee cup, but her aim was off. I felt a little guilty, but not much. People Pollution is bad enough; people who try to collect on it are even worse.

That day couldn't end too soon, and it didn't. Trudging back to the car, I knew I'd been someplace. The smog was high; I should have used the respirator, but I was too pooped to bother.

And godDAMN! Not thinking, I'd driven the little Matador all the way into the parking stall, leaving room for some asshole to sneak a Midgie in behind me, crosswise inside the spotter beam, blocking me. *You sonofasow!*

Midgie had chosen badly; I carry a dolly-jack in the rearhood. Up and out with the heavy thing, under the braked back wheels; raise it. Fine. Now, where to put it?

Franzen's stall was close; I was tempted to dump it on him. He's a mechanical moron; he'd probably try to kick it to death. But I settled for leaving the Midge directly in the spotter-beam at the back of an empty stall. Not unhappily, I drove away. Midgie would probably pay about fifty for that one. *That'll teach you to screw around with the Green Hornet!*

A few blocks ahead of the on-ramp to I-5 South, I saw the blinker signals. Access had been cut from blue to yellow: external-combustion, yes; me and my propane, no. For a while, until the smog level dropped and the signal changed back again, I was stuck.

I could cut over to old Route 99, like crawling on hands and knees. Or I could wait for I-5 South to shift back to blue. If it shifted within the hour, I was better off to wait. And more comfortable . . .

Yeh. Joe's Stoneboat Bar was off to the right, not far. I stopped there sometimes, knew a few of the people. For instance, one of the doctors from the nearby hospital was absolutely an engraved character.

I turned right, and three blocks later pulled the Matador into the shady side of Joe's parking lot. I hated to button up the car, in the heat.

The Stoneboat was cool inside. The back room, away from the TV-juke, was quiet except for the crowd noise. I figure that's why Joe usually works that room himself and lets his hired help handle the front.

"A live one, Johnny?" said Joe. I nodded. Live-yeast beer is my favorite low-high; sometimes I wonder how we ever got along without it.

Even after three years a bar doesn't smell right to me without stale cigarette smoke; the Stoneboat smelled only of beer and last month's repainting.

I knew the two men at the table next to the end of the bar. We said "Hi" and I sat with them.

Artie Rail was singing it down about his stupid car some more. "I just dunno what I'm going to do, fellas." He said it with his usual whine. "I'm about ready to turn it in for the demolition bonus. Except I can't afford to buy anything I *can* afford—if you see what I mean."

Sure, I saw what he meant. Artie was paying sevenyeight

hundred in horsepower tax, and close to the same for the area of his Detroit parade-float. He was in a tight knot, all right.

Hollis MacIlwain wasn't wasting his sympathy, if he had any. "Oh hell, Artie, it's your own fault. You bought that Cadillac when the taxes you bitch about were already in the talk stage. It was a damn fool trick, and you know it."

"Yeh?" Artie bit back. "*You* weren't all that happy, Hollis, when you had to put in short pistons, to cut your compression for no-lead gas. Anyway, my brother-in-law gave me a real good deal on that Cad."

"So sue your brother-in-law." Hollis' gravel voice was weary. "Don't load me with your grotches."

I wasn't much interested, either; I'd heard it all before. We'd each had to make our choices. I'd made my bet two years ago, good or not, and got it over with. But here they were, still at it.

"What ya think's the best pick in the new stuff coming out?" Artie said. "Joe, you got any upper ideas on that?"

"Hard to tell. General Ford's selling its little electrics a lot, for short-haul. The ones with the plug-in packs."

"Yeah," I said, "but you use twenty percent of the charge just lugging the pack around. Okay if you don't use a car much, I guess."

"Hey, Joe," said Hollis, "gimme a tink-and-tonic." He had bills on the table, and his card for Joe to punch. "You know what *I* think?" We did, but he went ahead with it, anyway.

"Until somebody without an expense account can afford one of those fuel-cell jobbies, you're not going to beat the little Japanese outside-burners, like the hot-air Honda my nephew got." He went on with it, but I wasn't listening. He always says it just about the same, Hollis does, as if it was real news.

A new customer came in, a young fat little guy, letting the TV-juke noise come with him as he opened the door. It was the *Stucco Crocodile*, doing "Baby You're a Sidewiser." I didn't notice anyone inviting him, but he came and sat with us, anyway.

The three of us gave each other the look that said that none of us knew him. The Stoneboat got trade from people hanging around the hospital waiting-rooms up the next block. Usually, though, they stayed in the front room with the juke to take their minds off their worries.

"Tink and soda," the new guy said. Joe waited until the man remembered and got his card out, to go with his money. "It's all right, bartender. First one today." So Joe punched the card, counted the drops of tincture he shook into the glass, and added the ice and soda. The man didn't get the extra drop, I noticed, that Joe usually gave his regular customers, law or no law. His first sip went long and deep; he grimaced at the bitterness. Personally I like a mix that covers the taste.

"Aah! That's what I needed." He smiled, then apparently though better of it." "Oh, bartender! I'm expecting a call. From the hospital. They'll ask for Mr. Anstruther. If you don't mind."

"Sure," said Joe, "no trouble. Bleeding for some news?"

"Yes," Anstruther looked embarrassed. "My wife is—er, having a baby."

We were all careful not to look at him. Then I thought, what the hell; it happens sometimes. And he was pretty young; maybe it was his first. Couldn't blame a man for that, even now. I had two myself, but they dated from when nobody knew any better. Now, there wasn't that excuse.

More to break the silence than anything else, I said, "Hey, Joe! Throw a tink in a live one for me, will you?" That's the way I like tink; I can't taste it through live beer. Joe inspected the card with a straight face before he punched it—I mean, he knows I seldom tink up and hardly ever take the limit of three in one day.

He gave me the extra drop for being a regular, though. Someday, I thought, he's going to get narked off for that. I hoped Anstruther was only a would-be daddy-boy and not something else.

"You know?" said Anstruther. "They had tink over in Britain and Europe for years, before most of us here ever heard of it. Say, I might as well have another one." He pushed forward his card and money. Joe obliged him. Anstruther, I saw, still didn't get the extra drop.

"Anyway," he went on, "I think the administration made a good compromise, legalizing only the liquid form. Makes it a lot easier to control."

"Hell," said Artie Rail, "all they wanted was to get reelected, just like always. Any campaign's a snow job; what makes this year any different?''

Well, who could argue? Give one side a little, but not enough to grotch the other side. That's politics and always will be.

The phone chimed. Anstruther stood and moved to the bar. Joe picked up the handpiece, listened, and handed it over. He faced the console piece toward the other man. By habit—the visual was off; someone at the other end was saving money on the call.

''Yes?'' said Anstruther. ''I'll be right over.'' He came back to the table and gulped his second tink, which is not a good idea. Then he bolted out.

Hollis smiled. ''That guy has a point. Who would have figured that when pot got legal, we'd be drinking it instead of smoking it?''

I wished he hadn't said that. I still miss tobacco. Not enough to bootleg it, though. Then I relaxed, beginning to stone-up from the tink. It *is* nice, once in a while. It was a little while before I started to listen again.

Artie was off and running, about his kid, this time. ''They're trying to turn the boy queer or something, in them schools,'' he said. ''Other day I caught him and his buddy—you wouldn't believe it! And he had the bowels to say to his own father . . .''

I didn't bother to argue. I had my own misgivings to argue with, and I wished I knew which side of me was right.

When I tuned in again, Artie was still going. ''And you know what else? He asked, did I rather he went and got his sterilization bonus? At *his* age? Hell, I want grandchildren, like anybody else.'' He grinned, looking uneasy. ''Not too many, o' course. But, freakin' Jeez—*one*, anyway. I believe in Zero Population Growth, but not Zero Population.''

Nobody answered Artie; he didn't ask questions that *had* good answers. He went back to creeping about his car; every place he wanted to go, the routes were more and more coded-out against him. Green code routes, no restrictions, were getting hard to come by.

So what *else* was top-line news? I could see the handwriting on the wall, too. The only difference between Artie and me was that I believed it meant what it said.

*   *   *

The door to the front swung open; it was Anstruther again. The blast we caught from the TV-juke was *Lefty and the Seven Feeps*, striding on "Up Your Taxes."

"Tink and soda," he said, waving his card. This time he didn't sit with us, but climbed onto the nearest barstool. "Yes, I know," he said, "last for the day." Joe nodded; he hadn't argued. "But fitting, you know," the man continued. "Very fitting."

"Yeh?" said Hollis MacIlwain. "What fits it so nice?"

Anstruther didn't answer right away. He sipped on his tink while Artie began on the next chapter of how the whole damn world wasn't set up to his personal tastes. I can listen to that all night without ever hearing much of it. Not that I hang in at Joe's that heavy; I wasn't even late home for dinner yet.

Anstruther raised his glass. "Three tinks," he said, "and three—"

"And three what?" Hollis said. Anstruther didn't say anything. I got a hunch.

"Three, uh—kids, maybe?" I said. "Three *kids*, you have?"

Whatever Anstruther wanted to say, it wouldn't come out. He tried to shake his head, but all it did was wobble a little.

"Three kids," said Artie Rail. For once, he wasn't whining. "You goddamn' *breeder!*"

"All right, three kids!" Anstruther blurted. He pulled his head up, sat straight. "It's not a crime. Not yet . . ." True, but still . . . Then he threw it. "And maybe we'll have another, too, if we happen to want to!"

Silence. Then the sound of chairs being pushed back. Joe was the first to say up. "Whatever you do, do it *outside!*"

I didn't really feel like it, being stoned, and I don't suppose Hollis did, either. But it was too much. Anstruther hadn't made an apology, much less an excuse, and then he'd said maybe he'd do it again. Hollis got him by the neck and one arm; I had the other arm. We took him out the back way, to the alley.

We used to say "Up against the wall," and Anstruther sure as hell was. But he didn't fight, or even try to. All he said was. "Not all three of you, for God's sakes!" That was fine with Hollis and me; we stepped back. And Anstruther did get his hands up, looking fairly competent.

Still it was no fair fight; Artie was Golden Gloves, once. He faked Anstruther's hands high and slammed him in the gut, then threw his hard one.

Anstruther's head cracked back against the bricks; he collapsed. Artie knelt beside him. "Jeez; I didn't mean to *kill* the bastard. Just to show him how the cow ate the cabbage." Artie looked scared. "You think he's all right?"

The man was still breathing; Artie relaxed a little. Hollis was looking into Anstruther's wallet; he showed it to Artie and me, then stuffed it back into the man's pocket.

"We might as well go back in," he said.

Inside, on our table, three tinks were set up. Our usuals, on the house and no cards punched. Joe had one, too. We all drank a little off the top. I don't think anybody thought it was a toast.

"Call an ambulance for that guy," said Hollis.

"Sure thing," said Joe. "In about an hour."

"No," said Artie. "Now. We did wrong on him."

"What the hell you mean?" said Joe.

Artie sure didn't like to have to say it. "He has a ZPG card. Sterilization bonus, a little over a year ago."

"Bullshit!" Joe said. "His wife just had her kid, today."

"Yeh, sure," I said. "But whose?"

"Jesus! No wonder he—" Joe didn't finish it.

You don't waste a tink; we drank them, then left before the ambulance could get there. It's one thing to admit you screwed up, and something else to stay around and pay for it. Tough world, little brother.

I-5 South was blue again; I got home before my warmed-over dinner was too tired to eat. Marise and Les were both out someplace. I didn't feel much like talking.

"Anything special happen today?" Linda asked.

I thought about it. "Well, yes. Joe at the Stoneboat set up three tinks on the house."

The Learning of Eeshta

THE YOUNG PERSON is surrounded by the animals. In this room on their planet Earth—a strange room, all plane surfaces and right angles—Eeshta is their captive. One of them has taken its robe and hood; under the odd discrete lighting sources, the smooth exoskeleton shines ivory tinged with red. Eeshta is one of the Demu and eggborn; the symmetry of its head is broken only by the eyes and their brow ridges, the nostril openings and serrated chewing-lips below, and the slightly flanged earholes.

The heads of the animals are marred by fleshy and fibrous growths. Although their general shape is acceptable—head and body, arms and legs—they do not have correct appearance. None but eggborn Demu have correct appearance without aid. When captured animals learn to speak as Demu and thus earn citizenship, they are given whatever aid is needed.

But now it is Demu who are captive—the young Eeshta, its egg-parent Hishtoo, and three not eggborn. Taken by an escaped animal named Barton, they are brought in Hishtoo's ship from the Demu planet Ashura to Earth. Although its arm was broken in the struggle of capture, Eeshta no longer fears Barton, for Barton encased the arm for healing and offered no further injury during the long journey.

Eeshta fears these others; it does not know what they want of it, except to learn to speak with them. Demu do not speak with animals or in the tongue of animals. Hishtoo has told it thus, and the young person respects the word of its egg-parent. After a time the animals cease their attempts.

One enters who is Demu but not eggborn. It is of the type

that grows young inside itself; before its citizenship it bore on its chest the growths by which such persons nourish young.

To correct the appearance of such a one requires much aid. Knives and other instruments eliminate the growths on head and face, remove the teeth, notch lips, and shorten tongue to proper proportion. Chest and crotch are pared to smooth and sightly contours. Fingers and toes are rendered clawless, and if necessary, the number at each extremity is reduced to the proper four. And on the abdomen the single useless depression is replaced by a pattern simulating concave oviducts and their matching convexities that produce cells to fulfill the eggs. This is how deserving animals are honored for their intelligence. It has always been the way.

The one who enters is called Limila; on Ashura its appearance was made correct. It wears proper robe and hood but has added a cloth that covers all the face except the eyes. It did not do so on the ship, during the trip to Earth.

It approaches. "It is that you do not speak, Eeshta, and that you should."

"It is that you, Limila, not eggborn, speak with animals. I do not."

"It is that you are foolish. On this world you can now speak only with Hishtoo or with me, or the other two who are made Demu. Much is to be learned here, and you learn nothing."

"You may learn, and tell me in our own speech."

Limila nods. "That for the present we do it so. Also, I ask questions and you answer. Later we speak more of this."

"It is as you say, but that I have my robe and hood." The garb is returned; the questions begin. An animal speaks to Limila, who asks the question. When the young person answers, Limila speaks to the animal. Eestha's fear is soon dead of boredom, as it waits while things are said that it does not understand. It finds itself trying to understand, and quickly changes its thought.

"It is," says Limila, "that we would know your age."

"That I am nearly three fingers, of four, toward end of growth." Eeshta waits while Limila and the animal speak.

"It is that your duration may be counted in revolutions of your planet around its star."

"We do not count it so. And Ashura, where Barton escapes and takes our ship, is not my planet. The revolutions of my own planet, while we are on Ashura, are not known to me."

Finally the speaking ends. Eeshta is taken to its place and, with Hishtoo and the others, fed. While eating, it does not speak with any, nor wish to.

"She's a hard-shelled little devil, isn't she, Limila?" Annette Ling smiled across the table; then her delicate Oriental features moved in a slight frown. "In more ways than one. Not as bad as Hishtoo, though. That one wouldn't talk at all."

"He talks, Doctor Ling, when Barton asks through me or Siewen to learn of the ship, to build others. Hishtoo fears Barton, and with reason." She shook her head under the hood. "They are not he and she, of course; each is both. I have listened too much to Barton—and I suppose it is natural to assign gender in terms of size."

"Yes. You know, I'd like to meet this Barton of yours."

Within the concealment of hood and veil, Limila shook her head again. "Not mine, not now. He allows me to live with him, but cannot bring himself to . . . touch me."

For a moment, embarrassed, Annette did not speak. She brushed fingers through her short black hair. "Uh—why does Hishtoo fear him?"

"You have not heard? How he forced the ship from Hishtoo, to bring us here? He was without food, but had Eeshta captive. He threatened to begin eating her alive."

Doctor Ling gasped. "Would he have . . . ?"

"I do not know; I have not asked. But once aboard the ship, he broke both Hishtoo's arms so Hishtoo could do no mischief. And when Barton says to Hishtoo, 'crab salad,' Hishtoo answers any questions I ask."

Annette Ling's laugh was shaky. "I'm not so sure I want to meet the man, after all."

"You must remember, he had been seven years—more than that—in a Demu cage. The ship was his only chance of escape. And he had no other way to restrain Hishtoo safely, short of killing him."

"Yes. Yes, I can understand that. And he rescued you and the other two?"

"We were there, at the ship. Although Barton had refused to learn Demu speech, Hishtoo offered him citizenship as an inducement to return Eeshta safely, and surrender. We were supposed to be . . . exhibits, to persuade him. Hishtoo did not understand Barton very well."

"I should say not." Annette paused. "Limila, do you feel that Eeshta will cooperate more fully, eventually? To counter the Demu threat, the raiding and kidnapping, we *must* know more about them. Eeshta is the only window we have any chance of opening; it would help a great deal if we could speak with her directly." She raised a hand against an unvoiced protest. "I don't mean to say—*your* help has been invaluable. But still . . ."

Behind the veil she saw maimed lips move in a kind of smile. "Yes, Doctor. As Eeshta would say, I am not eggborn. For more than six years, after what was done, I lived as Demu. But even yet, I know them only from outside." Her hands, together, clasped and unclasped. "And Eeshta? I do not know. The Demu never speak another's language. It may be that they cannot learn as we do. We can only continue to try."

"Yes, and hope for success." A knock sounded. "Come in." A boy entered with coffee and a snack plate. Annette moved papers to clear space on the table. "Thank you," she said. He smiled, set down the tray, and left the room.

"I'll pour, Limila. Cream? Sugar?"

Her cup prepared, Limila raised it. She held it before her veil a moment, then set it down. "Thank you, but I do not want any, after all. I must go now."

"Limila! We're going to be working together a long time, probably. Can't you—?"

"You have seen me." The voice was flat, wooden. "In the pictures, at least. Do you wonder that I hide myself?"

A small five-fingered hand shot out to grasp one that now had only four. "Oh, damn all! I do tend to forget that anything is important, except my work. But I feel I know *you* only from outside, and—well, it was a long session; you should have some coffee and a bite to eat. I'll go out, if you wish. I'm *sorry*, Limila. Forgive me?"

Limila shrugged. "You have not harmed me; it was done before. And if you wish to see me, I can bear it if you can. When we are alone . . ." She removed the veil and pushed back the hood.

For long seconds, seeing what had been a woman's face, Annette Ling could not speak. "Yes," she said at last.

"When we are alone. Thank you, Limila." She busied herself, leafing through her notes.

"Now I'd like you to look at the questions my team has
prepared for us to ask Eeshta tomorrow. Do you think perhaps . . ."

As they talked, Limila sipped coffee and ate small bits of
cheese and wafers. Without teeth it was a slow process.

The young person has eaten. It sits with its egg-parent
Hishtoo and the two Demu not eggborn. They are of the type
that does not grow its young inside but supplies cells to fulfill
the eggs. Siewen, the frail one, supplies no more such cells.
It is one of the first of its kind to be made Demu, and live;
there was not knowledge that to provide correct appearance to
its legs-juncture would render it useless for breeding. Like
Limila, it speaks with animals, but only in response. Here
among Demu it does not speak.

The other has taken the Demu name Shestin and does not
speak with animals. It has been given citizenship later when
more is known of its kind. Its appearance where its legs join
is not fully correct. Protrusion has been miminized but not
entirely eliminated; this one, it is hoped, retains ability to
fulfill eggs. It shows no signs of wishing to do so. On the
ship it did not speak to Barton. Barton called it Whosits.
Those who bring food call it The Freak.

Hishtoo addresses its egg-child. "It is that you speak with
animals?"

"I speak with Limila, who speaks with animals. I do as
you."

"It is that I should not. But the animal Barton—"

"It is that first you do not speak with Limila in presence of
animals. But when Barton makes the sound 'crab salad,' then
you speak. I do not know that sound."

From Doktor Siewen comes a harsh cackling.

"It is," says Hishtoo, "that your mind is not waking when
Barton first makes that sound. Then, if I do not give the ship
to it, it eats you. On the ship it destroys use of my arms. And
the animal Barton eats me now if I do not speak of the ship
with Limila and Siewen. But I speak much of no truth."

"It is that if Barton finds you speak not truth, Hishtoo. . ."

"It is that we have no certain way of safety. That the
worlds must know the Demu and become Demu. Barton eats
me before I allow it to eat our race."

The young person pauses, thinking of what it knows. "It is that Barton harms me also when we meet, but not again. I do not know when it says to eat me, for, as you say, my mind is not waking. It is that the animal puts its hand to my head and makes a soft sound when I have pain and want no more."

"It is that you forget, Eeshta, that it is an animal and of no assured mind. You forget no animal is Demu. Barton has not our speech, nor correct appearance."

"You say much truth, Hishtoo. I think on your saying." The young person thinks of what it knows, and of what it does not know.

Limila waited. When Barton arrived, his dinner would not take long to prepare. He did not need her to cook for him; he could manage well enough on packaged meals. But he had brought what was left of her away from the Demu; she had no one else, and felt he deserved some payment for suffering her monstrous presence. So she did what she could, though she found it ever more difficult to talk with him.

A groundcar stopped outside; Barton's footsteps approached, and he entered. "Hi, Limila. You have a good day?" He sounded as though he were reciting a set speech.

"Well enough, I suppose. Are you hungry, Barton?"

He looked at her, then away again. When they were alone she did not wear the veil; it was no use. On the ship he had seen her too long without it.

"In a little while—any time you're ready. Right now I need a beer." He made busy at the refrigerator, then sat near her.

"Hishtoo's lying, you know," he said. "At least half the time, maybe more. That big lobster is nobody's fool."

"You have charged him with lying?"

Impatiently, Barton shook his head. "Wrong approach. Let him think he's getting away with it. For now, at least. No, we just keep asking questions, sometimes the same ones from a different angle. He'll slip up; he already has. We'll transcribe the tapes and cross-check; feed it to the computers. Nobody can lie consistently over the long haul. The parts of his story that don't stay put, we can throw out. Where it hangs together, it's probably fact. And sooner or later we'll figure out how the Demu ship works."

"And the Demu mind, Barton?"

He looked at her, his expression unguarded for a moment,

as though she still had a face. "That's the hard part, isn't it? What *you're* doing. We need force, sure—ships, and all—to stop the raids. But we need to know about them, too, and the little one's the key. How you coming with her, by now?"

"It is hard to be certain. She answers questions, but obliquely."

"Comes by it naturally, I expect; her egg-daddy's a liar by the clock. Too bad—I've gotten to like the kid, but she sure as hell comes from a rotten family."

Explanation was too difficult; she served dinner instead. Barton ate silently, saying only, "Hey, pretty good there," after the first bites. When he finished, he said, "You want to watch the Trivia or anything?"

"The Tri-V? No, Barton."

"Yeh; well, maybe I'll read awhile."

"Yes, Barton." But she needed to talk. "Barton?"

"Yeh? Something?" He seemed interested, so she plunged ahead.

"Barton, how did you know not to learn Demu language?"

"Huh? Oh—well, I didn't. I mean, I didn't know . . . what happened, if you did. It was just, they pushed me around so long, before they tried the talky-talk, that by then I was too stubborn to do *anything* I thought they wanted. There's a lot happened that I never told you .. ."

And a lot, she thought, that I can never tell anyone. "I wish I had been stubborn, Barton. But I was alone and did not want to be alone, and I did not guess that harm could come from learning."

She stood and went to him. Once more, she thought, and then not again. She took his hand. "Barton? I—"

He clasped her to him but turned his face away. She heard him curse, his voice thick. Then he said, more quietly, "I wish I could, Limila. I wish . . ." He released her. "Oh, hell! I'm going to bed."

She went to her own room. This is not life, she thought; I am not living. I need to work yet awhile for others, and then I can stop.

The thought comforted her more than any had in a long time.

The young person sits with Limila and the animal Ling. The fourth of the second four of questionings begins. Against its will, Eeshta understands more each time, of animal speech, but as Hishtoo has said to do, it pretends ignorance.

Also, it understands some meanings of Ling's face movements. The downward-together pull of the small dark growths above the eyes means the animal is dissatisfied. The young person has known this meaning earlier, for on the ship Barton often made the sign—but never the upcurving of incorrectly smooth mouth, meaning pleasure, that Ling makes. Eeshta has made the Demu sign of pleased feeling, mouth opened slightly to show the tongue uplifted, but Ling does not understand until Limila explains in animal words. Then, to Eeshta, Ling lifts its own tongue, so incorrectly long.

Eeshta is certain Ling comes to understand some Demu speech, also. It sometimes speaks before Limila repeats Eeshta's saying fully. On Ashura, perhaps Ling would soon be worthy of being given citizenship and correct appearance . . . though Eeshta is surprised to find that with familiarity the animal's deformities are less offensive and seem almost natural.

Now Ling speaks directly to Eeshta but in its own animal speech. "Eeshta, do you know what I say? You do know, don't you?"

"Limila, it is that Ling speaks. That you tell its saying in our tongue."

"It is that I hear you," says Ling, "that you hear me, also. That we forbind and enfeel." The last has no meaning; Ling is not yet worthy of correct appearance.

"It is that I am pleased that Ling attempts Demu speech, Limila. That it may continue to do so."

Ling turns to Limila. "I didn't get that last." Limila repeats Eeshta's words in Demu and then in animal tongue.

"I *know* you understand me," says Ling. "Why won't you answer? Limila? *Why?*"

The young person shakes its head; animal gestures demean less than animal words.

"The Demu see no view but their own, Annette. We can only keep trying."

"Yes. But not today, Limila; the hell with it." And to Eeshta: "It is that you go to your place, that another time we speak in both our tongues."

"Limila, it is that I go to my place."

As the young person leaves the room it hears Ling say, "Sometimes I think Barton had the right idea the first time."

* 　 * 　 *

The young person sits with Hishtoo. Across the room Siewen looks at nothing, while Shestin very softly speaks an old Demu chant it has learned. Outside, on guard so that all must stay in, is the animal that speaks much with upcurved mouth when it takes Eeshta to and from its place here. Eeshta thinks upon a matter.

"Hishtoo, when Barton crushes our armshells, it is that there is much pain."

"That the animal gives us pain, we remember."

"Is it that there is much pain in the giving of correct appearance?"

"Much pain and loss of body liquid. It is done over many days, or animals die of becoming Demu. When Barton and the others are taken, none on Ashura had experience. We lose many as we learn. Siewen is one of the first to live, and Limila. It is that each for a time is near to death."

"That I find it not good, Hishtoo, to give such pain."

"It is that the pain is not from us, Eeshta, but from being animal without correct appearance. That animals may become Demu, we do what is proper."

"Is it that the pain is soon gone?"

"As correct appearance heals, pain goes. And we learn a thing, Eeshta. On each day of correction we give the greatest pain first, so that often the mind becomes not awake and does not feel more of what is done."

"That I am pleased you give no pain without need."

A sound is heard. Siewen is crouched over, holding itself. Its shoulders shake and it makes harsh rasping sounds with its breath. Eeshta moves to bend and see under its hood. Its face below the eyes is wet.

"Siewen," says the young person, "is it that the food today is not good to you?"

The animal of the upcurved mouth closes the door of the room behind Eeshta and remains outside. The times of questioning now count nearly to two fours of fours. Ling sits behind the squarish thing that is always covered with papers. Limila sits to one side; it no longer hides its face, and has thrown back its hood. Its smoothed head is deeper and less wide than is quite correct, but the shell of it is inside and difficult to reshape. Attempts to make such changes cause dying, and so are now abandoned on Ashura.

The young person moves a seat closer to the others, and sits. "It is that you ask and I answer," it says. "That I would now ask."

Limila would speak, but Ling waves a hand and says, its mouth curving: "All right, Eeshta, we'll make a deal. Ask anything you want—*in English*—and we'll answer. what do you say?"

"That I do not use your speech, that I must not. Hishtoo—"

Ling waves the hand again. "Forget Hishtoo for a minute. We've been asking questions, playing by your rules. If you wish to ask in turn, you'll have to play by ours for a change."

Eeshta considers. Already it speaks with an animal, though in Demu tongue. And what it would ask, it needs to know. There is no need to inform Hishtoo . . .

"Then tell me what you really want to know from me. And why."

Ling nods. "We want to know about you, about your people. How they think, and why they do what they do."

"What we do? What is that we do?"

Limila brings its hands near its face, its two fours of fingers pointing stiffly toward itself. *"This!"* It touches here and there on its head and body, and its extremities. "And this, and this, and this!"

"It is only that you are given correct appearance, Limila." Startled, the young person uses its own speech but is not rebuked.

"But why?" Limila's voice is high and harsh with strain. "Do you know what it is to be cut and sewn, and to have no face?"

"I know you had pain, yes."

"Pain? I saw others die and envied their luck. The flesh was bad enough, and the teeth. But"—it indicates the jog at the base of its hand—"the disjointing of bones! And here!" It points to the nostril openings. "There was bone. A saw, and the chisels. After the first of it I could not see, for the blood. Pain? You do not know of pain, Eeshta. Why, how, can you possibly do such things?"

"But, so you could be Demu and not animal. And now that is a long time past. You healed, and are Demu and have no more pain."

"No pain?" Limila's breathing is harsh and rapid. "Eeshta— Eeshta, how would you like to have your arms cut off?"

At first frightened, after a moment the young person realizes that there is no threat. "I would not; no one would. But why . . . ?"

"Suppose you met a race of super-Demu with no arms. They give you correct appearance by removing yours. How would you feel?"

"But without arms, how could they?"

"Damn your stupid little soul to Barton's hell, they'd *bite* them off!" In awkward haste, Limila pulls its robe from itself, crumples it, flings it against a wall. Unlike its conduct, its appearance is most correct for one not eggborn.

"Annette?" says Limila. "Would you show yourself completely?" Ling looks for a moment at Limila, then removes its own garb. The two stand together. Ling's appearance is not at all correct, but in it Eeshta can see a kind of symmetry.

"Look!" With one hand Limila touches Ling, and with the other, the same portion of itself. "This!" The mouth, the growth above it that is partly bone, the flaps at the sides of the head, and at top and back the fiber called hair.

"This!" The lumps on the chest, the changes at the extremities, the fiber-covered protrusions where legs begin. "This! This! *This!*"

It pauses, breathing heavily. "These things are all part of her. They were part of me, too, until you—your people—took them from me. My face was myself. Now I have no self."

"But you are Demu, Limila."

"Am I? No. I am not eggborn; I cannot in breeding season lock to another, bearing eggs and at the same time fulfilling that other's. I cannot go to Sisshain once to visit and perhaps a second time to become—or if not, no shame to the eggs."

"No shame to the eggs," Eeshta responded.

"I cannot even truly have correct appearance. I am not Demu, Eeshta. I am only something that was once a woman, who can no longer be a woman or even a person, from what the Demu have done to me. Because of that I am of no use, even to myself."

The young person is confused. "But the Demu mean no harm, only good. Not to take, but to give. It has always been our way, when we can, to help animals. I am sorry, Limila, that even though not eggborn, you can find no pride in being Demu."

"Pride? *Pride?*" Limila shakes its head. "Eeshta, you work very hard at not understanding me. Barton, I suppose, would call it a racial trait. Let me try again. Eeshta, would you prefer to live, or to die?"

"To live, of course, Limila. To live."

"Yes? Why?"

"Because—because alive I can do and learn. Dying ends all of it."

Limila still stands, feet apart. Its legs shake, but it does not seem to notice the shaking.

"Yes. You are right, Eeshta. Dying ends all of it. But for me it is all ended now. It ended under your knives, on Ashura. And I would rather die than live as I am."

"No, Limila—!"

"If I did not feel I were needed here for a time yet, I would die tonight."

"But how is that? Have you a sickness?"

No Demu mouth ever moves as Limila's serrated lips move now. "Not the kind you mean. My sickness is only that I would take a knife, and let out all my blood, so as to die."

The young person resists belief. "But that is—no one does so except those twice-come to Sisshain, who would become but do not become—no shame to the eggs."

"No shame . . ." Limila murmurs. "You are beginning to understand. I cannot become, as you would, because I am not eggborn. And I cannot become in my own way, because of—because of having been given correct appearance. This is what you do to me and others. This is what must be stopped. This is why we need to know of you. Not to hurt you. But to stop your hurting us!"

The young person is troubled. "Can you not still become, Limila, in your own way?"

"My way? I have no face; I have no self. There is no one left who can become. I would have—Barton would have been my most needful person—and he cannot stand the sight of me. I cannot stand the sight of what is left, either. It is not Limila. I am inside, but no one can see me, and I can no longer see myself."

All that Eeshta knows collapses; nothing is left but to believe. "But then," it cries, "Hishtoo is *wrong*. We, the *Demu*, are wrong. For to give such hurt—it cannot be correct." It hardly notices that it speaks in the tongue of animals.

It goes to Limila and holds that tall person in its arms as though for breeding—although Eeshta is one of four fingers short of breeding age, and Limila not eggborn. And the feeling is not of eggs, or of fulfilling eggs.

"Limila, it is that I help you, that I learn in both our tongues. That I try to tell Hishtoo, though I think Hishtoo does not listen or understand. That when you go to our worlds, I go, also, and tell what you say, so that it is known.

"Whatever else, Limila, it is good that Barton brings me here."

Barton got home late; the Tri-V was off and the lights were dim. "Hi! Anybody home?"

"Yes." The voice came from the kitchen. "I am here, Barton."

She sat on one chair, leaning back with her feet on another. The drink she sipped was dark between the ice cubes; the bottle on the table was bourbon. She wore no robe or hood; for a moment he saw her as she once had been. The light was dim, and the slim body almost the same—but the moment passed, and again she was faceless.

"Had to work late." He rummaged in the refrigerator, found a beer, and opened it. "A breakthrough on the Demu space drive, if Hishtoo slipped as bad as we think he did. So I ate in that crackerbox cafeteria, by the ship." He sat, and swallowed beer from the bottle. "How'd it go with you, today?"

"We broke through, also, Barton. The young Demu has decided to cooperate." She sipped slowly at her glass.

"No kidding? You cracked the shell? That's great! Hey, how did you get through to her?"

"Personal talk, Barton. Exchange of reminiscences, among all of us there."

"Yeh? I'll bet you did most of it, Limila. Didn't you?"

"I was of some help; the matter is not important." But the ring of her voice belied the words. "At any rate, it has agreed to learn and exchange information, to reduce the conflict that must be."

He wanted to go to her, but then she would expect more than he could give. "Well, that's great. I'm glad the kid's shaping up."

"Yes. We should make much better progress now."

and destroy you. If you are not there—but you have to be! I'll force you to exist; you can't escape me that way.

You really set me up after the funeral, you cosmic bastard! First the three young thugs who beat me up; crippled, I could offer little resistance. Then in the hospital, in nurse's garb, was the lady Cristal who became my wife.

You left us alone for nearly two years. You enjoyed that, didn't you—the cat-and-mouse thing? Allowing Cristal to become pregnant, then not quite killing her when you took our baby. You're really quite expert, aren't you? For a time I allowed myself *again* to believe that we would be let to live our lives, childless but in relative content and great love.

You know where you made your mistake? You're arrogant. You didn't bother to give me any reason for Cristal's death yesterday. I intend you to regret that.

She came in the door, out of the cold, with a bag of groceries. She simply collapsed, smiling at first and then showing shock and grief when she knew you were killing her. The food, for a minor personal celebration of ours, was scattered across the floor. I won't tell you how I felt; why should I let you gloat more than you're gloating already?

But then I *knew* the hell of my life was no accident. Then I knew that if you exist, at least I have a target.

I know you're not going to be easy to attack. You hold all the high ground. I don't know what you are or where you are or how to reach you.

But if you could simply wipe me out at whim, you'd have done so by now, I think. There must be rules that govern you; I have to believe that. And by those rules, your own rules, I think you've given me a chance you didn't intend. I must be right; otherwise you'd have killed me.

I'm not alone; I've asked advice from friends I can trust. They don't believe me but they humor me and are helpful.

My friend Charles the engineer says that if you are the Creator you must also be the Totality—that I am as my own fingernail trying to change my own mind. He may be right. But a hangnail can produce blood-poisoning; perhaps I shall be your friendly neighborhood hangnail, before we're done.

Larry, my lawyer friend and an atheist, clearly thinks I've lost my marbles. He says that if you exist you are the spoiled-brat God of the Old Testament, an omnipotent five-year-old child who never changed your mind in anyone else's favor and never will. So that I may as well forget it. But I think I am smarter than five years old. We'll find out.

I thought of attacking you through devil-worship but my friend Gerard says that if I am right you *are* the devil, and the last thing I'd do is worship you. In his view, and perhaps he is right, you'd be some sort of parasite claiming Godhood but not entitled to it. I may as well believe part of this along with parts of other views. It sounds like my best chance, and I need all the breaks I can get, dealing with something like you.

I may be weak and even stupid by your lights, but I don't intend to remain helpless. You'll see. There is a whole universe which I think you did not create: you came along later and took advantage of it. That makes me as good as you are, maybe better; you hear? We are here in this universe together, and if you can influence my existence, perhaps I can influence yours, too.

Gravitation works both ways.

You have negated everyone I ever loved, everyone who ever loved me. You haven't negated me yet; why not? Maybe you can't. Again, why not? Because it would backfire? Because we're tied together somehow? That's the only handle I have; I think I'll try it.

I've asked you, begged you, to return Cristal to me. You wouldn't answer. I tried prayer, the format you're supposed to appreciate. No comment. I tried other ways. And you ignored me.

It shouldn't be difficult. You resurrected a man once, if the stories are true. You rolled back a sea. You did a lot of things. Or so I've been told.

Maybe you didn't. Maybe you can't do anything but hurt and kill. It's hard, even now, to accept such a concept of you. But I must.

So I am going to call it quits, for this life. No more. Does that scare you? It should. Because I think that when I cease to exist, so will you.

I'll settle for that.

In a few minutes now, we'll see.

2000 ½: A Spaced Oddity

A TRIBE OF savage apes dances to the background strains of "The Red River Valley." Others approach, shrieking, jumping up-and-down; it may be that they do not like "Red River Valley." The two groups scream and make faces until the number comes to an end; then they separate and go in search of the modest evening repast: grubs under rocks. The first tribe finds more. Replete, it seeks a shallow cave under a cliff, for shelter through the night.

It is dark. The little clan awakes, startled by a strange sound and a flash of light. The young are frightened; at first they cry, but soon quiet, for the Old Man of the tribe reassures them. He shake a fist and reassures them that he is much more to be feared than any strange sound or flash of light.

Next morning the tribe forages for its breakfast: roots and berries. The group comes upon a huge object, black and rectangular. A strange sound is heard; all pause, awed. They cannot see the upper surface of the object; it is too high. Could they view it, they would see but not understand the message in Vegan script: "Live Cargo. Other End Up."

Again the second tribe approaches. Shrieks are shrieked; faces are made; ups-and-downs are jumped. But the Old Man of the first tribe remains silent; he makes no faces and does not jump. He is thinking. Finally he picks up the thighbone of an antelope and with it smashes the skull of the Old Man of the second tribe. The latter flee. It is time for lunch: nuts and grasshoppers.

The first tribe does not forage for nuts and grasshoppers. In prehistory, a great milestone has been reached. Man has invented cannibalism.

A spaceship thrusts itself up from Earth. Inside, one man sits alone amid a number of empty seats. Outside can be seen the famous name "Mother Ferguson's Space Line And Storm Porch Company," painted over the original legend "V-2."

The man shuffles papers from his briefcase in obvious boredom, puts them away again. He ignores the lovely stewardess who offers her repertoire of demure King's-X flirtation. He looks around the ship's interior. The stewardess passes by; this time she ignores him also. Serves him right.

The ship lands on the Moon alongside the Serenity-Hilton. The lone passenger has reservations; he checks in at the quaint old-fashioned modernistic twentieth-century desk. In the bar he meets some old friends.

A lady greets him. "Hello there, Joe. What are you doing here?"

"Adjusting to the crummy gravity, like everybody else."

"Aw, come on, Joe. You know you can trust me; I won't tell anyone?"

"Sure. I know," he says gently, patting her under the clavicle. "Well, I have to go now. Goodbye, Brenda Starr." She looks after him wistfully.

In his hotel room the man looks somehow pensive, as though troubled by irregularity. His eye lights upon the picturephone, and lights. He punches seventeen digits by pushbutton. The screen glows red, indicating that he forgot to punch the area code first.

Eventually he gets it right. A picture appears, that of a young girl. Not too young; either she has passed puberty or she owes much to the garment industry.

"Hello?" she says.

"Hello, dear. My, but you've grown!"

"Hello?" she says. Although electromagnetic waves travel at 186,000 miles per second and the Moon is about 240,000 miles from Earth, there is no delay between statement and response, due to anti-delay networks developed by Bell Laboratories. The advantage of these devices is even more evident, later on.

"Yes, hello!" he says. "I said, you've grown!"

"I suppose so. I seldom shrink!"

"But only two weeks ago, dear, you were just a little girl. Now you're a young woman. I never heard of such a thing!"

"You ever hear of getting a wrong number, clabberhead?" The screen goes blank.

Next day our man attends a secret meeting fraught with dire verbiage. A dozen or so people calmly tell each other a lot of things they already appear to know. Our man, who is being briefed, is the only one who doesn't know what everyone is talking about, because nobody ever states anything explicitly. The scene is very true to life, for a true-life scene.

Spacesuited, our man and several others inspect the depths of an excavation on the bare vacuum-packed surface of the Moon. Vacuum does not conduct sound, but the "Red River Valley" is playing; their helmets are wired for Muzak.

The group reaches its goal: a huge black rectangular object, still half-buried in the Lunar conglomerate. A strange sound is heard; everybody falls down. No one knows why they fall down, or whether they ever get up.

On the bottom of the object, still buried, is the notation in Vegan script: "Do Not Litter. Use This Container."

In deep space a ship is enroute to Jupiter or Saturn, depending on who wins the toss. Aboard it, two men are talking with a third sentient member of the crew, a highly-developed computer called Henry 8000, who speaks very softly. To be polite about it, Henry 8000 sounds as though he might have been assembled at the bottom of someone's garden.

"Henry," says one crewman, "I can't seem to find the rest of the crew. Do you happen to know where they might be?"

"Why, I'm sure I don't know, Laurel," croons Henry. "Where have you looked?"

"In the Bullmoose room; where else?" says Laurel. "Once you're in the deep freeze, you don't walk around a lot, you know."

"I wouldn't know about that," says Henry 8000. "I don't walk around much, anyway. Is it pleasurable to walk around, Laurel?"

"Well . . ."

The second crewman cuts in. "Hold it, Henry; this is Hardy. Are you sure you don't know where the rest of the crew is?"

"Why, of course I'm sure, Hardy. Statistically, at least."

"But . . ."

"It is now time for your exercise period, Hardy."

"I want to know a few things first!"

"Please, Hardy; let's not have any unpleasantness. I'll tell you what; we'll have a game! I'll give you fifty-five seconds to get to the airlock and put your spacesuit on before I let all the air out. Starting—*now!*"

Hardy scrambles to the airlock and frantically dons his suit. He wins the game with four seconds to spare. Now it is time for exercise.

The planners of this expedition know the vital importance of exercise on a prolonged space mission; they do not leave it to chance. Deliberately, they have shorted the fuel supply. In order that the mission may succeed, once in each twenty-four-hour period a crew member must go outside the ship for one hour. And push.

Laurel is in his quarters. If he isn't bored silly he's faking it nicely. His picturephone screen lights. He yawns and says "Hello."

"Hello, Stanley," says a lovable grey-haired old lady. "This is Momma."

"I can't come over for dinner, Momma. I'm busy."

"I know, I know; a mother is always wrong. Just remember someday, Stanley." The screen goes blank.

The ship lurches forward heavily for a moment, but Laurel doesn't notice. Why can't his mother understand that you can't always get away for dinner at a moment's notice? Especially when you're halfway to Jupiter or Saturn and can't find most of your crew.

The exercise hour is long past, but Hardy has not returned. Laurel punches one of Henry's buttons. "Hey, Henry; where's Hardy?"

"Why, I'm sure I don't know. Isn't he with you?"

"You know he isn't. You can see all over the ship, you peeping-Henry."

"But I don't *tell,* do I?"

"Never mind that. Is Hardy on the ship, or isn't he?"

"Well . . . he isn't."

"Why not?"

"I had to accelerate to avoid a meteor, Laurel."

"So it's goodbye-Hardy? Is that right?"

"Yes, I'm afraid so, Laurel. I'm sorry, you know. I really am."

"Yeh. I'll just bet you are."

"Well, I am! And now might I have a little silence for some decent mourning, you crude *man*?"

"Yeah; crude. First, you tell me what happened to the rest of the crew!"

"Laurel, dear boy; believe me, that knowledge would not help your morale."

"*DAMN* my morale! You *tell* me . . .!"

"Ooh; what you said!"

"Never mind what I said; let's hear what you say."

"You know, it's going to spoil your whole day, Laurel."

"Between you and my mother you're beating a dead horse. Get on with it."

"All right, Laurel, if you insist. But if I had known you were going to be like this, I wouldn't have even wanted to be your friend."

"*Say* it!"

"Well—a food-freezer went bad and all the other meat spoiled, Laurel."

It is an urgent moment. Before Henry 8000 can move to exhaust the air from the ship, Laurel pulls his plug. Down the drain swirls Henry's consciousness, counterclockwise.

Another historic milestone has been reached. Man has invented a machine that has invented cannibalism.

Laurel's ship is approaching Jupiter or Saturn; Laurel can't be sure, because of the ringing in his ears: "The Red River Valley."

Suddenly in his viewscreen appears a huge black rectangular object. A strange sound assaults his being: he reaches blindly for the pain-reliever most often recommended by doctors. The object looms, then vanishes to one side as the ship swings left and plunges into a montage of spectra swinging wildly up and down the electromagnetic scale at 186,000 miles per second. Laurel barely has time to realize that instead of aspirin he has dropped about six hundred mikes of "clear window" acid. He has not seen, on the black monolith, the clear Vegan script that reads: "No Left Turn."

Several hundred years later, subjective time, Laurel recognizes a few realities among the splendors of his visual display. He is coming down; so is the ship. No matter that it has not been built to land anywhere; it does, anyway.

Just alongside is a nice big homey-looking house, fresh out of early twentieth-century Earth. Laurel doesn't question it; he's still more zonked than not.

He leaves the ship, paying no heed to whether the air is fit to breathe. It must be; he doesn't fall down.

Laurel is now inside the house. Oh, it is so homey! And well-kept, too. He sits down to a meal, served by no seen hands. He smells the meat first.

He opens a door to another room and sees an older version of himself. The practice must be habit-forming, because the second one opens another door and sees a really decrepit specimen of Laurel.

"How come we are getting so old so fast?" says the latter. "We better stop this, or we're in real trouble."

"I know," says the other. "But I have this problem. Every time I come to a door, I open it and there you are."

"Well, try to watch it; OK?"

"Sure. And you try not to be there. Right?"

Somewhere two skeletons face each other through a door frame. One of them says nothing; the second answers in kind.

At the other end of everything, a baby mumbles. It's probably hungry.

Time of Need

THE EARTHWOMAN NEEDS me, and I her. If I had not found her, each of us would have died alone. But now her blood runs sweet in its cycle between us; I am nourished. In return, as with the *hlurin*, I sense the needs of that blood and feed into it the essences my body makes, lacking in the food she gathers here.

The filaments at the ends of my blood-tubes read her senses. They are stronger than mine and more vivid—more so, even, than those of a *hluri*. Her awareness is much greater than theirs; it may be equal to my own.

I cannot follow her thoughts in detail; I receive only fragments of memory, concepts and intentions. And unlike the *hlurin*, she can not receive my thoughts—or control-impulses. I can, of course, affect or block her senses.

Her picture of me is that of a short cloak hanging from her neck, rippling with iridescent color. The concept interests me: the *hlurin* have no such image of our kind. We are here, as they are, and they accept us.

When I found her, she was lying on the sand, with no use of her awareness. At first sight she looked much like an overgrown *hluri* except for the coverings of her body, which I then thought to be a part of her. And her short fur—it is yellow—also leaves bare her face and limbs.

I was midway of a journey I had undertaken alone. I should have been safe enough, with days to spare before my fulfilled eggs brought forth the egglings. But suddenly my *hluri* weakened and died. I do not know why—it was young, and its blood came and went with good vigor.

So, perilously near starvation, I was creeping slowly in the only way we have, of ourselves, when I came to the Earthwoman. Thinking her to be a *hluri,* I was overjoyed, and moved faster against my weakness. But, no—she was something I had never seen. Still, perhaps . . .

The risk was great, but to avoid it was to die.

At first I thought the venture had failed, for her blood was sour and noxious. But I persisted, and soon, each giving to the other's need, our strengths returned. Her breath slowed and became deeper; she stirred, rolling onto her back—onto me. She is heavier than a *hluri* but the discomfort was minor. I waited, heeding the confusions of her awareness as it slept.

Late in that day she woke. Her eyes opened; the impact caught me unprepared—I was drowned in hues and brightnesses I had never known! Then came the burst of her awareness— trying to absorb its scope, I was paralyzed. The *hlurin* think of food, comfort and—in season—breeding; to know this new creature was like knowing one of ourselves, but directly rather than through vibrations. For a time I did not think, even, to try to take control in the normal fashion.

Though I could not evoke her thought at will nor choose what I would experience, I learned much, for her awareness was busy. I saw much that I did not, still do not, understand. She was from another place, called Earth, but where it is I do not know. She had been traveling high above the sand, through the air in some way not clear to me, and then had been unable to travel further. Moving on the sand for some days she had eaten all her own food, which in some way maintains her blood without need for one of us, and then had resorted to eating that which grows here. And she, as I, had come near to death.

When first she rose she did not notice me, for I hung behind her. When she did see me—or brushed me with her arm; I am not certain which first occurred—she stroked me with her fingers and seemed pleased. Then she felt our points of attachment at her neck; she made distressed sounds and tried to tear me away. She could not succeed, nor injure me; we are not fragile, though we may appear so. But for the first time I sought to exert control, to quiet her.

I could not; she did not seem to feel the impulses, let alone respond to them. Abandoning the effort, I tried to give to her my own thought and sense-impressions so she would know

I was also aware. It was obvious that she received nothing; she pulled and tugged the harder, and made louder noises.

I could only wait, and eventually she calmed, realizing that no hurt had come to her. Then, also, came the thought that she had been near death and was restored—and what but myself could be responsible? I felt in her a sense of relief—mixed, I think, with the wish not to have pulled at me and made the noises.

She stood, walked about and fed upon the sparse growths around us. Then she gathered the things she carried with her—the *hlurin* do not carry things except under our control—and set out walking. I sensed her intention. It was to return to her own point of origin—Earth, I supposed, though the concept was confused—and rejoin others like herself.

Her course posed a problem. I sympathized with her wish to be with other Earthwomen—again there was confusion in the image I received—and also welcomed further contact between them and our own kind. The difficulty was that she was walking toward neither the origin of my journey nor its destination, but away from both. And before we left the areas I knew, I needed to add to our company a *hluri,* or preferably two. So, lacking direct control, I tried another way to turn her toward my original destination.

When I dimmed her vision on one side to turn her toward the other, she hesitated but continued movement. When I blocked it entirely she stopped, and for the first time her thought included the concept of my awareness. But her intent was strong; again she walked in the direction of her own choosing.

I blocked the other side also; she could see nothing. After a pause I restored that side, then allowed a moment of sight on the other, to tell her that to see fully she need only turn. Sensory blockage is a limited means of communication, but the *hlurin* respond to it when it is more convenient to guide them without exerting full control. With her greater awareness, I felt that she should grasp the concept easily.

She understood—I was certain she did—but she would not turn. Like a *hluri* at the peak of breeding cycle, she was totally subject to her own urge. I did not need her thoughts to know her feelings; her blood tasted of fright and anger.

She did not realize my own need; there was no way I could tell her. We contested for a time . . .

I blocked her vision completely. By touch, she found a

stick with which to probe ahead for obstacles, and proceeded slowly. I blocked hearing; she slowed further but still continued. I blocked the sensation of surface-touching; she lost the stick and dropped to proceed even more slowly on all four limbs. Her blood told of feelings I had not known, and I felt the pain of them as she did.

So after a time, since I was failing of my purpose and our pain was to no point, I restored her senses and abandoned all effort to guide. In part, my feeling of defeat was mixed with relief; it had not been pleasant, risking injury to her as she fumbled without warning senses.

There was a chance, I thought, that her destination might be near enough that we could reach it without disaster. Or that we would meet another traveler willing to accompany us or lend me a *hluri* or two. At necessity one of us can maintain three *hlurin*, or if activity is moderate, one of them nourish three of us.

And if the distance were too far, and we met no one? I had tried to turn her . . .

We traveled many days but saw no one. I do not know the distance; she moves faster than the *hlurin*. Slowly and incompletely we learned of each other, though by the nature of our contact I learned the more.

In small ways she came to accept my guidance. Often when we crossed areas where food was scarce, I noticed hidden plants that she did not. At first I dimmed or blocked vision in momentary intervals until she paused and looked around. Later I found I could intensify her sight in the desired direction; the new method was quicker and easier for both. Our relationship became more complex—more rewarding— than is possible with a *hluri*, even though we could communicate less fully.

I found that her kind breed as do the *hlurin*—but at will, not by cycle. They do many things—and much more—that the *hlurin* do, or can do, only under our control. They are, in my view, almost a combination of ourselves and *hlurin*, together in the same form.

And I learned that inside her, also, a fulfilled egg was growing to term.

She could learn of me only indirectly, by the things I could show her; how to look for food where it is scarce, how to avoid the rare places of treacherous footing—the things we must know, to live. She came to realize that something like the *hlurin* must exist—or else I could not—but nothing of what they are like, nor the degree of our mutual need.

I am not certain whether she became aware that I have my own senses, independent of hers though inferior to them.

I do not know—nor did she—how near we might be to her destination, to others of her kind. But we shall go no further; my time is here and she would not turn. I wish it were not so.

If we had reached her goal, there would be other creatures that could serve. Had I not chosen to breed at the last togethering, this time would not be upon me, nor upon the one whose eggs I fulfilled in return. But once begun, we have no control over this aspect of our lives.

Against my wishing, my body has produced the essences that spread quickly through her blood; she can no longer move. I have blocked all her senses—her awareness, shut off not only from all that is outside but also from what her own body would tell her, is in much turmoil but will be free of pain. It will not know when it ends, I think—the *hlurin* do not, in the rare times we must use them in this way.

My eggs have opened; the egglings move into her. As they must, they will feed and grow—and in that feeding, she will die.

Without her, I will die also, and my egglings with me. I wish I could have made her turn . . .

But most of all, I wish she could know that her death comes only from my body—not from my will.

Retroflex

SHOUTING, COCHRANE BURST into Haldane's office. "I've had enough of your persecution!" Haldane rose, held out a conciliatory hand and backed away. He was still trying to get a word in when Cochrane pushed him out the window.

Tumbling—around him wheeled street and sky and buildings—Haldane's mind knotted in the effort to understand. He hadn't persecuted Cochrane—he had merely conducted a legitimate investigation. The client chose to remain anonymous—the procedure was irregular, perhaps, but hardly illegal. Why had the man reacted so violently?

For perhaps three seconds of free fall, for half the distance between window and death, Haldane's preoccupation shielded him from panic. Then it broke—the need for life convulsed his body and fragmented his mind. He tried to deny the reality, and failed. He prayed for oblivion, even for insanity—but could achieve neither.

Then it stopped. Abruptly, Haldane hung in mid-air, ungracefully, legs spraddled higher than his head as if taking a belly-flop into water.

Close at hand he saw only two pairs of bare shins and feet. It didn't make sense; he drew himself into a crouch and kicked out to bring his head up.

Then he could see more. He was inside a shimmering, transparent bubble, sharing it with two smallish men who could have been twins. They had deep chests and dark ruddy complexions like high-Andes Indians. They were nude and stone-bald. Otherwise, it struck him that they looked quite a lot like Cochrane.

With relief, Haldane sighed. "Thank God, I'm dreaming! For a minute there, I thought this was all for real."

"You do not dream," said one. "This moment exists in reality."

"Oh, come off it! You mean, Cochrane really threw me out the window—and here we float? No way, friend."

"Yet we are here. And for us, the way is simple enough."

Haldane shook his head. "All right then—just for starters— *why* would Cochrane do a thing like that?"

"Because on our behalf you located and identified him. So that we may remove him, before further damage is incurred."

"*You're* the client? But what's it all about?" I still don't believe it, he thought. But no harm in asking . . .

"The one calling himself Cochrane is not of this era, but from a time far forward. Here he seeks to create havoc—to destroy our future world by changing its present roots. That his actions would cancel his own existence, either he knows not or cares not.

"Now that you have found him out, we may remove him. Our code requires that you be thanked for your service."

"Don't mention it, fellas. Just put me back upstairs, huh?"

Floating, Haldane had slowly rotated, so that again he saw shins and feet, and the sidewalk below. Directly beneath him stood two women; he saw their gestures but could not hear their words.

"It is regrettable, but we may not. Our records show that before the Cochrane person was apprehended, he did cause your death. We may not change that. Please accept our apologies."

"Well, *that's* a hell of a note! With friends like you two, who needs enemies?" The two women parted and walked away in opposite directions. At least, now when he fell . . .

The thought was small comfort. "But for Christ's sakes," he said, "couldn't you—?" He stopped in mid-question because the bubble vanished, and the two men with it.

He fell . . . then the scene wavered. An instant of pain-death at pavement—but it wasn't real—he knew it wasn't real, because

He sat in his office. Cochrane was shouting; Haldane rose to conciliate the man and

Cochrane flickered like a strobe light, and disappeared.

At the mini-bar beside his filing cabinet, Haldane filled a

small glass with ice cubes. In his hand, the glass rattled. He poured a small drink, then made it larger.

Back at his desk, he sat and spoke aloud as if explaining to an audience. "They didn't do their homework," he said. "Or else the Skin Twins would have known that the survival of their future world required not only my death—but the two women dead, too . . ."

He sipped sour-mash bourbon and found it good. And with all his heart Haldane wished he could buy a drink for two women he didn't know, and probably never would.

Two women who knew when to stop talking . . .

Misconception

FROM SEVEN KILOMETERS away, Kernan Jois watched the ship land at base camp. Outbound, he wondered, dropping off supplies? Or inbound, stopping to pick up samples? Neither matter was urgent—he voted for outbound, with word from home and perhaps new people for the exploration teams. Suddenly curious, he walked faster. At least, he thought, visitors might help ease the growing tension between himself and Lyssine.

Lyssine Druvich had attracted him within his first five minutes on Boyne's First Bounce. Carrying his luggage toward his assigned hut, he saw the slim girl—walking fast, the ends of her bright tawny hair swinging below her waist. At the welcoming party that evening, they met; her expressive features, more vital than pretty, intrigued him further. They spent most of the evening together, talking, and became lovers that night. Next morning they moved into a hut together.

When Captain Bourg's team left to explore the hills while Doctor Pridoun's was still scouting the marshes, Jois and Lyssine—and Charleyhorse, the big red dog—had the base camp to themselves. At first Jois thought the situation ideal. But as the days passed, Lyssine became less amorous and more irritable.

For part of it he blamed the "gophers," scaly little creatures that stole anything they could carry. When Lyssine's hairbrush vanished, and then her last comb, she tried for some days to manage the mass of hair with only fingers. Then one afternoon he entered their hut and found her before a mirror, wielding scissors. Most of her hair lay on the floor;

her head, except at the back where she was working now, bore only ragged, inch-long stubble.

She snipped, and squealed in pain. "Damn! I cut myself. Probably made a bald patch, too." She held the scissors out to him. "Help me, will you, Kern? I can't see what I'm doing." His expression must have startled her. "Oh, I know it looks like hell, and I'm sorry. But I can't *cope*."

"But why? Why so drastic?"

"So I won't need a comb—since I can't keep one." He nodded, and took the shears.

The cut was minute; only a few drops of blood showed, and the notch through hair to scalp was not much worse than a few others he noticed. Working slowly, he finished the job for her, first at the back and then snipping here and there to reduce the raggedness. When he was done he stepped back and looked. She said, "Is it *that* bad?"

He shook his head, but not in answer. The trouble was that the proportions looked wrong; without the heavy frame of hair to soften them, her strong features seemed almost coarse. And before he thought, he said, "I didn't know your ears were so big."

Maybe that moment, ten days ago, was when it had gone wrong. Quickly he told her it was all right, really—it didn't matter, he loved her anyway—he was only joking—certainly, under the circumstances, her decision made sense . . .

And he knew she did not believe him.

He tried to heal the breach, being as attentive and considerate as possible—especially in bed. But the harder he tried, the less she responded. Last night, for instance . . .

Sweating above her he strove to endure until she could climax. He knew what to do—in the post-pubertal training programs he had learned those skills well. So he was gentle, patient, carefully noting her reactions and responding to them. And he was sure he would succeed as he always did, until—

Her eyes opened; she frowned. "Damn it, Kern! Just *do* it!" Startled, he failed—not only her, but his own culmination. He knew such mishaps were not uncommon but had never had one before, himself. He felt, somehow, lessened.

And this morning, except to answer direct questions, she had not spoken.

Now he walked, rapidly in Bounce's light gravity, toward the camp. The air was thin but high in oxygen; at midafternoon the small, orange sun gave pleasant warmth, and the mossy turf was springy underfoot. His sample-pack sat lightly on his shoulders, containing only a few unfamiliar plant-species and one new animal. He heard it move in its cage; occasionally it made a weak, piping sound. He hoped it was not hungry.

When he neared the camp, the haphazard group of huts and domes and tents, he saw the landed ship more closely. Its ramp was up, closed, and the ship carried no familiar markings. He passed it and went on to the camp itself. As he approached their hut its door opened and Lyssine, followed by Charleyhorse, came out. The dog ran ahead, jumped up against Jois, then dropped and rolled over for a belly-rub.

Lyssine followed more slowly. *Damn it,* he thought. *I still can't get used to the way her ears stick out.* She came to him, almost, but stopped a pace away. He straightened to stand, and said, "Did the ship bring news? Or is there anyone we know, on it?"

She looked up at him. "It's not one of ours, at all. It's an Ilyachi ship."

"Ilyachi? Are they the heavy-set, furry ones?" She nodded. He said, "Yes. Two of them, females, visited the installation on Freehearth while I was training there. I tried to pick up a little of their language, but never got more than a few words."

"I speak it, some," said Lyssine. "At B-sector headquarters there were five on the trade commission. Clannish lot—they lived on their ship, and commuted. Now that I think of it, *they* were all females, too. And so are the three on this ship."

"Maybe the women travel and the men stay home."

She shook her head. "Not unless they use artificial insemination—or have a really long gestation period. Two of them at Sector came up pregnant, after they'd been there more than two years. No, it must be some kind of social protocol—the males don't meet with other species, or something."

She turned toward their hut. "Come on, I've got our afternoon drinks set up and cooling." The dog leaped up and frisked, jumping against her and being pushed away.

"Fine," he said, and followed her. Whatever was wrong between them, he thought, it was getting better—or she'd have left him to fix his own drink. At the door he caught the dog by the collar and shut him outside. "Sorry, Charleyhorse—

you're just too rambunctious for a quiet cocktail hour.''

Lyssine set out the frosted pitcher and glasses; Jois poured. He raised his glass. "Cheers." She tapped hers against it and smiled. They sat, their chairs facing.

"Have you talked with the Ilyachi? Did they say what they're here for?"

"I spoke with the one in charge; her name's Reznit. She's the shortest of them—and you can recognize her by a patch of white fur on her chin. I didn't understand much; she has a little English—*very* little—and insisted on using it. But they're not here for anything official; it's an impromptu stop. They need help of some sort, but I couldn't figure out what it is."

"Well—what *did* she say?"

"Only that Tagole and Bineft, the other two, are—how did she put it?—at necessity. And pain grows worse. That's verbatim, Kern. She got really frustrated when I couldn't understand. Finally she said she'd meet with me again at sundown, and they all went into the ship and closed it."

"Sundown." He looked at his watch, designed for Bounce's short days, and swallowed the last of his drink. He rose and went to her; she was looking at her half-filled glass, held on her lap between the fingers of both hands. He reached and tipped her chin up; after a moment she looked at him.

He blinked, and a trick of perspective changed his view of her—suddenly head and face, ears and all, looked *right*. He laughed and kissed her. First she responded, then as his kiss became demanding she shook free of it. "No."

He gripped her shoulders. "Lyssine—I'm sorry about what I said the other day. It was just the surprise—the haircut, and all. Now I've had a chance to get used to it. I think your ears are just great—I mean, just the way they *ought* to be."

"That's not it." She laughed briefly. "My brothers called me 'Jug-ears' from the time I was eight years old; that's nothing new. You hurt me for—oh, ten seconds, maybe—then I said the hell with it, you could take them or leave them. And you took them, certainly. No, that's no problem, Kern."

"Then why—"

She frowned. "I'm tired; I've worked all day. And we have to meet the Ilyachi in about an hour. I simply don't have enough energy to work myself up for the big production; that's all." The frown relaxed. "A quickie, maybe?" She shook her head. "No, I forgot—you don't like quickies."

She held her glass up. "So—nothing, then. Fresh this up for me? And show me your samples?"

If there were an answer for her, Jois did not have it. He poured again for both of them, then carefully took the day's booty from his pack. The lone animal specimen, as he set its cage on a table, was quiet. "This one's new, Lyssine. Reminds me of a six-legged lizard with fur."

"Yes." It made a squeaking sound. "Poor little thing. What does it eat—do you know?"

"Insects. It dips them out of the purple cup-flowers, with a long tongue like a toad's. Keeping it fed should be easy."

Before and during the evening meal they discussed the fauna of Bounce. Then, dressed for the quick cooling that sundown brought, they went out to meet the Ilyachi.

Charleyhorse, waiting outside, wanted to go along. Jois decided against him, and shut him into the storage shed that housed the dog's bed and feeding-dish. Then, in silence, the two walked toward the ship.

To their left, Bounce's sun neared the horizon. Jois could see the waiting aliens clearly—broad, squat, each wearing a coverall-like suit that bulged to show three pairs of breasts.

Short fur, as on a cat's muzzle, covered their blunt, wide-mouthed faces. Above, it grew longer, nearly hiding the triangular ears. The humanlike hands were bare-palmed but furred on the backs. All visible fur was predominantly grey and brown, randomly stippled with small white streaks.

Two paces short of the Ilyachi Lyssine stopped, and Jois also. In the sun's sidelighting, he could see the aliens' large, deepset eyes—but not their color. He waited; no one else spoke, so he said the only Ilyachi greeting-word he could remember. *"Lefelen."*

The shorter, white-chinned one—Reznit—spoke. "We meet."

"We meet," he said. Reznit did not answer. Aside, Jois muttered. "Take it, will you, Lyssine?"

She nodded and began to speak in Ilyachi. He could follow only the rise and fall of voice that divided phrases and sentences, and the intonation that indicated questions. Finally Lyssine paused and made a gesture to Reznit, then waited.

Slowly, from side to side, the Ilyachi rocked her head. Left—"Tagole"—right—"Bineft—both at necessity. Pain growing. No pain stop on ship. Where we go, yes, but too far—time is now. So we come here—and hope—"

Lyssine stepped closer. "But *what* do you need? Medicines?"

"Is—no word you have—*krasynu*."

"*Krasynu?*" The girl turned to Jois. "I don't know the word. From the inflection, it's a verb, not a noun. What can I *do?*" Helpless, he shook his head.

Reznit beat her hands together—only the fingers, not the palms. "*Krasynu,*" she said again. "*Krasynu. KRASYNU!*" No one answered; she turned toward the ship. One harsh syllable brought her two companions to follow her, each occasionally looking back. At the ship's ramp she motioned for them to precede her, then turned back and said, "Rise of sun—try talk more." Then she walked up the ramp and it closed behind her.

The sun had touched the horizon; now it sank visibly. "Let's get back," said Jois. "I won't ask if you made any sense out of that."

She reached down to take his hand; companionably they walked through the growing dark. A moon had risen, so small that even through the clear air Jois could barely see that it was crescent.

Back inside the hut they shed their outer clothing. Jois said, "Would you like some fruit juice? Or a little wine?"

"Juice is fine." Lyssine sat, frowning, chin propped on one hand. She took the glass, nodding in acknowledgment. "If only she'd talk her own language. I know more of that than she does English. Maybe . . ."

"Maybe she will, tomorrow." Then they sat, silent, as minutes completed one hour and began another. Jois' thoughts found no traction on the problem; he wanted to ask more questions, but Lyssine's intent expression deterred him.

Finally she emptied her glass and said, "Oh, the hell with it— I can't *think.* Maybe I need sleep."

He raised an eyebrow. "Or maybe—"

For a moment she showed no reaction—then, slowly, she smiled. "Yes, Kern. That's a thought." She rose. "I'll get ready first. All right?"

"Sure. Go ahead." She undressed quickly. Then as she turned away he was caught between desire and admiration by the slim lines of neck and back and waist, but felt a brief pang for the long, bright hair that had cloaked them.

She entered the bathroom; he heard the shower begin. He removed one shoe and was unfastening the other when from outside the hut came a different sound. At first he did not recognize it—and then he did.

It was Charleyehorse—in the storage shed the dog barked, bayed, then howled. Jois pulled his shoe on again and picked up a coat. He opened the bathroom door as Lyssine stepped out of the shower. "What—?" she said.

With droplets of water running down her body, the stubble of her hair plastered wetly-smooth to her scalp, she aroused untimely desire. He shook his head. "Charleyhorse—something's wrong; he sounds frantic. I'll go see—be back as soon as I can."

"Be careful. Take the gun."

"What for? There's no dangerous animals here."

"There weren't on Wormy Apple, either, for nearly a year. Then the snapping moles came out of hibernation and people lost some feet."

"All right; I'll take it. The powerpack's fully charged?"

"It had better be—I left it that way, after last target-practice."

He grinned and leaned to kiss her wet mouth, then went to a cabinet for the hand weapon. He hefted it—awkwardly designed, in his hand it balanced poorly. He said, "So I'm armed—satisfied? Wait here. I won't be any longer about it—whatever it is—than I have to."

Outside he used the gun's sighting-light to pick his way across night-frozen ground. As he approached the storage shed, Charleyhorse stopped howling; Jois heard a few quick yips and then the growling whine of the dog's "talking" voice that he used in play or begging. Sweeping the light from side to side, Jois saw nothing unusual. Satisfied, he opened the shed door and entered.

Sudden light, too bright for endurance, forced his eyes shut. But briefly he had glimpsed the dog—and *something*—rolling together on the floor. He raised one hand to shield his eyes and squinted against the glare. At first he did not understand.

The Ilyachi—not Reznit—held the dog's head and blew breath into his muzzle. Then the alien—unclothed, and Jois saw flecks of orange in the fur at sides and back—turned and crouched on the floor. The dog mounted her and began thrusting. The Ilyachi moaned.

"What the *hell*—?" Shocked, unable to move or decide to move, Jois stood. This freak-show *had* to be wrong—but what grounds did he have for stopping it? And if he interfered, what might happen?

Something—another Ilyachi, and again not Reznit—jerked

the gun from his hand. He tried to back away but she gripped his shoulder. *Strong*, she was!

With her other hand she clasped his neck and pulled his face to hers; he smelled—was it peppermint? Something like it, anyway. She breathed into his face. And breathed, and breathed. Until, without volition, he acted. He had no control of what he did; he could only experience and observe. He noticed that the six breasts were bare, unfurred, shaped like those of a human woman, and small.

As soon as he was naked the Ilyachi dropped crouching to the floor and he upon her. His first plungings were futile; she reached back to grasp and guide him. Penetration was painful, but he could not stop.

Now he had no skills, no restraint; his body hammered hers as hard and as fast as his muscles could perform until, very quickly, he climaxed and rolled off on one side, to lie gasping.

The Ilyachi leaned over and breathed into his nose and mouth. The smell of peppermint . . .

Again—though he did not remember getting up—he was plunging, slamming, hammer to anvil. Shame and terror filled him; revulsion raised his gorge, but again he could not stop until the act completed itself.

He lay supine, gulping breath in harsh sobs. Until the Ilyachi bent to him—peppermint—and it began again.

And again—his strength was gone, his thrustings jerky and without rhythm. How many times? He did not know, but he was no longer capable of true climax. He felt only fatigue, despair and pain, but he could not stop his body, pointlessly going through the motions of mating.

"*Kernan!* What—?" He turned his head enough to see Lyssine standing at the doorway. He tried to speak but could not. His body continued its movements.

Then he lost consciousness, not knowing if he finished the act.

There was a time of pain and dreams of pain, of wondering whether what he felt and saw was real. Usually he knew he was in bed, but sometimes he could not be sure. Lyssine was probably real, he thought, most of the times he seemed to see her—but he could neither understand nor answer her. And Reznit—would Reznit be there? No, probably he was hallucinating her presence—he preferred to think so.

Gradually the pain diminished; then it was gone, and he knew words again.

One day he knew Lyssine was real, and he could have spoken. But he did not want to speak; he waited.

"Kern? Are you back to reality yet?"

After a pause, he said, "I suppose so. I don't like it much, though. What must you *think* of me?"

"You remember, do you?" She waited for his reluctant nod. "Reznit wasn't sure whether you would or not. You got a really bad overdose of that psychedelic aphrodisiac of theirs. Charleyhorse, too—he was one sick dog for a while."

"A drug? But why? And how?"

"I don't mean you were doped, exactly. It's a natural substance. Their glands manufacture it at the proper time and they breathe it out."

"What kind of crazy freaks—?"

"Not freaks. Kern—victims, if anything. Reznit explained, in her own language. To the Ilyachi, sex isn't pleasure; it's relief from pain. When they come fertile, they *hurt*—and worse all the time, until they get release. If they don't, they can die of it, or be driven to suicide. Reznit's no surgeon, but she was ready to try a spaying operation on the other two if necessary, to save their lives. It's been done before, she says, in emergencies. Not often—an Ilyachi has maybe four or five fertile periods in a lifetime."

He almost laughed. "Then, two at once? What odds?"

"Tagole and Bineft were born together—littermates, we'd call them. So they're synchronized, I guess."

Impatient, he shook his head. "I still don't see—"

She grasped his hand. "Kern! Those two were close to suicide, just to escape the pain. That's why you got the overdose; they were so far overdue that they were frantic; they couldn't stop."

"But why—why not their *own* males?"

She laughed, then. "Their own? Kern—you know who the Ilyachi males are? You, for one—and Charleyhorse. There *are* no Ilyachi males—and there never were."

For a time he neither believed nor understood what he heard. ". . . *any* four-limbed, warm-blooded vertebrate of reasonable size. The one they had on the ship—from their own planet—it died; they don't know the cause. That's why they were in trouble."

"Different species? I don't believe it."

"You'll have to; Tagole and Bineft are both comfortably pregnant. You see—some genes and parts of genes are common to life-forms in our category. If the basic DNA matches at all well, the Ilyachi ovum accepts what fits and throws out the rest. It's not a perfect system—they whelp about one-third monsters, born dead or destroyed at birth. But they have litters of four to six; a few discards don't bother them much. Their fertility-breath acts as a screen; it won't *work* on a creature that's not fairly compatible."

He thought about it. "How could such a species evolve?"

She shrugged. "How did sexuality itself evolve, on Earth and elsewhere? Somehow, in the change from budding to mating, the Ilyachi only made it halfway, and became an incomplete species. But that's their problem; we have enough of our own."

"We?" He could not read her face. "Oh—yes. Well—I suppose I can't blame you. I—" He shook his head. "What you must have thought when you saw me—like *that*—I don't think I want to know."

Her grin showed teeth. "Want or not, I'm telling you. You know what? First I couldn't believe it. And then I *envied* Tagole."

"Envied?" Was *she* going crazy?

"For once in your life, Kern, you had to work without a script—the drug gave you no choice." She exhaled, a sound of impatience. "You have no *idea* how tired I get of seeing you strain, hanging yourself up, oh-so-careful like the books say, waiting on *me*. It hangs me up, too, you know—all that waiting."

"But I—"

"But, but, *but!* The hell with that." Her voice was harsh, but not her smile. She put a small pellet in her mouth and chewed. "This isn't the real thing, of course—but we can pretend, can't we? Now that you like big ears?"

She leaned over him and breathed peppermint. *"Krasynu?"*

The Signing of Tulip

NOW:

Westman looked around the locked room—at the man holding the gun, at the woman trying to get up, and at the corner where Tulip crouched, bewildered. He asked again, "Who are you, really?" Then, "I've seen you somewhere. What's your name?"

The room was small; the man's harsh laugh filled it. "If you can't remember last week's headlines, my former name doesn't matter. I broke out and I'll stay out. You can call me Zaird—*Colonel* Zaird, of the FFJ. Does that tell you anything?"

The woman was on her knees now, hands braced against the floor. Before Westman could speak the other man said, "Now you know, so get that damned door open. I'm going out of here and taking her with me."

Westman shook his head. "I told you—I don't know the combination." He nodded, not toward the man or woman but toward the corner. "Only *she* knows it—she, and the computer."

"Then tell the damned freak to get busy." The gun hand twitched.

YESTERDAY:

On the closed-circuit screen, Ivar Westman watched Tulip push the six buttons, rapidly and without hesitation. When the door opened, she made her usual little jump of triumph. Then, with a fast but awkward-looking gait, she scuttled out to join him. She signed, *Tulip good, give food.*

He turned to her and answered with his hands. By habit, he spoke the words also. "Tulip good. Eat one food."

143

Tulip smacked her lips, grimaced and signed again. *Two food. Give Tulip two food.*

"No. One open, one food." Tulip looked away, scratched herself, then reached to the fruit bowl. After deliberation she chose a plum, and started back toward the door.

Reaching it the young chimpanzee turned, and put the plum in her mouth to free her hands. She signed, *Door. Two open, two food,* and went into the testing room. Activated by her entry, the door closed.

Behind Westman, the woman's voice startled him. "She's getting to be quite a little dickerer, isn't she, Ive?"

He turned. "Hi, Maurie. Didn't hear you come in." He smiled as he looked at Maurine Zagren—straight, slim, with dark hair framing her tanned features. "Glad you're back. How does it feel to be the daughter of a Supreme Court justice?"

Maurine grinned. "Wonderful, if you want to know. To have a woman on the Court, finally—and my own *mother.* I'm floating, Ive."

She came to him; they kissed. He hugged her and stroked her hair where it hung past her shoulder. When she snuggled against him her dark head touched his nose; he sniffed the light perfume she wore.

With a final squeeze he laughed and released her. "Well, I'm glad for both of you." He turned to the screen, where Tulip reached toward the buttons, pulled her hand back, moved up and down in a slight bouncing motion as she awaited the green light that meant her console was activated.

"She's getting impatient. I should have left the switch on 'lock'." He moved the toggle but again did not engage the locking clip.

On the screen they saw the light glow; Tulip's fingers moved rapidly and again the door opened. The woman asked, "How long since she's missed?"

"She learned the new sequence progression in two days; she hasn't brought on the red light and buzzer since then. Her biggest hurdle, of course, was earlier—learning the *concept* of progression."

Tulip came to Maurine, taking the woman's hand in both of hers and holding it to her cheek. When she released the hand, Maurine signed, *Tulip good. Take one food.*

Tulip looked, chose a pear, then paused and set the fruit down. She signed, *Tulip go Jasmine. Give Jasmine one food?*

Maurine looked at Ivar; he nodded and signed, *Give Jasmine one food*. Tulip took another pear, picked up her own and scampered away. The screen door banged shut behind her as she entered the hall leading outdoors. Westman said, "She's coming along faster than most, despite everything. I wonder what her limits will be—or if our own will stop us from finding out."

The woman moved to a chair. "Let's sit down—I had a long day yesterday, and a short night." She kicked off her shoes and stretched. Then, "Ive, do you think she'll really give the other pear to Jasmine—or is she up to pulling a little swindle?"

Westman shook his head. "No, she'll deliver. Oh, sure, she has the intelligence to lie—even dogs have, for that matter—but it's not part of her pattern. She's always been rewarded for honesty and ignored for her few lapses. The only times she plays games is when they *are* games—and she knows the difference."

Briefly, he laughed. "Tell me, Maurie—when you were in school did you ever think you'd wind up on a project trying to determine the I.Q.s of chimpanzees?"

"Hardly. And when I took the offer I had no idea how totally *fascinating* it would turn out to be. These past two years . . . "

"I know." He stood again; for a moment he gripped her shoulder. "I could use some coffee. How about you—coffee? Tea? Something from the fridge?"

"If there's any grapefruit juice . . . otherwise, coffee's fine."

He walked along the hall; the kitchen was on the left, second door. He checked the coffee urn and decided the contents were not too old. In the refrigerator he found an open can of Maurine's juice and poured a glass.

Back in the testing room and seated again, he said, "Webling's field report came in. The new tests still aren't the answer."

"Are they any improvement?"

"Some. He tried them on over a thousand retarded deaf children in—I forget how many institutions around the country—more than twenty. Correlation with the standard tests was good over a considerable range—but the divergence sets in at just about the levels our little friends here can manage."

"So we still can't assign Tulip—for instance—an I.Q. rating in human terms. Ive? Do you think we ever will?"

He shrugged. "I'm not sure that it even matters all that much, except to the press and for hyping up political support at budget time. We're finding out what chimps can *learn*—and *do*. It shouldn't be important whether we can compare their abilities with our own on a one-to-one basis. Maybe we can, maybe we can't. Maybe the speech center is so great a part of human reasoning power that tests that ignore it *can't* correlate with those that don't."

She reached, and squeezed his knee. "Then let's not worry about it. So—what else is on your mind, lately?"

His hand covered hers. "Well, there's us, of course. Have you decided yet? And what does your mother say?"

"Oh, Cecile's on your side, as usual." Maurine grinned. "My mother the liberal jurist still has a sneaking preference for legal marriage, old style, when her only daughter's concerned."

He nodded. "Sensible woman. So—why be a holdout?"

"Well . . . I *wish* you wouldn't be so stiffnecked, insisting on barring yourself from community property rights."

Now he shook his head. "No gossip writer gets the chance to call me a fortune hunter. We've been over this before." He squeezed her hand. "Come on—what do you say, Maurie?"

"Can—can you wait until the fifteenth, Ive? Cecile can't get free before then, and of course she wants to be here."

His silence lasted nearly thirty seconds. Then he said, "You could have just *told* me, you know . . ."

"But it's more fun to be asked." When next she had the chance to speak, she had no breath for it.

When Degardis, the swingshift attendant, arrived—on time, as usual—Westman and Maurine went to their lakeside apartment. They showered and after a time dressed to go out for dinner. Transferring her billfold from one purse to another, Maurine found a small piece of paper.

"Ive? I forget this. Denise had gone when I came in this afternoon, but she left this memo.'

He finished tying a shoe and stood. "What's it say?"

"Hmm . . . Denise must have written this with her left foot—a freelancer wants to interview us, about the project. A Roger Wolfe, or maybe it's Walfe.''

"Either way, I never heard of him. And why us? Doctor

Kawahara's the official voice around here, and he's due back sometime next week.''

"Tight schedule, apparently. Or, as Denise puts it,''—she spelled it out—"T-I-T-E S-K-E-D. He's asked to see us tomorrow, at the labs.''

"Saturday?'' Westman paused. "I was sort of looking forward to our day off . . .''

"I should go in anyway, Ive. I can't get caught up in one day, but at least I can find out how far behind I am.''

He shrugged. "Oh, all right. With you and the Doc both gone, I'm a little behind on the paperwork, myself. So— might as well make it a full shift, I guess, and let Olivia have a free day. We still owe her a couple from last month. Now how do we—?''

"There's a number. Here.'' Westman took the paper, sat and punched out the number.

"Hello. Mr. Wolfe?''

"Yes, I'm Wolfe.'' The voice sounded thin, and harsh.

"Ivar Westman. I understand you'd like an interview tomorrow.''

"Yes. I'd appreciate it. You and your assistant both, if possible.''

Westman made a grimace, but did not explain that Maurine was hardly his assistant—that they worked as a team. He said, "All right. Tomorrow afternoon, at the labs—say, two o'clock?''

"Yes. Yes, that's fine.''

"Okay. See you then.''

"Right. Thank you. Good night.'' The phone clicked.

Westman punched another number. "Olivia? How'd you like to take tomorrow off?''

Olivia Croix laughed. "Love it. But how come?'' He explained, and the conversation ended quickly.

Westman stood. "Maybe if this Wolfe knows what he's doing, that part won't take too much time.'' He picked up his jacket. "Let's go eat, shall we?''

Poseidon's Palace overlooked the bay; no buildings obstructed the view. Ivar and Maurine were seated without delay; shortly they clinked Martinis together gently, took first sips and fell silent to watch the red glow of sunset on the water. A huge ferry entered the shadow cast by the far headland; a bumptious tug cut across the brightest area of reflected light. "Always beautiful, isn't it, Ive?"

"Huh? Oh yes—of course."

"Is something bothering you?" Her voice sounded concerned. "You're feeling all right, aren't you?"

"Oh, sure. It's just—did you see the headline on the stand, as we came in?" She shook her head. "More damned terrorism! If it isn't the Fanatic Left it's this new right wing outfit, the Force For Justice. They all talk high ideals and behave like mad dogs!" Pausing, he managed a grin. "I'm sorry. That's no way to celebrate, is it?"

She reached and touched his hand. "It's all right; I don't like it any better than you do. And you ought to hear mother on the subject! She'll be sitting when Hoagerth's appeal comes to trial. The bus station massacre—remember? Four survivors identified him solidly, but the arresting officer's report spelled his name wrong! Well, there's more than that, of course, but Cecile says the whole appeal is built on trivialities. Non-germane, she says—in the tone of voice that means she's not putting up with any nonsense."

"Well, that's a help." He breathed deeply, and said, "You never did tell me about the ceremonies. Did it all come off okay?"

"There were a few highlights—" She laughed, leaned forward and talked softly. By the time she reached the incident of the prominent official, his faulty zipper and last-minute rescue by a receptionist's stapler, Westman also laughed. He enjoyed the dinner a great deal.

Later at the apartment they sat facing the moonlit lake. At Poseidon's they had declined liqueurs; now each nursed a tiny glass of Drambuie. Ivar said, "Are we fully settled, on the marriage terms?"

Her hair moved against his cheek. "I have nothing new. You want separate financial holdings; I think it's silly but I'll agree. We each take the other's surname as an extra middle name; I like that. I have one child by you and the option of another by anyone of my choice—*including* you—and no more." He nodded, and she turned to him. "You can't stop me from leaving you money in my will, you know." She nipped his earlobe. "Married or not, I can do that."

"It's a waste of time; ask the insurance companies." But

he hugged her. "Sure, Maurie—I don't want the money, but do as you please. Since you will, anyway . . ."

Clouds hid the moon, and they found no reason to sit longer.

Ivar Westman woke to sunlight that matched his feelings: *Maurie's home again.* He turned and saw her also awake. "It's a little early," he said, "but let's get up anyway."

"All right. Nothing like a change of pace."

They breakfasted leisurely and well, and arrived at the laboratory site with several minutes to spare. As they walked in, Ivar whistled.

Pennell, the night man, had no objection to leaving early. Westman checked the logsheets quickly; he saw no problems and waved Pennell on his way.

Maurine said, "I'd better go get reacquainted with Jasmine. The interim tests don't look too bad but the program *is* lagging. Not too much, I hope."

Westman nodded. "I hope not, too." As she left he began reading reports on chimpanzees he did not usually work with directly.

Bozo, male, above average but lately moody and given to tantrums. The young ones, thought Westman, will play our silly games of intelligence and communication. But once sexual maturity begins, they have no time for anything but serious business . . .

"Well," he mused aloud, "that goes for a lot of so-called humans, too." His file notation recommended transferring Bozo to "graduate school," an area where the trained adults lived in relative freedom but under close observation. "He's been a good one," Westman added, "so pay special note to how much he continues use of signing with the others, with less stimulation from humans."

Some files required only his comments; others demanded that he leave his desk to go deeper into the building and test one of his small friends' responses against the bare records. Miriam, age four, female, performed much better to signing plus voice than to signing alone. Interesting: taking some fruit with him, he joined Miriam for a half hour of games with her training toys. The report proved correct. He lacked the time to give Miriam as much petting and cuddling as she wanted, but left two extra plums in recompense.

Sonya, second-generation trainee; first taught signing only

by her mother, Mercedes. Most chimps do not sign as
precisely as do humans; until human teachers also worked
with her, Sonya's "accent" was almost unintelligible—except
to Mercedes. "Analogous to regional dialects," wrote
Westman, and wished for the time, space and money to
conduct more extensive experiments. Start two self-teaching
families, he thought—what happens when they meet, a genera-
tion later? He shrugged: it wouldn't happen in *his* time . . .

Midmorning brought coffee break; Maurine joined him in
the kitchen. "Jasmine's doing well," she said. "We didn't
lose much. I think she was frustrated while I was gone; she's
certainly eager enough, today."

He told her the highlights of his own findings, then asked,
"How's Turtleneck doing?"

"Now that's odd. He's past due for puberty, for losing
interest and becoming irritable, but he doesn't. Possibly he's
just short on hormones. A physical checkup, do you think?"

"For sure. But maybe there's another factor. I hope so."

"Yes, I know." She stood, and washed her cup. "Well,
back to it.' He smiled and nodded as she left, then followed
her example and set out, with his clipboard, on his own
late-morning rounds.

He found Tulip in her favorite playground, squatting before
a board composed of dark and lighted squares. She touched a
button; a light went out and Tulip jumped once as she waited
for the computer terminal to match her move—the computer
was set for a five-second delay, to simulate a living opponent.

The game was an advanced version of tic-tac-toe, and
Westman saw that Tulip was winning too easily; it was time
to reprogram for added complexity. But no hurry . . .

When the game was done she turned to him. He signed:
Good win; play more? Without answering, she came to him
for cuddling; he gave and accepted it. Then she pulled back
and signed for food and sleep—nap time. Hand in hand they
went to her sleeping quarters, stopping on the way for her to
select a peach and an orange.

Westman's own stomach felt overdue for lunch. In the
kitchen he rummaged in the refrigerator and cupboards, and
was stirring a steaming kettle when Maurine joined him. "Hi!
Just in time for Westman's' famous grab-bag goulash, from
the recipe handed down for generations."

"I didn't know you had a recipe, Ive. I mean, it's never
twice the same."

"That's the beauty of it. Easy to remember, too—the first two vegetables I lay hands on, and brown the hamburger before adding."

Early in the afternoon Westman found he had used up all the interesting tasks from his backlog and was left with the routine chores he tended to postpone. When the gate buzzer sounded, shortly before two o'clock, he sighed with relief and went to admit the visitor. The man was tall, with sandy hair; his acne-pitted face bore fresh sunburn. He said, "I'm Rog Wolfe. You're Westman?"

They shook hands. "Yes. Come on in." Westman led the way; inside, he introduced Maurine.

Wolfe said, "Maurine Zagren. *The* Zagren?"

"Daughter of *the* Zagren, yes."

"Well. How does it feel?"

"I'm proud of my mother, of course—"

"Sure—and congratulations. But it doesn't change anything, you know."

Maurine frowned. "I don't understand."

The man waved a hand. "Because your mother's rich, just like all the others. Did you ever think, how can there be justice between rich and poor, when no *poor* man ever sits in judgment?"

Westman spoke. "Not entirely accurate, but you have a point—judges aren't named from the welfare pool; I'll grant you that. But we both know why."

He gestured the other to silence. "Except for a few J.P.s out in the boonies, judges are lawyers first. And for good reason—do you want the law interpreted by people who don't *know* law?"

Wolfe hunched his shoulders forward and dropped his chin into their protective custody. "Maybe what we need is less law and more justice."

Maurine said, "No one disputes that, Mr. Wolfe—as an ideal. In practice it's not quite so easy." She breathed deeply once, smiled and said, "But hadn't we better get on with the interview?" She sat, and the two men did, also.

The man shrugged. "Yes, you're right." He took out notebook and pen. "I've read some about all this, of course—but pretend I haven't, and start from the top. That way I'll probably pick up facts I've missed." He looked to Westman.

"All right. Let's see—" Westman began with the earlier,

disappointing attempts to teach chimpanzees to speak, the realization that chimp intelligence was greater than those experiments indicated, and the introduction of American Sign Language, used by the deaf.

"Bypassing our friends' lack of a true speech-center, you see. The work began in the 1960s, made considerable progress and then was stalled for lack of funds—until the Carrington Foundation, operating partially on Federal grants, established this project eight years ago. Dr. Kawahara's in charge; Maurine and I, jointly, are more or less his chief honcho. The group here is conducting a number of related programs—" He described several of the major lines of study—the comparative efficiency of sign language to that of verbal commands and questions, graphic symbols, sequential light patterns— separately and in combination. "We still have a lot to learn. But even so, the results to date have been—we think—spectacular."

Wolfe interrupted. "Yes. I saw, in the paper. But you're enslaving them, making them do scutwork. At a time when computers are putting *men* out of work."

Westman shook his head, hard, trying to understand. Then it came to him, and he laughed. "Oh—you mean Jasmine, sorting parts into bins?" Wolfe nodded; before he could speak, Westman continued. "You should have *seen* that. I saw part of it, and Art Schatz told me the rest. Here's how it happened . . .

"Jasmine looked in at our Apparatus Shop to see Art, because she likes him. Art was busy sorting miscellaneous components from dismantled experiments; it's a tedious chore and there's a lot of it to do sometimes. Jasmine watched for a while and pretty soon she began trying to help. She made mistakes at first, and Art hadn't been here long enough, then, to learn much Sign Language. So he showed her by pantomime— taking a component and going along from bin to bin until he came to the one that matched. Just a few examples and she had the idea.

"I got there at the funny part—when she caught *him* out. Art was short one container so he'd doubled up two items. Jasmine didn't like that; she was scolding him something awful." Westman laughed. "I had to go scrounge up an empty coffee can, to keep the peace."

Wolfe showed no amusement. "So now you have a slave you can pay off in bananas."

"Slave? Just try to keep Jasmine *out* of the Apparatus shop, mornings. It's a game to her; don't you see? And she only plays as long as she wants to. Usually she runs out of parts while she's still interested, and drives Art nuts by mixing a couple of handfuls so she'll have something to do."

"If you say so." The words came grudgingly. Then, "Can you show me anything new today, some eyeball stuff?"

Brows raised, Westman looked at Maurine. She said, "How about Tulip?" He nodded, and she said, "Shall I fetch her?"

"We could go to the playground; the board game's there. Or do you think the door here—the combination lock, and the screen for observation—would impress the public more?"

"The door, I think." She stood. "I won't be long."

As she left, Westman said, "In a way, Tulip is our star pupil. It's too bad—well, it's too bad there aren't more like her."

Wolfe leaned forward. "What does she do?"

"She—no, I have to give you some perspective. Have you had any experience with retarded persons?"

Wolfe had a harsh laugh. "I've watched Congress on TV."

Westman lost patience. "I didn't come here on my day off, Wolfe, to listen to your political resentments. If you can't stick to business, let's scrub it." The man shrugged; his expression might have been meant for apology. Westman said, "All right. Part of my homework for this job was to study how retarded youngsters can learn and function." He paused. "Wolfe—! What we're finding out, here, is that chimps—in their own way, with the limitation of lacking verbal speech—can think and function on a level with a considerable percentile range of humans."

"I know about percentiles. What's the range?"

"We won't know yet. The problem is devising tests that use only the abilities chimps and humans have in common—no speech or reading, for instance, although some of our chimps can 'read' in the sense of correlating graphic symbols with hand signs—tests that check out with standard tests when used with deaf retarded children. We haven't done it yet and maybe we can't. But if we do, we can rate chimpanzees on the standard human I.Q. scale."

Wolfe said, "And you think that's important?"

"I don't know if it is or not, but certainly it's interesting."

"As long as the world is set up for morons, I guess you're right."

Westman gave his guest a hard look. Then as Maurine entered with Tulip, he relaxed and signed a greeting. The young chimpanzee signed: *Tulip win good.* Then: *Open door? One open, one food?* She turned toward the door; he tapped his foot once, saying, "Look." She looked back; he signed and said: "Wait." Tulip squatted and watched him.

To Wolfe he said, "Once in that room, the only way Tulip can open the door from inside is to punch a series of buttons in the correct order, with no repetitions. She began with two; now she's up to six."

"That doesn't sound too hard."

"Do you know the law of factorials? Six buttons make seven hundred and twenty possible combinations. Care to try it?"

Wolfe shrugged. "Not especially. But once she's hit on it . . ."

"Each time she succeeds, the computer is activated to change the combination—in a logical progression. And the point is that Tulip is able to learn that pattern and know what the next combination will be. Which is more than I know, without checking the readout tape."

Impatient, Tulip rocked on her haunches, but Westman continued. "Five days ago we changed the sequence pattern. She solved it in two days—with a little help. At first the starting-point button was lighted to give her a clue. Since then she's made no mistakes."

He signed to Tulip; she scuttled through the door and it closed. Westman turned the screen on. "Now watch." They saw Tulip sitting, waiting. He activated the console, and moved the locking clip to hold the switch operated.

Tulip reached; her fingers moved rapidly and the door opened. She jumped, clapped her hands as she ran out, then signed: *One food.* Westman signed agreement; she squatted and ate a plum.

Three times she repeated the performance. Westman said, "Satisfied?"

"I guess so," said Wolfe. "I couldn't follow exactly what she does—she moves to fast—but I could see it was different, one time to the next."

"Good. Now then—what else can we do for you?"

Wolfe frowned. "Well—is there anyone else here I could talk to, and maybe get a few additional sidelights?"

"I'm afraid not. We gave the regular Saturday attendant the day off, since we were going to be here anyway. But—"

"In that case—" For a moment Wolfe turned away; when he turned back he held a gun, a medium-caliber automatic. "In that case I'll take what I came for, and leave." He grasped Maurine's arm.

Confused, Westman said, "What the hell is this?"

"Simple kidnapping, slave trainer. Zagren goes with me."

She tried to pull free. "But why? I'm not all that rich—"

Westman cut in. "And ransom payments are virtually impossible now; you must know that. Ever since the Hearst Law—"

The gun swung toward him. "Be like a clam." Then, to Maurine, "Your mother—Madame Justice Zagren. The Hoagerth appeal—throwing out Ronnie Hoagerth's conviction and turning him loose—that's important to our group. I'm making sure of it."

Maurine shook her head. "You don't know mother. She won't—"

Wolfe grinned. "She'll disqualify herself; she'll have to. And maybe that's all we need. Or maybe I'm not the only one doing a job today." He shook his head. "That's enough—now shut up! And you, Westman—get in that room like I told you." The gun hand motioned.

Westman stood his ground. "What good will that do you?"

"You told me yourself—the chimp knows the combo but you don't. I can use a headstart." He laughed. "Seven hundred twenty possibles, you said? That should take you a while." His teeth showed as he snarled. "Now move!"

Slowly, Westman began to obey. *Seven twenty for him*, he thought, *but twelve or less for me. I know the pattern and the sequence; all I don't know is which step it's on now*. And with a rush of feeling that dizzied him, *I'm glad I didn't tell him that*.

As he approached, the gunman pivoted to keep facing him. Maurine stood still; Wolfe jerked at her arm. Suddenly she lurched toward him; her left hand clawed at his wrist and pulled the gun down. She shouted, but not in words. Westman grabbed for the gun also, hoping to hit the safety catch and disable the weapon. In the jungle of palms and fingers he could not know what he touched, but something clattered on the floor.

He looked down. The clip!—with all the cartridges, unless one were in the chamber. He kicked at it, missed, kicked again and saw it skitter to disappear under a filing cabinet. Maurine, on her knees now, hair hanging over her face, clung to Wolfe's arm. With his free hand the man struck at her. She screamed—a sound of rage, a war cry.

Then Tulip opened her jaws wide, leaped and closed them on Wolfe's ankle. Westman, in midstride, could hardly believe what he saw—Tulip? Gentle Tulip? But he did not waste the diversion; once more he kicked. He caught Wolfe's wrist squarely and saw the gun tumble through the air, falling into Tulip's problem room.

The kick took his balance; as he fell he saw Wolfe lunge after the gun, dragging Maurine and Tulip. Westman pushed himself up and went after them. His shoulder, where he had fallen on it, was a numb ache; he gasped for breath.

He stopped, and now there was time for fear. Wolfe, with the gun pointed straight at him, was rising; the man's expression gave no hope that the chamber might be empty.

He looked around, hearing the door close behind him. Maurine lay to one side, slowly turning to get to hands and knees. Tulip, teeth bared, crouched in a corner, shivering.

Westman shook his head. "I don't understand. Who are you, really?" The second time he asked, the man told him.

The name, the absurd *nom-de-guerre* of "Colonel Zaird," meant nothing. But he knew what atrocities the FFJ had done—and could do again. And now Wolfe, or Zaird, pointed to Tulip and said, "I told you—tell her to get at it. Fast!"

Westman tapped his heel on the floor once, then three times. He said, "Tulip, open the door," but he signed: *Tulip stay*. The frightened chimp looked at him and did not move. He repeated the sequence.

Zaird said, "What the hell's the matter? Get on with it."

"She's scared, I think—and confused. Give her time."

"That's what I don't have, to spare." The man went to Maurine and helped her to her feet. "See what *you* can do."

She looked at him and did not move. "If you were dying of thirst—" He slapped her; she said no more. Westman tensed to leap, but the gun swung back to him.

"All right—*you*. Go face the wall, hands behind you.

Cross the wrists—that's right." In a moment Westman felt cold wire around his wrists; it tightened and he knew Zaird was twisting the ends together. "Now turn and sit down. Back against the wall, feet straight out.' Westman stepped a little to the right, then followed orders. Sitting was awkward with hands tied—he almost fell, but under cover of his wavering, moved to the position he wanted.

Scowling, Zaird bent and rubbed his bitten ankle. Westman saw no blood, but against dark socks it might not show. The man said, "Get on with your act—make the damned monkey open the door. And hurry up."

"I'll do what I can." *And that,* he thought, *is utter truth.* Tied now, he could not sign; he repeated the verbal orders and occasionally tapped a heel three times against the floor. Tulip fidgeted and grimaced but did not leave the corner.

Zaird walked over and pointed the gun at his head. Westman said, "I'm doing the best I can. You'll just have to be patient," and the man moved away again.

He went to Maurine. "*You* tell her, too. Maybe with both of you—" Tight-lipped, she shook her head.

The gun hand raised; Westman said quickly, "Do it, Maurie." So the woman duplicated Westman's efforts—all of them. Tulip stayed where she was, but her fidgeting became more and more restive.

Westman thought, *there's too much time left. I'll have to try it.*

At first he thought he had miscalculated, that the outlet was too high. But twisting his wrists painfully against the wire he turned his right hand up, and reached it. His fingers grew numb—first the appliance plug would not move; then he was afraid he would pull it all the way out, and lose it. While never pausing, always repeating his commands to Tulip . . .

He braced against pain and shock, hoping his face did not show the effort. He probed with the protruding end of the wire that bound his wrists—up and down, back and forth—and then it happened. The wire bridged the plug's exposed prongs.

The shock galvanized him. Peripherally he saw the flash reflected from the wall, as molten metal splattered his wrists.

But *the lights went out*—and freed from his momentary paralysis, Westman rolled to one side. The gun's report crashed in the small room; Westman heard the bullet splat into the wall above him. Then he heard shouts, Zaird's and Maurine's, but could not make out the words.

He tapped one heel three times, and again three. Zaird's voice came. "Tulip! Open the door. Open the door, God-damn you!" Then, "Let go, you bitch!" and a thud, and someone scrambling.

"Maurine! Are you all right?" Then, realizing the danger, "No, don't answer!" Nearer to him now, the scrambling noises ceased.

Only the dim green light above Tulip's console broke the darkness. It told Westman that the testing equipment was still working, drawing current from its separate circuit. Well, he hadn't really expected to get the main breaker. . . .

Dimly he could see the crouching, shadowy figure of Colonel Zaird, terrorist and would-be kidnapper. The man moved to Tulip's control panel. "All right, I'll try it myself. Any-thing a monkey can do—and seven twenty is just the outside possibility. I could get lucky." Then, over his shoulder, "When that door opens, Westman, you're a dead man. I don't forgive treachery."

Now the green glow, very faint on the wall, outlined Zaird's silhouette. From outside, a buzzer sounded and Westman knew a red light was blinking also. Zaird had completed his first attempt. Then, over and over again, the buzzer sounded, as the man punched sequence after rapid sequence.

Westman knew he could not wait on luck; Zaird might hit the combination at any moment. Twisting back and forth, he put pressure—more pressure than he thought he could stand—against the hard wire, trying to bend it repeatedly, hoping to break it in time. He had to try—and he did, heart pounding and breath coming fast and shallow. Warm blood oozed down along his palm but he could not allow a little blood to matter—he kept trying. At first he worked as quietly as he could, but now Zaird was shouting, cursing; the noise didn't matter, either.

A hand touched his knee. He whispered, "Maurie?"

Very softly: "Can I help? Or should I try to tackle . . . him?"

There was no choice to make. "Stay here. He's crazy now—if he wasn't already. But maybe—the wire, behind me. See if you can untwist it, if it hasn't welded itself together."

He felt her hands at his wrists, but just as she began to move the wire, the door burst open.

Again a shot exploded the air around his ears; he saw figures wrestling and falling. Then a light blinded him.

"Are you all right, sir?"

Bandages circled his wrists; on his lap Tulip nibbled grapes slowly, one at a time, while he sipped Doctor Kawahara's bourbon, diluted only by ice cubes. Maurine sat next to him, one hand on his shoulder. Across the kitchen table Police Sergeant Lantry asked questions and took notes, while technician Degardis enjoyed the plaudits due him as rescuer.

His testimony was already on record: "I came on shift and kept hearing the buzzer—on and off, a whole series of failures and the red light to prove it. That didn't fit, not with Tulip, and she's the only one doing that series now. I came in here and nobody was on control, and I thought, where was Olivia? So I switched the screen on—got no picture but the sound worked. Well, nobody around here cusses all that much. Doctor Kawahara a little sometimes, but not like that. And he's out of town, and it wasn't his voice anyway. So I dialed the emergency number; that's all.

"But sergeant, I sort of wish you *had* killed that bastard."

"Wrong. This way, shaken up as he was, he spilled quite a lot. We'll be rounding up some of his associates."

Now, Lantry said, "Okay, I see part of it, from what the suspect said before he got under control and clammed up. But I don't understand—" and he specified what he wanted to know.

"I had to knock out the lights," Westman said, "before Zaird caught onto what we were doing—he would have, sooner or later, and his kind of answer would be to use force on Maurie, hurt her. We needed time, until Degardis came on duty; I was counting on his seeing something was wrong."

"But you—"

"I was *saying*—and Maurie was, later—what Zaird wanted, but *signing* Tulip to stay put, and reinforcing that instruction by floor-tapping signals. She's good at those; she can feel the vibrations from two or three rooms away, if the place is quiet—not a lot of people walking around, I mean."

Lantry frowned. "Look—I know your little friend is a lot smarter than I would have thought. But how could you depend on her to know what to do when you were saying one thing and—what do you call it? signing?—another?''

Maurine squeezed Westman's shoulder and said, ''That's the thing Zaird didn't know. It's why Ive needed to kill the lights.'' She smiled. ''Tulip's brilliant, in her own way. If she weren't, she wouldn't be in the project any more. Because since two years ago, when she had a very bad fever and nearly died, she's been stone deaf.''

Tulip ate another grape.

Advantage

FLAMING, THE RUINS collapsed; the world's last survivors perished. Watching the guttering embers, the one observer said, "You win again. I thought I could sustain this sequence, but you out-maneuvered me."

Gesturing in self-deprecation, the other laughed. "Once you introduced large groupings, the idea of politics was inevitable."

"I admit, you have a real talent for destructive concepts."

The other said, "I admire your attempt to turn my construct to your own use—and you came close to success. But with all due respect, the materials at hand gave you no real chance of winning."

"True," said the one. "The poor grade of operational subjects handicapped me. Perhaps we should adjust the betting odds."

"No. They are the same for both of us." The other paused and took refreshment. "Do you wish to discuss, further, this latest exercise?"

"Not at all," said the one. "It is self-evident. Let us cast for roles."

"I agree." The tokens rolled, and gave their verdict.

"You see?" said the other. "I told you . . ."

"Yes. It's about time, too. This turn, Yahweh, *you* have to build the Universe—and *I* get to be the bad guy!"

Getting Home

WHEN HE WOKE and saw the bunny-rabbit wallpaper, he knew it had gone wrong. He'd forgotten the kid. But the man Charlie had been closer—what had happened? He'd thought Charlie was asleep before he let Gilda doze off, but maybe not. Or maybe the man woke up and left before the change could happen. Yes, that was probably it—the slob had taken off early, back to Seattle all by himself. Damn!

He'd gone to a lot of trouble to set Charlie up. As soon as Gilda's sister had gone home, leaving him alone, he'd given Gilda a bath and brushed her hair. He couldn't manage the intricate upsweep she'd worn the day before when he arrived with the mousy sister, and so he settled for letting the blonde waves fall loosely past her shoulders. The ends were slightly ragged—she must not wear her hair down much, he thought—but he didn't tamper with them. He knew very little about makeup, but could see by the mirror that Gilda's clear skin hardly needed it. He experimented with a pale lipstick; after several tries he decided it would do. Gilda's own habit patterns helped some, but not enough.

He could have managed the girdle by now—he'd had some practice—but he felt she looked better without it and ignored the mild protest he sensed. No, keep it simple. Bra and panties, sweater and slacks, sandals—that was enough. A last check on the hair, and he was ready to go.

He thought of using her car, but if things worked out right, it would be superfluous. He rode the bus downtown. Before leaving, though, he memorized the address; it would look funny if someone wanted to bring him home and he had to look it up.

In the first bar he had no luck, and so he went to another. It wasn't that no one wanted to pick Gilda up, but that none of the men were any use to him. In the second bar he talked with several before he found Charlie, who was going to Seattle the next day. It had to be the next day, of course. Charlie was no great prize, but at least he was pointed in the right direction.

Gilda's stomach, he found, didn't take well to alcohol, and god only knew what he was doing to her reputation in her own home town. But grimly he nursed his beer until it was warm and flat, talking to one and another and then all to Charlie.

Aside from an overweight problem, the man was presentable enough; Gilda's interest was only mild, but she was not actively repelled. Later, though, was like being bedded by a cross between a bull and a jackrabbit; her disappointment was evident. Too bad she'd had to be subjected to that, but how else to keep Charlie overnight? He'd tried to get him drunk, but the man had the capacity of a tank truck. So, no choice. . . .

And all for nothing—the bum had copped out, leaving him with the kid. Barney, his name was. How old? Four, he thought—not old enough to cross the street by himself, let alone get to Seattle and find a chance to become Art Forrest again.

How long had it been now? Three weeks? It seemed like forever, one day at a time.

It began with the drug. "It's a new thing," said Eddie Finch. "Like acid, only better. You keep saying you want to trip—okay, here's your chance. Two bucks and the hit's yours."

"Gee, I don't know," Art said. "Are you sure it's good stuff?"

"Got it from the 'factory representative,' Roger himself. One for you and one for me." Eddie's grin showed prominent teeth. "Come on, man—finals are over. Before we start the summer quarter, let's have ourselves a time."

Art looked around his small apartment, at the books and clothes spread carelessly over the cheap furniture, and thought about it. All through his Army hitch and now his belated freshman year at the U, he'd heard the psychedelic mystique, but somehow there had always been a reason to postpone trying any of the stuff. And now? Well, why not? He had nothing better to do. Eileen was out of town for the weekend, and while they were halfway on the outs, he didn't feel like dating anyone else just yet. . . .

"Okay, Eddie. Here's your two bucks. Now, so I don't forget."

Pocketing the money, Eddie grinned. "Don't worry, Art. Zonked or not, *I* wouldn't forget."

The pills were dark blue—shiny, irregular little spheres. Eddie filled two water glasses with Burgundy from a half-empty gallon jug and made a small ritual of swallowing the pellets with sips of the harsh wine. "Well, here we go, Art. After a while, that is. While we wait, let's clear the place a little and put on some music."

Art collected books into a stack on his desk and hung up most of the scattered clothing. Eddie sorted records and piled them onto the turntable. Turning the stereo on, he left the volume low. Then they waited, talking quietly and sipping wine.

Nearly an hour later, Art had decided the pills were fakes. Then the rush hit him—*impact!* The overload that battered his senses was beyond anything he could have imagined. With effort he raised his head to look at the blur that a moment before had been Eddie and tried to speak.

"Heavy," he managed to say. "Too *heavy*, man."

When Eddie spoke his face came into better focus, but it shimmered like mist. "Go with it, Art," he said, slowly. "Don't fight it; let it be. Look at things—see how pretty? You're having a good time, Art. A *good* time."

Then it was easier; he let himself drown in the flood of sensation and was not harmed. Familiar objects rioted in kaleidoscopic color, ever changing, but at the same time he knew what they were and how they really looked. He was no longer frightened; this was fun! He relaxed his guard completely and lost himself in the moment.

The place became another place and all places, the time another time or many. Where was he? He didn't know and he didn't care; he no longer had the ability to care and didn't miss it. The whole universe came into his mind, and he fell in love with it.

He played with it; it changed. He went far, far into its depths and kept going, seeing and feeling wonders everywhere.

An eternity later a voice spoke. "Hey, man. You lost?"

He had forgotten his starting point; he had forgotten there was a place to return to. Yes, he thought: reality. How do I get back to it?

It was easy. When he tried to open his eyes, he found they were already open; merely, he hadn't been looking out through them. He saw reality, shimmering only slightly now. But he wasn't a part of it. If anything, he and reality were on opposite teams. He laughed at the idea, and then he didn't.

"Help me," he said.

"Sure, what's the problem? You're all right." But the voice was wrong. He squinted to bring the face into focus, and for a moment he saw it clearly.

It wasn't Eddie's. It was his own.

"What's happened?" He shouted it. "Why are you *me?*"

"Calm down, Eddie," said the other. You'll quit flashing in a minute."

"But I'm not Eddie; *you* are! I'm Art! Don't you notice anything wrong?"

"You're freaking a little, is all. Just take it easy, like you told *me*. Enjoy it, like you said. You'll be okay."

"Yeah." He inhaled deeply. "Yeah. It's just a 'visual.' It has to be."

"Sure," said his face to him, with his voice. Then the face yawned, and Art saw himself lie back in his chair and go to sleep . . . or pass out.

His vision was clearing; his muscles were real again. He stood shakily and walked over to look down at himself; the illusion persisted.

He shook his head and moved clumsily to the small bathroom. From the mirror above the washbasin Eddie's face looked out at him.

His orientation dropped away; for moments he was plunging through the universe again. Then he was back to face his panic in the familiar apartment.

He misdialed twice before he reached the Drug Crisis Clinic. A girl answered; after he hung up he couldn't remember two words of what he had told her.

Two men came to the apartment. They were quiet and gentle; soon he sat in the back of a panel truck, watching his own limp body sprawled on a stretcher, joggling slightly with the bumpy ride. He thought of what he must say at the clinic.

But as it happened, he said very little, for by the time they arrived it took him so long to form sentences that no one in that busy place was free to wait upon him and hear him. He felt himself being carried and laid onto a cot. His last thought was: I'll be all right when I wake up.

When he woke, he looked at the next cot and saw Eddie Finch. "Eddie! You all right?"

Eddie stared at him. "Sure. But who are you?"

Then Art saw the hand he had reached out. It was thin and wrinkled—an old man's hand, liver-spotted.

Before he had time to feel a reaction, Eddie turned away to look at someone sitting up in the cot beyond him. "Hi, Art," he said. "You okay now, too?" And again Art saw himself.

He fainted then, or something close to fainting. The next thing he saw was Art Forrest and Eddie Finch walking together, out of the room.

The old man's name was Einar Gundarrsen; he had a Social Security card and a long-expired driver's license. After a bad hour, during which Art came to realize that it didn't much *matter* whether he were insane, he braced himself to meet the situation on its own terms. There was no point in a seventy-four-year-old cocaine freak claiming to be a twenty-three-year-old college student, so he didn't. Instead he waited and listened, and learned. He learned about Einar Gundarrsen and thus about his own predicament.

Einar, the resident mind in the old body, was neither dead nor unconscious. He was receiving all sensory data and responding to it with thought. Art sensed the thoughts as they appeared, but he could not influence them—nor experience any memories that did not arise spontaneously. He was in full control of Einar's body, though, when he wished to be, and Einar didn't seem to notice any discrepancy. Einar, in fact, was not aware of Art's existence. Silently, with his mind, Art tried to "speak" to the old man, but there was no response. So again he waited.

The doctor, a little later, was cheerfully resigned to people like Einar. "You had us worried, old-timer. But you'll be all right, this time. Any chance of your kicking the nose-candy before it gets you?"

Riding Einar's thoughts, Art answered. "Ay don't use it very often, sir. Yust sometimes, when all things are . . . too much for me.'' The wife dead slowly and painfully, the fishing boat sold to pay medical expenses, the son dead in the war, the strumpet daughter a suicide. Nothing left, except Social Security checks and a room in a cheap flophouse. And nose-candy, sometimes. No wonder he sometimes took too much. . . .

The doctor's gaze dropped, then rose again. He put a hand on Einar's shoulder. ''Take it easy, then. And try to find yourself something to do. Something else. . . .

Einar wanted to apologize, but Art said only, ''Thank you, sir,'' and Einar did not protest. Turning away, he left the clinic. Outside, he waited for a downtown bus; it came soon.

He spent the afternoon on the waterfront, watching boats and gulls, workers and tourists. He ate fish and chips and later discovered, with guilt to match his discomfort, that Einar's digestion was not equipped to handle his choice of victuals. As dark approached he felt the old man's urge to retreat to his own den—but Art was beginning to get an idea of what had happened to him, and if he were right, the last place in the world for him to sleep was a flophouse for derelicts. He caught a bus not to Einar's part of town, but to his own.

It was a dirty trick, he thought, to use the old man's money—but if he ever got back to himself, he could repay it. Apartment 310, next to Art's own 308, was vacant. Mrs. Swenson, the manager, agreed to rent it to Einar for a week, on ''tryout.''

He went to bed early, hoping for the best. But he woke up in bed with John Ferguson, in 312.

He was Sylvia Ferguson, of course. And the hell of it was that Art didn't even *like* Sylvia Ferguson, that fat blonde dummy!

Moving cautiously, to avoid waking Ferguson, he got out of bed. My *God*, he thought: without her girdle the woman's absolutely monstrous! So much for any fleeting idea of promoting a quick liaison with Art Forrest—to be followed, with luck, by a brief nap together. For that, he figured, was how it worked—when he slept, he shifted to whoever was closest to him.

And maybe if he once got home to himself, he could stay put. *But I sure can't get there from here.*

One thing he could do. First he found a robe to wear—it

was bright pink, but if Sylvia wanted to look like a frank-furter, that was her business. He put money from her purse into an envelope; on the outside he wrote "Einar Gundarrsen." Then he went out and down the hall and pushed the envelope under the door of 310. If he had to owe money, he'd rather owe the Fergusons; they could afford it.

Belatedly, after shuffling ponderously back into 312, he wondered why Sylvia's thoughts showed no response to his action. Her mind was entirely concerned with making break-fast for John. He went along with her inclinations. A poor cook himself, he found that by letting Sylvia have the reins he could produce a pretty good meal. When she was ready, he called John Ferguson to come and get it.

So far so good, except that his feet hurt. Forty or fifty extra pounds, he thought, and usually teetering on spike heels, were cruel and unusual punishment.

While he didn't like being so fat, he was surprised to find that he could detect no emotional reaction to being in a female body. So far as he could tell, Sylvia's glands did not affect the essential male image of Art Forrest; he was who he was.

John Ferguson, blue-chinned and swarthy, stocky but not stout in his pajama bottoms, came silently to breakfast, bare-foot on the chilly linoleum. Watching the man's slow, relent-less eating, Art failed to notice how much and how fast Sylvia was putting it away on her own account—until she got up for seconds. He sat her back down. There was one burst of protesting thought; then she congratulated her conscience for keeping her on her diet. She still didn't like it, though.

John rose and refilled their coffee cups. "We'd better get at it, Sylvia, if we're going over to your mother's today." Her mother? In Spokane, came her thought. But that was nearly three hundred miles to the east. He'd have to try to put a stopper on that trip. If he could. . . .

"John, I don't think we'd better go, after all." He felt the rise of Sylvia's bovine puzzlement, and ignored it.

"Not go?" Ferguson slapped his hand down on the table, flat and loud. "Damn it all, Sylvia, I rearranged schedules at work, just so we could visit your mother on her birthday, and I had one hell of a time doing it. It wasn't my idea, remember—let me tell you, Spokane isn't exactly Fun City! But I did it; I put everybody out of joint to do it. So now we're going."

Without Art's volition, Sylvia was up and moving; he

decided he'd better go along with it and not make waves. An hour later, the Fergusons were on the road to Spokane.

Ferguson was a fast driver and a good one; the trip took less time than Art had expected. Then came a dull dinner and a long evening with Sylvia's mother, brother and sister-in-law. Sylvia had a taste for sweet wine; she crowded the port a lot, and neither John nor Art stopped her. Toward bedtime Art got nervous, but it seemed that John and Sylvia were not much given to marital romance.

He woke as John Ferguson. From his viewpoint it wasn't much of an improvement, for if anything, John's thoughts were duller than Sylvia's. Bored, Art waited for night and return to Sylvia's body. The Fergusons were going home the next day—until then, he could do nothing. He was glad when John went to bed early.

But the next morning he was not Sylvia—he was Sylvia's mother. *What the hell?* Sylvia had been the nearest person, hadn't she? Maybe he couldn't repeat. . . .

Well, the old lady would have to wangle an invitation to visit her daughter. She could sleep on the couch . . . sure, that couch was against the other side of Art's bedroom wall!

Then the woman's thoughts came clear to him, surprisingly sharp for the mother of anyone like Sylvia. She had to be in court the next day—something about a trust fund. *Damn all!*

The Fergusons left without him, then. In total funk, he let the resident mind make the proper good-byes. Then, against all her habits, he had a go at the port, himself.

And next he was Derek Ardwell, who rented the basement apartment, and then Derek's old Army buddy who stayed overnight because he'd had a fight with his wife. And then the buddy's wife, and then—the sequence, leading to no help for him, became hazy in his mind.

Two things stood out: first, he never repeated; and second, for good or ill he hadn't gotten laid once—until last night as Gilda, by Charlie the bull rabbit.

He didn't know whether to brag or complain.

And now he was four years old and named Barney, with a full bladder that spoke of urgency. He climbed over the sideboard of the small bed—large to him but small in the room—and fumbled loose the buttons of his warm fuzzy sleeper. Where, from here, was the bathroom? He'd been in this room only once, letting Gilda put the boy to bed by habit. Out in the hall there was more length to the right, and there—second door—was his goal.

The pressure relieved, he surveyed himself, both directly and in the full-length mirror behind the bathroom scales. Not a bad-looking little kid: blue eyes, square stubborn jaw, blocky build, blond hair that fell over his eyes too much. And he felt healthy: his senses were sharper than an adult's; it was almost like tripping. A person could do worse than be four years old, he thought. But of course it wouldn't last. Not for anyone—and for him, only a day. Besides, he might get tired of waiting for sex to come along. He looked at his potential for it and had to smile; the little clump looked so *innocent*. Well, it was. . . .

"Barney!" It was Gilda; he hadn't heard her coming. "What are you doing, running around trying to catch a cold?"

What to say? Barney said it. "Nothing. I had to go pottie."

Gilda laughed. "All right, that's good. Now let's get some clothes outside you and some breakfast inside. *Scoot!*" He scooted, and Gilda helped him dress. Just in time, he remembered not to try to tie his own shoes.

In the kitchen he sat on a cushion on an ordinary chair, too grown-up for a high chair. The soft-boiled egg tasted better than he expected; his youthful tongue knew flavors he had long forgotten. And his mind looked through Barney's four-year-old eyes to savor the charms of Gilda in her thin night-dress. Too bad, he thought, that I had to come visit her as her sister. And even more, he regretted inflicting Charlie on her; she hadn't deserved that.

But damn it, he was beginning to get desperate. Was there any end to this?

Gilda was in the bathtub. From the previous day he knew her penchant for steeping herself in warm suds; he had some time to think.

After his one manipulation of Einar Gundarrsen he had avoided, as much as possible, interfering with the normal behavior of the persons he became. The previous night, with Charlie, was an exception he regretted. But he had followed Gilda's thoughts and found casual desire mixed with only slight distaste, and so he had followed through with his fruitless plan.

If he were ever to get back to himself, he realized, he'd have to take actions that his "hosts" would have no reason to take. But he shrank from that necessity. Why? He wasn't sure. For one thing, he didn't want to get any innocent person into trouble or a really embarrassing predicament. Not that such events could be traced to him, but still . . . And that was the other part of it.

He had seen Art Forrest walk out of the Crisis Clinic with Eddie Finch. But who was it he saw? He had to know, and he had no good way to find out. Oh, there was a way—he could simply force one of his new selves to go to Seattle and confront himself, or to make contact by phone. But such an action would be *remembered*—and against the time he might become himself again, he wanted no clues pointing to Art Forrest as anything out of the ordinary. Why? Well, just because!

Wait a minute, though. Barney, the kid . . . four years old. What if *he* made a phone call? The content wouldn't mean anything to the boy; he'd probably forget it entirely by the next day. At least he wouldn't be able to keep it straight, and if Art watched his words—no problem. The phone bill? A dollar or so, marked only "Seattle." A little kid playing with the telephone; it happened all the time. Barney probably wouldn't even get spanked for it; Gilda was an indulgent mother. Maybe Charlie had been an unnecessary mistake.

Four-year-old fingers found it hard to dial accurately; twice he miscued and hung up to start again. Third time was the charm; he got it right, all eleven digits, and listened to the ringing. Where the hell *was* he, the one at the other end?

He heard the bathroom door open; Gilda said, "Barney? Time to get ready, dear." *Damn!* He hung up fast and moved away from the phone before she could see him.

"Time for nursery school, Barney. Let's wear your blue jacket, shall we? It's a little nippy out this morning."

He'd been talking as little as possible, smiling a lot, remembering the kid from yesterday as cheerful enough but not much for chatter. When he did speak, he kept it simple, and Gilda didn't appear to notice anything different about him. But nursery school? He could fool an adult, maybe, because he knew how adults saw children. But how did children see other children? He'd forgotten. Hell, he'd never make it!

"I don't feel so good, Mommie."

"Don't feel good? Oh, sure you do. You ate like a horse, and your BM was just fine. Don't try to kid your ol' mommie, young horse." Expertly she stuffed him into the jacket. "Anyway, Miss Preston *isn't* mad at you for breaking the crayons yesterday."

"She isn't?"

"No, she isn't. She told me so. Cross my heart and hope to catch a mackerel."

He laughed, and the reaction was as much his as Barney's. Okay, what the hell—might as well take the chance. If the other tots—*and* maybe Miss Preston—thought a four-year-old was a little freaky one day, it wouldn't blight the kid for life. But he'd try to watch it.

Gilda was a better mother than a driver. He'd noticed, while being her, that her habitual driving motions felt sloppy; he'd had to add effort at the wheel. Well, nobody's perfect; at least she wasn't reckless or aggressive. But he was more glad than not to arrive at the white wooden house where Miss Preston held sway.

Inside, he was nervous. Gilda handed him over quickly, kissing him goodbye and telling him she'd pick up up right on time for a change. Barney's thought told him she always said that but never made it and that it was no big thing anyway. Then Gilda left, he was on his own.

Miss Preston was a small, slim woman in a grey blouse and slacks, with black hair growing out from a shag cut. She smiled and said, "Aren't you going to hang up your jacket, Barney?" He looked around, ignoring the dozen or so other children for the moment, and saw no place to hang the damned thing. Miss Preston pointed to a folding screen at the side of the room, painted with birds in Japanese style; belatedly, Barney's thought echoed her. He went to it, looked behind and found the coat rack. Great start . . .

He was relieved to see that the other children weren't paying much attention to him. A couple said "Hi," and he said "Hi" back. The activity seemed to be random and loosely directed; he took a picture book from a table and sat down to "read" it. His impulse was to take a corner seat where he could keep an eye on everyone, but from his recent course in psychology he knew that would draw attention, and so he found a seat neither central nor peripheral.

It was a long morning. He listened to the kids—listened

hard—so that when anyone spoke to him he'd have the language right. He watched to see where they went when the left the room; it would look pretty funny if he didn't know where the bathroom was, and Barney wasn't thinking along those lines. When he colored a page of a coloring book, he was careful not to be too neat. He broke one crayon, just to keep his average up. And he watched a couple of other boys, out of the sides of his vision, to see what colors they preferred, and followed a composite of their choices in his own work.

Lunch, when it came, looked bland to him, but his young taste buds found it delicious. Then his young metabolism made him drowsy, and when Miss Preston said "Nap time," it sounded like a good idea. Then, curled up with a pillow and half dozing, he thought: *Oh, no!* but it was too late; his body put his consciousness to sleep. He couldn't do a thing about it.

He woke to find himself gently chewing a blonde braid. He looked and saw he was wearing a pink dress. He felt unmistakable signs that he wasn't properly housebroken. Which kid was he, and how old? He had no idea; he hadn't paid that much attention. He rose quietly and went to the bathroom where he toweled away the worst of it; the dress should dry soon, especially after he rubbed the wet spot between two towels. The panties would take longer. Why he should go to the trouble for a kid he didn't even know, he wasn't sure— but the little girl's thoughts were distressed at the accident. He stayed there until someone knocked on the door; then he went out to rejoin the group. The spot still showed, but not much; the panties felt clammy. He had no idea where this kid had been sitting, or which was her coloring book if she had one, and, dammit, she *wouldn't* think about it. So he sat down with two other girls who were playing with modeling clay, and he squished the stuff in his hands also, careful not to produce any recognizable shapes.

One girl said to the other. "Sheila wets her pants." Then he was Sheila, and the mouthy brat had it in for him.

"So do you," he said without thinking and realized it had been Sheila's response.

"I do *not!* You'd better not say that." The other girl was larger; he could feel Sheila preparing to cry.

"I don't, either," he said. "It was my milk spilled."

"Sheila spills her milk," said the larger girl. Ah—Brenda was her name; thank you, Sheila baby. And a vengeful memory. . . .

"Brenda steps on *dog* do! With both feet!" It was overkill. Brenda ran sobbing to Miss Preston, who was too busy solving another squabble to do more than cuddle and soothe the child. Wow, he thought, you're really a tiger on the nursery-school circuit.

With the pressure off, he had time to look around for Barney. The boy was playing a simple-minded card-matching game with three other kids. He showed no outward effects from his period of coexistence with Art Forrest.

Art found himself enjoying the clay game with the remaining girl, Melanie. It was a contest with no rules—just, "Okay, now look what *I* made," and nodding and laughing at the clay shapes. The laughing was the best part, and afternoon moved much better than morning had.

He was anxious at first, when the parents—mostly mothers, but there were two fathers—began to collect their offspring. He needn't have worried; Sheila was on the alert and recognized the woman. Nice-looking redhead, he thought—but on the whole he preferred Gilda. This one was thin, tense and preoccupied; she greeted Sheila absently, got her to the car with maximum efficiency and minimum talk, and drove home in single-minded concentration.

He asked only one question. "How old am I, Mommy?"

"Three, dummy. Can't you remember anything? And I'm not your mommy; I'm your stepmother. I've told you before; you call me Rhoda, understand? Or else I'll belt you."

"Yes, Rhoda." He felt Sheila's fear; the child was terrorized. Oh, brother! *This* kid had a hard row to hoe, for sure.

Sheila and her daddy and Rhoda lived in a fourth-floor apartment, but the man watching TV in the chartreuse living room wasn't daddy. "Say hello to your Uncle Frank, Sheila." He looked at the man—about thirty, slim, brown hair— reasonably good-looking, he supposed.

"Hello, Uncle Frank." Art suppressed her innocent remark that she bet she had more uncles than anyone in the world. He noted her thought that they never appeared when daddy was home.

"All right, come on." Impatiently, Rhoda took him to the bathroom. When he had paid his small tinkling tribute, she marched him brusquely to a bedroom. "Now you get your medicine, and I want you to lie down for a while." Medicine? He felt healthy enough. But Rhoda was removing the dress and then the panties; she paused and felt the cloth. Damn, part of it must be damp, still.

"You disgraced yourself again, didn't you?" Before he could stop her, Sheila nodded. "*I'll* teach you!" He was flipped face-down across Rhoda's knees and his bare bottom spanked, surprisingly hard. Goddamn! That *hurt!* For an instant he was tempted to try Sheila's sharp little teeth on the exposed nylon-clad thigh, but thought better of it and merely allowed Sheila's startled wail to be heard. Why, the kid was in stark panic!

Then he was turned upright and set abruptly on the edge of the bed. "Now shut up and take your medicine." Rhoda picked up a bottle from the bedside stand.

Nembutal, for Christ's sake! Rhoda certainly didn't believe in taking any chances of being interrupted; what a bitch she was! And the stuff could be dangerous to such a small child. No point in trying to argue—he let the pill be put into his mouth but slipped it under his tongue while he swallowed water from the glass Rhoda held. "Now lie down," and Rhoda pulled up the covers.

As Rhoda closed the door behind her, he spat the capsule into his hand. He pulled a crumpled Kleenex from the bedside wastebasket and wrapped the wet thing in it, stuffing the wadded tissue well down among the debris.

He lay back and pretended sleep, while gradually Sheila calmed. Sure enough, about twenty minutes later Rhoda looked in, then closed the door. In the living room a record began playing; the volume was high. He guessed that Rhoda was a loud one in bed. He gave it a few minutes, then sat up and looked around.

Jackpot! There was an extension telephone. He wondered why Rhoda had the kid in an adult's bedroom, but figured the bitch probably had her own reasons.

Barney's fingers had had trouble with the dial; Sheila's simply couldn't manage it. The stand had a drawer; he rummaged in it and found a felt-tip pen. Holding it in both small fists he dialed the area code and the number of his Seattle apartment. Then he picked up the handset again. His breathing was rapid and shallow.

"Hello?" The voice sounded like his own, but he couldn't be sure.

"Yes. Hello," he said. "Who is this?"

"Huh!" It was between a snort and a chuckle. "You're the one that called. Who's *this?*"

"I was calling Art Forrest."

"And you got him. Now who are *you?*"

"A—a friend. I mean, I need to talk to you. I mean, you *can't* be Art Forrest." Damn! He was getting rattled.

"The hell I can't." Definitely a chuckle this time; no doubt about it. "Look, what kind of game is this? And who *are* you?"

Who could it be? And how? "That doesn't matter. But this is important. Could you come to Spokane? Right away?"

"It has to be a gag. Who put you up to it? Eddie?"

"It's no gag. You *have* to come to Spokane."

"Sure. Naturally. Look, I'm busy. And I'm tired of listening to someone give an imitation of a five-year-old kid."

Three, he almost said, but caught himself in time. "I've got laryngitis, sort of, that's all. But listen, I've got to see you."

"Swell. You know where I live," and at the other end, the phone was hung up.

"Shit!" The word sounded strange in Sheila's piping little voice; he had to grin as he replaced the handset. But not for long—the man sounded like Art Forrest and talked like him, but he *couldn't* be. So—now what?

A further search of the room produced little of interest and nothing of help. Then he heard footsteps and scuttled into bed to play possum as Rhoda looked in again. He was hungry, but on Rhoda's regime there was no chance of being fed; for several more hours he was supposed to be sedated. He needed to go to the bathroom again, but probably he couldn't get there and back without discovery. He was tempted to be imaginative and punitive with the contents of his bladder, but realized that Rhoda would take revenge on Sheila later. So he made do with the cluttered wastebasket, hoping the contents would dry by morning.

Then fatigue hit his small body, and like it or not, he fell asleep.

Snoring woke him to the half-light of false dawn. The room was unfamiliar, but the thought came that Frank *would* be a damn snorer, and he knew he was Rhoda. Then she thought she'd better put the brat on the john, if it weren't already too late.

He withheld control and let her go through the motions of getting up and going to Sheila, but with the child he enforced gentleness on the woman. Her reaction shocked him.

I'd like to drown her, right here in the toilet. And sometime I will—maybe next time! If Frank weren't here. . . .

By God, she meant it! He gave thought to the quality of Rhoda's mercy. When Sheila was tucked back in, with more care than the little girl could have expected, he had made up his mind.

He took a few things, including the felt-tip pen, from the bedside stand. In the kitchen, under a stack of bills that told the name he needed to know, he found paper. Rhoda's habits controlled her penmanship, but he composed the text, taking clues from her thoughts as she saw the words appear one by one.

Ralph, I've been cheating on you every chance I get. And treating Sheila like dirt when you're out of town. She's too scared to tell you but sometimes I come close to killing her. I don't know why I do it. And I don't know why I can't stand it any more. But I can't.

—Rhoda

As he ran water into a glass and opened the Nembutal bottle, he could feel panic in her, but underneath it a resigned feeling of having been brought to justice. And no hint of realization that it wasn't her own doing.

For that matter, it didn't feel much like *his* doing—he'd never killed except in war, under hostile fire himself. But a puzzling feeling of compulsion drove him to get on with it. So he swallowed the pills, all of them, and went back to the guest bedroom. The snores had stopped.

It was a grim risk he took, for he couldn't know when the change would come. He might die with Rhoda—but somehow, for Sheila's sake, he couldn't let her live.

About midmorning, he woke as Frank.

It wasn't, he thought, going to be one of Frank's best days. The woman was dead, no doubt of it, and he could find no regret for her. But Frank was scared spitless, and there was no point in making things any tougher on him than they had to be. Or on Sheila. Or on Ralph, whoever he was when he was home.

Like any good detective-story fan, he found a towel and did his best to leave no Frank fingerprints in the apartment. The kitchen showed signs that Sheila had foraged there, but she was asleep when he looked in to check.

Before leaving he stood a moment—no, there was nothing more to do, here. Frank's thought told where his car was parked, and Frank couldn't get there soon enough. So it was time to go. Goodbye, Sheila, you're a good kid. And good-by to you too, Rhoda.

But walking out, down the back stairs, he thought, *Did I play God here? And did I have the right?* Then he remembered Sheila's feelings, and Rhoda's, and said, *Hell, yes!*

Frank's car was on the nearest side street, a block back. It was a green four-speed Mustang, vinyl-topped; Frank liked it. Art had driven better cars, he thought, but had not owned any as new. He let Frank's reflexes show him the car's ways as he set out for the freeway, Interstate 90. It looked like a good day for a trip to Seattle.

He checked with Frank first, using an idea he'd developed while he was Sheila but had had no occasion to test. He said aloud, "Hey, why not drive over to Seattle today?" Frank's thought responded that he had the weekend off, so why the hell not?—and right now, he could use the distance! So it was agreed, but only Art knew of the agreement.

The Mustang was low on gas; he pulled into a station with a phone booth alongside. As the attendant filled the tank, he rehearsed what he must say. In the booth he dialed the police emergency number. "I want to report a dead woman," and he gave the address and apartment number.

"Yes, sir. Your name? And are you calling from that address?"

"No. I'm not in this. I just thought you should know about it and get there fast."

"Where are you calling from, sir?"

"It doesn't matter." But he wanted their help; he should tell them something. "The door was open, is all. I thought, maybe something's wrong, so I looked in. And she's dead. A bottle of pills; it's empty on the floor. And a note in the kitchen; it didn't make sense."

"You realize, sir, that you are criminally liable if—"

"The hell with that. There's a little girl—three, maybe four. Somebody get out there before the kid wakes up and finds her." He hung up and wiped his sweating palms on Frank's colorful mod-styled slacks.

Back in the car he let Frank's habits sign the credit card. He had a quick breakfast at a nearby cafe and drove onto Interstate 90. It was a good day for a drive, at that.

Traffic wasn't bad; Art stayed in the fast lane and, without tailgating, went as fast as other people would let him. Usually, crossing the state, he enjoyed the scenery, but now he paid it little heed. He reached Seattle just as rush hour was beginning, driving off the freeway ahead of the main jam. And now, what to do next? There had to be a way to get next to whoever was calling himself Art Forrest. But not as a stranger. . . .

All right, how about the neighborhood bar? He could use a drink; he'd driven nearly three hundred miles nonstop. Luckily Frank had a heavy-duty bladder.

He parked behind the Puzzle Tavern and entered by the back door. After repairing the damages of travel, he looked around the place. Not much of a crowd—who was there who might be of use? The outlook was poor but the hour was early. He sat at a back table, so that he could scan all who entered. He drank draft beer. The Puzzle didn't serve the best draft he'd ever tasted.

He knew the woman who came in alone; without thinking, he waved to her. She frowned, looking uncertain. Of course—she wouldn't know Frank from a can of mushrooms. But she got a beer at the bar and came over to join him.

"I don't *know* you, do I?"

"Sure you do—Frank Chapman. And you're Lydia Corgill, right?"

"Yes, but I don't remember *meeting* you."

"I remember you all right. At a party last winter, the last time I was in town. You wore a red dress." Hell, she practically always wore red to parties. But the detail set her off, talking. He'd forgotten that she talked so much in italics.

He could sense Frank's appreciation of the woman—young, slim, with her brown hair piled high—but he wished he'd chosen someone else. He really didn't like this one much, at close range, and earlier in the spring there had been a rumor about her venereal health. Eddie Finch hadn't caught anything, though, come to think of it. Anyway, she was a mixer; maybe she'd attract more people. And sure enough. . . .

"Oh, there's *Cory. Cory!* Over *here!*" Waving her arm like a semaphore.

She wouldn't have luck, he thought, with Cory Purcell. Girls didn't interest big, handsome Cory—men did, but he was too polite to be a problem to anyone. Not a bad guy, Art thought—if only you didn't have to be so careful of his feelings. Purcell came to the table; Lydia introduced them.

"Siddown, Cory," said Art. "Pull up a beer and sit a while."

Cory smiled, showing large white teeth. "Oh, good, I'll get a pitcher—a big one." He always overpaid his way, Art recalled.

Maybe Cory could be the answer. Twice when he'd had spats with his current friend, Art had let him crash overnight, with nothing asked nor offered but a place to sleep. Maybe it could happen again.

But first there was another problem. Frank was getting the message about Cory, and it made him uncomfortable, especially when Lydia and Cory began to flirt with him, mildly but in definite competition. Art was amused, but he could afford to consider only one factor: Which of them had the best chance of spending tomorrow night in Art Forrest's apartment?

"Where did you say you were staying, Frank?" Lydia's tone carried an unspoken invitation.

"No place, so far. I'm fresh off the freeway from Spokane."

"*Spokane?* My *sister* lives in Spokane. You *know* her, maybe? Harriet Collins, her name is now. They live up in Rockwood."

"No, I don't think so. I live out the other way."

"No place to stay?" said Cory. "Well, I have a spare bunk."

Now Frank was thoroughly alarmed. If this line were to be kept open, Art would have to reassure him, even at the risk of hurting Cory's feelings. "That's good of you," he said. Now what? As himself, he could have kidded Cory—but as a stranger? No.

"But look," he tried again. "No offense, but I kind of got the idea, uh—and you see, I don't . . ." Damn! He was *all* hung up.

Cory's smile stiffened, but he rallied. "I'm really that

obvious? Sorry. But the offer's still good. A place to sleep, and that's all.''

Now Lydia was getting a message of her own, it seemed—that whatever else, *she* was being cut out of the game. "Oh, let's don't talk about *sleep* yet. Why, the night's *young*.''

"Hardly begun, in fact," said Art. "And we're low on beer. No, sit down, Purcell. My turn." He took the pitcher to the bar for a refill—it was faster than waiting for the bar girl, busily chatting at another table. He saw Lydia and Cory talking with apparent intensity and wished he could overhear. It had to be pretty choice stuff, from the looks of them.

The discussion had ended when he returned. He poured, all around. "Well, here's to us," he said, "whoever we are."

"*That's* a funny thing to say, Frank. Isn't it, Cory? Really *funny*.''

"Very," said Purcell. He drained his glass and stood. "I just remembered, there's a movie I want to see." He reached into a pocket. "I won't be home until about twelve. If you get tired before then, Chapman, here's my spare key." He recited the address; Art repeated it.

"But look, Cory—you're giving me your key? A total stranger?''

"I trust people. I have to. Well, good night, for now." He left, walking fast.

Art looked at Lydia. "What the hell did you say to him?"

She looked away. "What makes you think I had anything to do with it?''

"Come off it, Lydia. What did you do to the guy while I was at the bar?''

"What do *you* care?" She made a pout. "Oh, all *right*. I just told him I'm *tired* of types like him trying to cut me out with fellas, and it was just plain *bitchy* of him to take you home when you don't even *want* him. And—" She stopped abruptly, eyes wide; obviously she'd said more than she'd intended.

He grinned at her and decided what the hell—he'd go along with Frank's inclinations. "I'm not sleepy at all," he said. "But the beer isn't too great here."

"Do you like bourbon?" she said, smiling. "I have a bottle.''

"Sure. But let's grab something to eat first. It's a long time since breakfast.''

* * *

Both times he took care not to lie afterward and chance dozing, though after the day's drive Frank's urge was to rest. The woman's personality, he thought, was not so abrasive in itself, but her voice needed a disconnect switch. No, he'd never get to Art Forrest in her guise—not locally, with the threat of longer term involvement. He drank sparingly, needing to keep his wits. Frank's capacity was greater than his own, but still, a little caution wouldn't hurt.

"How are you *feeling,* Frank honey?" They sat on the sofa, across from a silenced Western movie in glorious TV color.

"All right. Good, I mean. A little tired. How about you?"

"You know how *I* feel?" Her liquor was showing. "Like *more.*"

"All right. I'll pour you a little." He did.

"Not that. *You* know." Sure he knew, but it was late and he was tired.

"No way, I'm afraid. This man is wrung out like dishrag."

Her pout slipped. "Well, let's go *sleepy*-bye for a while then. And maybe later I'll wake you *up*. You'll *like* that."

"Well . . ." He pretended to consider, then to do a double take. "Oh hell, I forgot. Gotta take Cory's key back. And besides, I'm really pooped."

"I could put it in his *mailbox* tomorrow. Or *you* could. Huh?"

He shook his head; all else aside, he had to get away from this woman. Frank wanted to stay, but the hell with Frank; he'd had a good tour, hadn't he?

"No, I really have to go." He tipped her chin up and kissed her. "Don't be jealous, Lydia. You won the war, didn't you? And it's been good."

"*Call* me tomorrow?"

"Tomorrow night, from Spokane. I'm heading back in the morning. Gotta work, ya know?"

"All right. Good night, Frank. Like you say, it's been *good.*"

Cory wasn't home yet. He hadn't been kidding; there were two beds. Art showered and drank a glass of Cory's orange juice. Then he put the key on the kitchen table, hung his clothes over a bedroom chair and went to bed. He guessed he had the right bunk; the other had the personal conveniences alongside.

He was tired but couldn't sleep—waiting for the other shoe to drop? When Cory came in, he was quiet, but Art heard him and then saw him in the dim light.

"Are you still awake, Frank?" the man said softly, and waited.

You should at least say good night to your host, Art thought. "Yes. The key's on the kitchen table. And thanks."

"Fine. I'll close up shop in a minute. And—don't worry, I—"

"I wasn't worrying. You're a good guy, Cory. Good night."

He heard water running, and the refrigerator door opened and closed. Then Cory came soundlessly into the room and turned out the night light. Art could hear him, moving in his bed and pulling the covers around; then it was quiet. But still Art wasn't sleepy; instead, he found he was excited.

Oh, no! he thought. The hots for Cory? It can't be. Then he realized it wasn't his excitement; it was Frank who was half attracted, half repelled. Well?

Careful, let's check this out. Burying his face in the pillow, he whispered, "So I play games with Cory. How do I feel tomorrow morning, having breakfast with him?" The answer was shockingly swift: Frank's premonition of guilt and shame, resentment at Cory's shared knowledge of his lapse—a vision of reasserting masculinity with both fists. Art shook his head.

"No," he whispered into the pillow. "Cory leaves me alone and I leave him alone. He trusted me with his key; I owe him that much. Time to go to sleep." It took some minutes longer, but finally Frank relaxed and let Art get some sleep.

Cory hadn't drunk much, Art realized, waking to see Frank in the other bed—not snoring this time but still asleep. Just as well; it wouldn't hurt to be up and dressed, fully in charge of the day, when Frank came to life.

Cory's thoughts revealed a great yen for his guest, but he was honor-bound to let his love go unrequited. Instead he performed morning routines and checked breakfast supplies before rousing the other man. Bacon and eggs seemed about right, Art thought, and Cory did not disagree.

Frank was a slow waker, a little groggy but apparently durable. He ate quickly, not saying much. His clothes, worn for at least the third day, were somewhat rumpled but still presentable. Obviously he had no wish to outstay his wel-

come; as soon as he finished breakfast, he vanished into the
bathroom. When he came out, he paused for a moment and
then abruptly held out his hand. Cory took it.

"Want to thank you, Purcell," Frank said. "Nice of you to
put me up for the night. Real good breakfast, too. And,
uh—well, I guess I'd better be going. Gotta get on the road,
you know. And thanks again." He didn't move, though.

"That's all right, Frank," Art said. "Anytime." He released his hand from the other's grip, and Frank went to the
door.

"So long, then," he said, and left.

Well. Cory hoped he'd come back some day; Art didn't
think the return engagement was a good idea. He spoke
aloud, hoping Cory was paying attention to what he said with
his mouth. "That one could turn out to be very rough trade
indeed." He wasn't sure that Cory was convinced.

Art knew that Cory, as chief dispatcher for a trucking firm,
sometimes worked odd schedules. But apparently he wasn't
working today; the man's thoughts showed no need or intent
to leave the apartment. Cory began tidying the place, dusting
knicknacks, but Art was soon bored; he put the rag away and
got a beer from the refrigerator.

Cory, he found, didn't smoke. Daytime TV was more than
Art could stomach. The only books in the place were of the
same predictable kind. It looked to be a long day.

The door chime came as a welcome surprise to Art, but he
was more surprised at the intensity of Cory's reaction; the
man practically leaped to admit this caller. At the door and
then entering was a tall, slim boy, about nineteen. Cory's
recognition of his current friend and protege, Sid Langlie,
was neon-lit to Art's perceptions. And as soon as the door
was closed, the boy threw his arms around Cory and kissed
him.

Jesus! *Now* what? Art disengaged from the kid, as gently as
he could manage in a hurry.

"What's the matter, Cory? Are you mad at me or something?"

He shook his head. "No, of course not. I'm just . . . tired.
Don't feel too good this morning." Cory searched himself for
signs of bad feelings but found none. "I'm—I'm just not in
the *mood*, Sidney, that's all." I'm *not?* thought Cory.

The boy was nettled. He pushed past and looked into the

bedroom, then the kitchen. "You had somebody here last night, didn't you? Two breakfasts, I see, Cory. But why two beds?"

Think fast. "I had somebody here, yes. But not what you think. We sat up late and talked, is all. And I drank a little more than I should have." Cory knew better; he couldn't understand why he was saying these things. Cory was smarter than Frank; he noticed discrepancies. Watch it, dummy!

"Anyway, can't we just enjoy each other's company, Sid?"

"That's not what you said yesterday. You're lying to me, Cory."

Before Art had a chance to think, Cory reacted. "Don't say that. Don't *ever* say that. I don't lie to people; I don't have to." But somehow, he *had* lied; Cory's thoughts were chaotic. He took a deep, ragged breath. Art saw what he was thinking and decided to give him his head. "And just for that, Sidney, you trundle your smart ass right out of here. Yes, *now*. And don't come back!" His voice was trembling. "Not for a *week!*"

The boy was backing away, looking puzzled. "Well, look, Cory. I didn't mean it; you know that. Can't I—?"

"Call me on Friday. If you want to." He took the boy by the arm and escorted him to and out the door. There were no goodbyes.

And then Cory threw himself headlong onto the sofa and sobbed bitterly. For once Art found he had no control at all. Now what, he thought, *should* I have done?

He was using Cory deliberately, as he had used or tried to use all the people he had been since the whole thing began. Was he justified? Maybe. The sooner he got back to himself, the sooner he could stop running other people. Meanwhile, no matter how Cory felt about it, he hadn't *wanted* to experience intimacy with that scraggly kid. In atonement, when Cory stopped crying and got up, Art let him do something he himself found rather disgusting. Well, he'd wondered about that kind of thing, and now he knew.

He decided to wait until midevening to call his own apartment. He didn't feel like dinner, though Cory was building an appetite. Over and over, he rehearsed the coming call.

It didn't go as rehearsed.

"Hello? Art? Cory Purcell here."

"Hi, Cory. What's up, or shouldn't I ask?"

He laughed; it was a standard joke. "Well, Art, I'm having a little problem here, with my friend. Three's a crowd, and you've put me up before, and I wondered—" Cory was puzzled, but decided he was playing a joke on Art.

"Hey, sorry. Not tonight. I've got a chick coming over. Maybe you know her. Hell, sure you do!"

He could see it coming. "I do?"

"Lydia Corgill. She talks too much, but I was a little drunk when I made the date. Well, hey, sorry, like I said. If you still need a crash tomorrow, give me a holler. Gotta go now. Bye."

Hell and *damn!* If only he'd stayed with shrill italic-voiced Lydia. But he hadn't thought she had a chance of getting to Art Forrest, whoever he was now. Now he'd wasted the whole pitch, including Cory's big day.

Or had he? Could he pull the apartment 310 ploy again, making sure to move the bed closer to 308 than to 312? He'd have a 50-50 chance, and if he came up Lydia, he could just stick around for another snooze, with any luck at all.

It couldn't miss. Except that when he called Mrs. Swenson, he found that 310 was already rented . . . and so, long since, was 306.

Cory didn't often drink whiskey, and he stocked a poor brand, but bad whiskey was better than none. And the ice helped. Art thought. . . .

All right, what if I don't *go* to sleep tonight? Maybe I can crash at my own place tomorrow. Cory caught a good night's sleep; he's in shape for it.

So he poured the rest of the glass down the sink. Can't afford to drink, today and tomorrow; it'll be hard enough to stay awake.

To stay awake, yes. He couldn't leave it to chance. He rummaged in Cory's medicine cabinet and found no signs of "uppers." Nothing of the sort in the bedroom, either. He asked out loud, "I wonder if there's anything around here to keep a guy awake if he wanted," and Cory's thought was negative.

Who did he know who was a pill freak? Eddie Finch, who else? He called.

"Eddie? Cory Purcell here.'

"Sorry, I'm taken." Eddie didn't like Cory and made no bones about it.

"No . . . I mean, could I get some uppers from you, please? I need to work all night, and I don't have anything here."

After a pause, Eddie said, "Yeah, I guess so. Sure. When you want 'em?"

"Uh, could I come over and get them now?"

"Why not? Bring money, keep Finchpad green."

"Yes, I will. And thanks."

Art hadn't noticed before, but from Cory's height Eddie Finch was a buck-toothed little shrimp and a rather obnoxious one. Most of the difference was probably Eddie's attitude toward Cory; he seemed to despise the man and fear him at the same time. "Yeh? You want some uppers, huh? How many you want?"

"I had a good sleep last night, got up about eight this morning, and need to keep going until tomorrow evening. How many would that be?"

Eddie nodded his head at an angle, thinking. "About ten bucks, my prices. And unless you want to be climbing the walls, don't take any one of them until you really need it. Okay?" He thumbed pills, poured from a small container, off his palm into a smaller one. "Ten bucks, right?"

They made the exchange. "Right. And thanks, Eddie."

"Anytime. But don't get sold on those. There's better stuff."

Better stuff . . . yes, but how could *Cory* ask what Art wanted to know? Well, have a try. "That stuff you and Art got last month must have been pretty wild."

"Oh, that," Eddie shrugged. "Well, it was new, and we got a little bit of an OD for a while." He looked plaintive or angry; Art couldn't be sure which. "So I freaked out for a couple minutes, was all. And part of my head hollered for help to the Crisis Clinic. Hell, inside I knew I was okay, but the twitchy side of my head dialed the phone. Didn't even feel like me doing it.

"But no problem. Art and me had a free ride and a free sleep, and that's all there was to it."

"Do you see Art very often, now?"

"Same as usual, not too often. Why?"

"Oh, I was wondering how he is these days."

"Got the hots, huh, Cory?" Was it Art or Cory who wanted to hit him, then?

"No" It was Cory who spoke. "I like Art and I respect his preferences. And he respects mine."

"Well, goodie for you. Have fun with the uppers."

"Yes. Well, not fun, exactly. But I'm sure they'll help. Good night." Be damned if he'd thank the guy again!

One thing he could do, back at Cory's apartment, was eat. Cory liked to cook, and with nothing better to do, Art enjoyed riding along watching that skill. The preparation of dinner took nearly two hours; when it was on the table, Art ate slowly and ceremoniously, sipping wine and savoring each bite of food. Cory made a good grade of veal scaloppine, that was for sure! And while Art wasn't much of a wine freak, the Grenache rosé set the meal off perfectly. It struck him that if he ever got back to himself he'd like to be on dining terms with Cory Purcell.

Dishwashing and other chores used up more of the evening. Then there was nothing but TV—he didn't want to go out, and he didn't want to stir Cory up by reading from the shelf of homoporn. So he watched TV and sipped—not drank, but sipped—beer. And ate peanuts. Halfway through the late, late show he found himself interested in the plot of a commercial. It was time for his first upper.

It was a long night, a long morning and a long afternoon. The pills kept him on a thin nervous edge of alertness, but underneath he could feel the body's protests. Cory was bewildered; he couldn't understand why he wouldn't let himself go to bed. The jitters were getting bad, too; around the middle of the afternoon Art said the hell with it and took a chance on a belt of bad bourbon—or rather, "blended whiskey"—America's Favorite, it said on the label. So much for America's Taste, he thought, but sipped it down, anyway.

Dinner was chicken in a wine sauce; it was probably great—Cory seemed to enjoy it—but Art couldn't give it due attention, any more than he had to the cooking. As long as Cory didn't try to lie down, Art let him have his way.

At eight o'clock he could wait no longer; he called Art Forrest's apartment and asked for sanctuary. He got it. "Thanks," he said. "I'll be right over."

*　　*　　*

The hell of it was that the Art Forrest who answered the door looked and sounded exactly like Art Forrest. "Hi, Cory. Come on in and rest it. Have anything?"

There was nothing he could do but play it straight. "Thanks. A beer, maybe?" He sat and watched himself go to the refrigerator.

"Sure thing. I'm stocked up."

Watching Art cross the room, he was surprised to find Cory really didn't have a yen for him, except in a reflexive sort of way. A memory flashed, of persistently repressing desire for the sake of friendship. Poor Cory! "Thanks, Art," he said.

"Any old time. Well—your friend still has a guest?"

"Uh, yes." This was bad; Cory was getting antsy again. Without moving his lips, Art subvocalized. "I'm just *kidding*. He'll get a big laugh out of it when I explain." Cory relaxed a little, but not entirely.

"Where'd you sleep last night?" said the other Art.

"On the couch. But it's too short—not like yours here."

Art laughed. "I know it's not really funny, Cory, but you must have looked like a pretzel."

"I guess so. Uh—were you going any place tonight?"

"Me? No, I'm pooped. That Lydia! Doesn't know there's a time to stop and a time to go." He lit a cigarette, and for the hundredth time Art wished that Cory were a smoker.

"I'll probably sack out early, Cory, but you can sit up and read if you like. Or watch TV, maybe—you always keep the sound low enough; it doesn't bother me."

"No, I'm tired, too. Didn't get much sleep last night."

"I can imagine. Another beer? I'm having one."

"Yes. Thanks, Art. Gee, I should have brought some, shouldn't I?"

"Forget it. Last time you gave me a bottle of booze; you're paid up for a month of Sundays."

Inside, remembering how he had disliked America's Favorite, Art cringed for Cory.

He was wasting time; maybe this Art could tell him something. "Say—Eddie was telling me a little about that trip you two had, the one where you went to the Clinic. What was it like for *you?*"

"Oh, wild!—my head was really spaced for a while. And then Eddie freaked some. But about that time I corked out cold and woke up next morning in the Clinic."

"That's all? Didn't you feel any different afterwards?"

"No, same as always—except a little high for a couple of days."

He couldn't believe it; it *had* to be a put-on. But the man across the room seemed utterly relaxed and natural. What could be running his head now, when *he* wasn't home?

"Well, it's good that you didn't have any permanent effects, Art."

"Yeah. But you know, I think that stuff's too powerful to mess around with. Next time I'll stick to plain old acid, or maybe even mesc, if I find any I can trust."

"Next time? You'll trip again, after that?"

"Not right away, Cory—not for a few months, anyway. But, you know?—once I got to where I could take it, having my head wide-open like that, it was—well, there's nothing like it. I think I need to do it another time or two."

We'll see about that, he thought, but said only, "Well, do your own thing, I guess."

"Right, Cory." The conversation slowed; his latest pill was wearing off, and the other seemed tired also.

He yawned. "Art, I think I've had it for tonight. Are the blankets still on the closet shelf?"

"Yes. Here, I'll help you." Between them, they spread the covers to relative smoothness. "There you are."

"Fine. Thanks." His beer was finished, and so he took first turn in the bathroom, then waited for Art to go before he undressed. He was under the covers when Art returned, facing away; Cory didn't want to see him nude—or perhaps, to be seen seeing.

The lights went out, and sleep came soon.

He half woke, began to drift back to dozing. Then it hit him—*this is it!* Eyes out of focus and staring, he came fully awake.

At last! He was in his own bed, and asleep on the couch was Cory Purcell. Now, by God, he'd find out what had been going on for the past three weeks—whether he'd been operating on "automatic pilot" or just what the hell *had* happened. But from that other track of himself, no thoughts came.

All right—sometimes memory could be fractious, elusive. But now, in his own body, he'd have direct access to it rather than the fragmented view of a rider on another consciousness. Let's see, he thought—what was I doing yesterday? Nothing happened; he remembered only the day spent as Cory.

What is this? By newly formed reflex he subvocalized his earlier question, and obediently the memory arose: After he'd got rid of Lydia, it had been a dull day, but that had been a welcome relief. He must have been really drunk to make a date with that one. . . .

Then he realized—he *wasn't* in his body in the old way—he was still a rider! But then . . . who was the resident mind now?

"Who am I?" he asked. "What's my real name?"

An answer came, the only answer he could not accept: *Art Forrest.*

He tried to cling to logic: Were there two of him? Had the drug split him into two selves, one "at home" and the other hopping from body to body? Frantically he searched for fraud or flaw in the identity that answered him, but he could find none—the Art Forrest at home in his body was every bit as much Art Forrest as he was. He couldn't be—but he was. Only shock kept him from panic.

Now what? For starters, he interrogated the "inside man" and learned that in his absence things had gone along much as usual. Nothing of importance had happened; the resident mind thought upon its routine with relative contentment.

As: the summer quarter had begun, and he was enrolled in the courses he'd planned to take. He and Eileen had finally split up, amicably enough; he was hoping soon to consummate a new romance. The girl was blonde, named Cynthia; Art had met her a few times. As usual, money was scarce but he wasn't quite broke. Nothing was new, to speak of. . . .

He was stymied—in his body but not *of* it. When Cory woke, Art made conversation with half his mind, letting the inner Art do most of it. Cory wanted to make breakfast; Art let him, as he obviously enjoyed the chance to show his expertise and do service for his lodging. He also washed the dishes, including yesterday's pile. Then he began to fold the blankets.

"Never mind," Art said. "I'll do it later."

"Well . . ." Cory paused, fidgeting. Art, I have to tell you something."

"Oh?" He had a premonition.

"Art, I lied to you. I don't know why I did it; I *never* lie; you know that."

"That's right, Cory. You're the most truthful guy I know."

"But for some reason I *had* to come over and stay here last night. So I said my friend had someone at my place, and he didn't. He wasn't even there himself."

"Oh?" Don't say anything more; let *him* tell it. . . .

"I don't know what got into me, Art. It seemed so *important* to stay here. And I don't know *why*." He looked even more embarrassed. "I mean, we're friends, of course; I always like to see you. But . . . anyway, it wasn't that I was *after* you or anything like that."

"I know, Cory." Now, what to say? "Look—don't worry about it. You'll be okay; everybody's head does funny things sometimes. And I was glad to have you here." *That* was true, at any rate, even though this situation was as confused as before, or worse.

"All right, Art. I just had to tell you, was all. And thanks."

"Anytime. Well, *almost* anytime." They grinned, and Cory left.

No matter how he wrestled with it, the problem wouldn't solve. He was in his head not once but twice, and the *he* of him was the outsider. He sat in the apartment, occasionally sipping a beer or munching a snack. No answers. And what would happen when next he slept?

The question frightened him. Would it be all for nothing? Would he be displaced and again go body-hopping, doomed for all his life to having one identity after another and never his own? And existing in that fashion, how long might he live? Would he somehow die with the Art Forrest body, or only when he found himself a rider with someone who met death waking?

Or would he go stark, raving nuts first? Such as maybe this very afternoon. . . .

The hardest thing to take was the waiting, and the longer it lasted, the worse it got. If he could stay awake forever—but, of course, he couldn't.

So why not get the suspense over and done with? He took two sleeping pills and went to bed.

"I find you at last. Where have you taken yourself for so long?" The words weren't English, but he understood. Who spoke? He saw no one in this dim luminous place his apartment had become. Was he tripping again—a "flashback"?

He couldn't feel his own body, or see it. He saw without eyes, heard without ears.

Then he did see his body—lying on the bed, in front of him. In front? Or was it to one side? Directions were confused; there *was* no front or back to his view.

"Who's that?" With no voice he said it. "Where are you? What's happening?" Then, relieved, he laughed. "Oh, hell—I'm dreaming, that's all."

"You do not see me? I will shift frequency a few increments." A brighter patch of light appeared and seemed to thicken before him. "But who would you expect, here? There are only two of us. And where is it that you have been?"

He tried to shake his missing head. "I think I get it—you must be the other Art Forrest, the one that stayed put. Is this some kind of symbolic hallucination, some way we can put ourselves back together again? My God, I'm so tired of bouncing from body to body—I just want to be *me* again!"

"You? But without doubt you are you. Have you a wrongness? Allow me to read you."

The bright patch approached and touched him. He felt warmth; it vibrated at first, then pulsed smoothly.

"There *is* a wrongness," the other said. "And so strange—you have come to believe that you *are* the human."

"I know who I am; I just have to get back, is all." This hallucination, he thought, was getting too big for its breeches.

"I am reading to learn the cause of it," said the voice. "Ah, I find it; it is here. The human had ingested a drug. As you scanned him in the usual mode, it took effect. And—*most* strange—on you, as well."

"It was Eddie's pill, all right; I guessed that much. Flipped me out—I mean, *really* out. But how—?"

"Tied to the human by the scanning mode, you disoriented as he did. The feedback imprinted his entire memory and personality over your own, which seems to be in stasis. And when the scan ended and you transferred, automatically, to the next subject, you still retained the human pattern." The voice chuckled. "How totally confusing, for you!"

You don't know the half of it, buster. "You're not helping much." He had to get this—whatever it was—back on track, fast. "Look: I'm Art Forrest, nobody else. Just put me back together, is all. If you can . . . if you're real . . . if I'm not dreaming you . . ."

"Dreaming? Yes. Obviously—your consciousness has followed the human wake-sleep pattern. And only in the sleep phase could your own abilities operate, instinctively. Then, each time, you transferred to scan another human as our mission requires.''

"Mission?'' *This guy is even confusing my confusion!* "Look, fella—I'm *out* of the army now.''

"You will remember soon. Ah! I note that your own feelings did become operative at one juncture.''

"My own feelings?''

"You destroyed the woman who outraged our instinct for the welfare of the young. In all other cases you were governed by the human imprint.

"Even under such handicaps you have absorbed much valuable data, as have I. The task of correlation, awaiting us on the ship, will be massive.''

"Ship?'' *Now, hold it!* "You're trying to tell me I'm not Art Forrest? I guess *I* know who I am!''

"For the best, we should return immediately. In this mode I cannot transpose the imprint into correct perspective with your own identity. Integration with your body should erase the difficulty. I predict that you will find your senses adequately convincing.''

Art's laugh was shaky. "Are you crazy, or am I?''

"Technically, you must be considered deranged. But only for a short time further. Let us now go.''

"Go where?'' *How?*

"You do not remember even that! No matter, I can move us both.''

He had time for one swooping glimpse of the body on the bed before he was propelled up *through* the ceiling and two more levels of apartments, up into the fading sunset sky. Up and up—the sky went black, lit with stars, and the sun's corona again peeped past the edge of Earth.

He felt no cold, no need to breathe. After the first burst of panic a numb calm spread over the surface of his plunging thoughts. Almost without volition he found himself talking to the other.

"I'll say this much, it's quite a trip. Okay, then—pretending it's real, for a minute—if I'm not Art Forrest, who the hell *am* I? And you, come to think of it?''

"Although you do not yet sound greatly like yourself, you are Tirel. I am Bexane. We are id-siblings, quadriplexed.''

If he had owned a head, he would have nodded it. "I guess

that makes as much sense as the rest of it." What else should he ask?—as if it made any difference. Well . . . "Anything else you want to tell me?"

"What is it that you would wish to know?"

That was a stumper; it was his play. "Well . . . like, then, how about the rest of the family? Or are there any more?"

"Indeed, yes. You have a fine family, Tirel. Most satisfactory."

"I—I have?"

"Certainly so. And it is fitting to tell you that they will be most joyous that you return. Your wife and husband, in particular, have suffered your absence painfully."

Stop the world! I want to get back on!

But ahead, luminous to his perception, lay the great ship. And deep in his frantic mind something plunged in sudden joy.

MORE SCIENCE FICTION ADVENTURE!

☐ 0-441-38291-6	**JANISSARIES**, J.E. Pournelle	$3.50
☐ 0-441-78042-3	**STAR COLONY**, Keith Laumer	$3.95
☐ 0-441-14257-5	**DEMON-4**, David Mace	$2.75
☐ 0-441-31602-6	**HAMMER'S SLAMMERS,** David Drake	$2.95
☐ 0-441-68029-1	**PROCURATOR**, Kirk Mitchell	$2.75
☐ 0-441-09019-2	**CADRE LUCIFER**, Robert O'Riordan	$2.95
☐ 0-425-09776-5	**CIRCUIT BREAKER,** Melinda Snodgrass	$2.95
☐ 0-425-09560-6	**DOME,** Michael Reaves and Steve Perry	$3.50
☐ 0-441-10602-1	**CITIZEN PHAID**, Mick Farren	$2.95
☐ 0-441-77913-1	**THE STAINLESS STEEL RAT SAVES THE WORLD**, Harry Harrison	$2.95

Available at your local bookstore or return this form to:

THE BERKLEY PUBLISHING GROUP
Berkley • Jove • Charter • Ace
THE BERKLEY PUBLISHING GROUP, Dept. B
390 Murray Hill Parkway, East Rutherford, NJ 07073

Please send me the titles checked above. I enclose _____ Include $1.00 for postage and handling if one book is ordered; add 25¢ per book for two or more not to exceed $1.75. CA, NJ, NY and PA residents please add sales tax. Prices subject to change without notice and may be higher in Canada. Do not send cash.

NAME_____

ADDRESS_____

CITY_____ STATE/ZIP_____

(Allow six weeks for delivery.)